Requiem *for the* Bone Man

R. A. Comunale, M.D.

05/09/08
To Alecia and Mike
young lovers forever
much too young to be retired
RA Comunale MD

Mountain Lake Press
Mountain Lake Park, Maryland

LIBRARY OF CONGRESS
CONTROL NUMBER: 2008920898

ISBN: 978-0-9814773-0-5

PRINTED IN THE UNITED STATES OF AMERICA

MOUNTAIN LAKE PRESS
24 D STREET
MOUNTAIN LAKE PARK, MD 21550

FIRST EDITION, FEBRUARY 2008

BOOK AND COVER DESIGN BY MICHAEL HENTGES

Requiem *for the* Bone Man

In memoriam: Leni, Cathy, Country Boy

Requiem for the Bone Man

CHAPTER I

The Calling

He was eight years old when the dead lady found him.

He and Angelo had been watching the old Mustache Petes playing boccie in front of Myers Tavern, their baggy patched pants held up by suspenders, twisting and turning like grotesque ballerinas as they pitched the wooden ball while the two boys laughed at the sight. But Youth is easily bored by Age, so they quickly ditched the game to sneak through the trash-filled alleyway between the tavern and the timeworn row houses that fronted the river. They slid down the muddy bank to walk along the shallow waterway toward the concrete bridge abutments. It was fun to hunt there for coins, buttons, and soda pop bottles to redeem at the store for money.

This time, in the shadows of the overhanging bridge, they saw a bundle of rags caught on a raised pylon. The increased speed of the water flowing venturi-like through the passageway stirred the bundle, and he noticed it had arms. One seemed to move, beckoning him forward, almost pleading.

"Angie, look!"

The other boy stared briefly before turning and running away, but he was drawn to it, moth to flame. He moved closer and saw her face.

Even in death, belly beginning to bloat from the gas in her bowels, she retained some of her beauty, her long golden hair framing an oval face and narrow nose. Traces of light-pink lipstick contrasted the death-blued lips and mottled pasty skin. Her long delicate fingers, artist's fingers, were a mixed palette of blues, reds, and grays. She registered the final rictus of agony frozen forever in those staring green eyes, with forearms drawn together as if to ward off Death's scythe.

Why was she here?

Surely she belonged in one of the big houses farther down the river where the people with money lived, not here in his neighborhood of soot-covered brick buildings.

Her eyes would not leave him, sunken, no longer vibrant, but planting within him a cry for help.

Don't leave me!

He ran back up the riverbank, trousers wet from stepping in the water. As he passed the old men spending their remaining days in pursuit of childhood pleasure playing the ancient game, one of them called out, chuckling:

"Hey, Gallini, you piss your pants, kid?"

He turned toward the old man.

"I'm Galen, Robert Galen."

"Yeah? You like you papa, boy. He too good now to roll ball with us, *con il suo nome Americano*. I remember him in old country, boy. Gallini good enough for him there. Good enough for him here!"

He didn't stop. He had learned early on that you don't argue with the Old. He began to run the final stretch to the four-story tenement where his mama and papa lived. He knew he wasn't fast like the other kids with their long, thin legs. His were what his papa called marching legs, thick but not fat—yet. Papa used to tell him about all the marching men back in the old country.

Mama would watch Papa as he told the stories of their former hometown, of the drums beating loudly and the young men marching through the streets, arms raised and waving flags wildly.

"Give us war," they had cried, and Papa now knew they had gotten what they wanted, and that all it had meant for many of them was death, and he was grateful he and Mama had escaped to America.

That was in 1914, Papa had said.

"Mama, Mama!"

"What's the matter, Berto?"

She looked at her son with pride. He was strong already and smart, just like his father. Antonio could have been a *dottore* back home, but they both knew they could not stay there. Now her Tonio ate the fire every day for them.

"There's a dead lady in the river! She's under the bridge, and Angie and me saw her! She's sad, Mama, she doesn't want to be there!"

"Antonio, come quick, listen what your son say!"

Antonio Gallini sat tired from his evening shift work at the foundry, but he rose from the patched-up chair his Anna had sewed and fixed. He had brought it home from where he'd found it in front of the rich man's house. His powerful arms, strengthened by countless hours forging the heavy metal tools at work, easily carried the chair atop his stocky body.

"Che cosa, cara mia?"

He listened as his son repeated the sad story. Then he put on his street clothes and walked the four blocks to the police station—they didn't have a telephone—and returned. Soon the boy heard the wail of the siren as the police wagon headed toward the river. By then his papa, too tired to do anything else, had returned to the old chair, which Anna stood behind rubbing his neck until he fell asleep.

Poor Tonio, she thought, but it was worth telling the police. Her Berto would be a big man, an important man, someday. He would live in a big house. He wouldn't live like this.

She smiled at her son. Already he looked like his papa did when they first met. She handed him the last apple from the bare table as he ran outside again.

But he wasn't going to play. He made a beeline for the police station, where he knew they would take the dead lady. That's where the *dottores* would examine her and try to find out what hurt her. He had read that in a book in the library, a book he wasn't supposed to read because it was in the grown-ups' area, but he had read it anyway.

He saw the police wagon in the driveway behind the red-brick building and ran to the large double-door side entrance. It was open and he looked each way before walking along the darkened corridor. He heard the voices of policemen in the different rooms, but he was careful not to get caught.

He saw a light shining under another set of big doors. He read the letters on the door: MORGUE.

Like morta, he thought.

Slowly he pushed one of the doors partway open and saw them, two men dressed in long white gowns like the priests at Easter Mass. They moved slowly, talking quietly to each other in words he didn't understand, their heads covered in white caps, their hands enveloped up to their mid forearms in heavy, dark-brown rubber gloves.

Then he saw her, lying stretched out on a table in the middle of the room. A sheet covered part of her, leaving her feet, stomach, chest, and head exposed. She looked like she was sleeping.

He saw one of the men in white take a big knife and make a cut right into her belly. The other man spoke strange words into a machine:

"From the gas distention, I estimate expiration occurred more than twenty-four hours ago."

"There it is," the man with the knife said. "Somebody botched the abortion."

Then they noticed him.

"Hey kid! Get outta here!"

He didn't move, his jaw set in determination.

"I found her. She was in the river. What happened to her?"

The two men looked at each other. The shorter man, the one who had been speaking into the machine, laughed.

"Why do you want to know, kid?"

They looked at the stocky little boy standing there in torn brown corduroy pants, tee shirt, and worn brown shoes, looking up at them so intently. *Strange little guy,* one thought. Then they both smiled as he said, "I want to be like you."

From that time on, he haunted the clinic where Dr. Agnelli worked. He watched him move from patient to patient, comforting some, scolding others, never stopping to sit or eat. He memorized the suture techniques the doctor used, went to his mama's sewing box and, putting thread to needle, practiced sewing two pieces of cloth together.

And he waited.

"Berto, there's a fight going down on Hamilton!"

Tomas and Angelo called to him late one Saturday afternoon soon after his tenth birthday party. Mama had saved to buy three cupcakes, one for each member of the family, and had put small blue candles on all three. Even his father had smiled and told him how grown up he looked now that he was ten. He had been so happy when his father reached under the table and pulled out his surprise gift: a brass belt buckle he had made from scraps at the mill, with his name on it! His father had taken the buckle and put it on his son's belt.

"Siete un uomo, Berto!"

He had run outside afterward to show his friends.

"Berto, come on, let's go watch the fight."

He hesitated, looking back at the door to his apartment building. Mama and Papa had warned him to stay away from trouble, but what ten-year-old boy could resist watching a brawl? He turned back to his friends and ran with them to the Hamilton block. Something was always happening there. It was the crux of the neighborhood territories, the nexus point where the different ethnic groups converged, so it served as the natural battleground for the frustrations of the immigrants and their children.

The three boys turned the corner and began hearing the shouts and curses of the older boys and men—spitting, kicking, and lunging at one another. The more vicious held back, waiting for the opportunity to mutilate their enemies with sharpened metal or spring-loaded zip guns.

The boys hesitated at the corner, peering around, afraid to go farther, but then they heard a loud scream and saw one of the teenagers fall to the ground, blood spurting in a narrow stream from his groin. The rest of the fighters stopped and then ran, fearing the arrival of the police or, worse, the neighborhood enforcers.

"Come on, let's help him," Berto yelled as he moved toward the fallen young man.

The other two remained transfixed.

He reached the victim and immediately began to press on the site of the stab wound, just as he had seen Dr. Agnelli do.

"Tomas, go get a bottle of your papa's *vino*. Angelo, get a needle from your mama's sewing kit—quick!"

He could feel the pulsation of the artery under his hand. So this was how it felt! How did Dr. Agnelli say it? *Blood runs down, walks up.* The blood was being pushed by the heart from above. He put more pressure above the stab wound.

"Here, Berto."

Tomas had returned with the wine bottle.

"Pour it over where my hand is."

Angelo arrived with a big curved carpet needle and a spool of heavy thread.

"Put the thread in it, then put your hand where mine is now."

He had never felt this way before. His whole body vibrated with excitement. With Angelo pressing above and Tomas pouring the wine into the wound, he was able to see the tear in the thick tube that wanted to spill its life-giving contents onto the cracked flagstone sidewalk.

He slipped the curved needle into the blood vessel, first on one side, then the other. He repeated to himself the mantra Dr. Agnelli would recite whenever he watched: *"Equal edges come together in prayer." One stitch, two, three! That should be enough.*

"Tomas, give me your knife."

He knotted the ends of the thread then cut it. No blood coming out!

As he started to stand up he felt a heavy hand on his back. His two friends had disappeared. Turning, he saw an enormously stocky man, a neighborhood enforcer, looking down at him.

"Good job, kid. We'll take it from here. What's your name?"

"Robert Galen."

The big man noticed the belt buckle with the boy's name on it and smiled, the jagged teeth in his jowly face glistening with gold.

"No, kid. From now on, it's *Dottore* Berto."

"Berto?"

"Si, Mama?"

"Berto, your papa wants to talk with you."

Uh-oh! All through his younger years he had never liked hearing those words, and it was still the same now. Was it because he had come home later than usual from his high school classes? He had been feeling increasing tension between himself and his father in the last few years, but he didn't know what to do about it. His father was a strict, hardworking man, short but powerfully built, with penetrating dark eyes framed by years of labor and suffering. His stare alone was sufficient punishment for transgressions. He demanded only the best of his son, no excuses accepted. Speak, read, behave, perform, understand, and just plain do better than the other kids—or else!

"Berto!" his father would typically start.

"Si, Papa?"

"Your report card. You got a B in English!" he would say, always speaking in his native tongue.

"Yes, Papa, but it's only a mid-term grade."

"I don't care. It's not good enough!"

He sometimes would raise his right hand strike the boy, who would wince reflexively, and then put it down slowly if he noticed his Anna was watching.

"Antonio, don't hit the boy!" his mother would call across the room.

"He must learn, Anna. He must always do his best."

He would turn and walk from the room, his wife following in his wake like a shadow.

"Antonio, why are you so hard on him? He is a good boy."

"*Cara mia,* you know what we went through in the old country. Look at me. Am I a hard man? I do it to give him a better life than we have. I don't want to see him sweat away in the mill, grinding metal, coughing up soot. He should not be like the other boys, hanging out on corners, trying to get in with those *Sicilianos* and their made men. Not my boy! Never!"

You don't have to worry about me, Papa, he would think as he listened to them talking about him. *I know what I want for my life.*

He would remember his first friend, Angie, now dead from a knife to the throat. He had tried to save him, but the wound was too severe. The boy's blood had spilled onto the street and into his lungs even as he had tried to stop its flow. So many others, his classmates from grammar school, were now dead, in jail, or hanging out. Not him. He knew what he wanted and was willing to work for it, no matter what.

When his father would smile at him, radiating happiness even through the mill-furnace darkness of his face, the boy would feel so proud, almost as if his father was treating him as an equal.

"Berto, go in, your father is waiting for you."

"Si, Mama."

He hesitated then walked into the small front room of their tenement apartment and waited for his father to recognize his presence.

"Figlio mio."

"Si, Papa?"

His father was standing near the window in a typical pose, facing away from him then turning his head toward him without shifting his body. It had taken Berto a long time to realize this was the parent-to-child posture of superiority used in the old country. He also knew that he had now grown old enough for his father to speak to him about something he considered a concern.

"Berto, *Dottore* Agnelli tells me you are spending a lot of time around his clinic. Are you sick, my son?"

"No, Papa."

"Good. He tells me you ask to watch when he works."

"Si, Papa."

Oh yes, Papa. It is like poetry to watch the dottore as he goes from one person to the next, his hands moving to set a broken bone, his fingers singing like Mama's sewing bobbin as he puts the cut skin back together. And how the little ones laugh as he taps their knees and runs his hand across their bellies to find out where it hurts!

His father had turned around to him and was smiling.

"What do you want to do with your life, son?"

"I want to be a doctor, Papa," he responded without hesitation.

The father stared at his son, looking so much like himself at that age, eager to meet the world but not understanding what it would do to him.

Tonio, do you remember how you also wanted to be a dottore?

Indeed he did, but war, lack of money, and his class had blocked him at every turn. Now he wanted to be sure his son was tough enough to deal with the realities of life, not the dreams. He and Anna had come to America for that very reason. So he was determined to administer a dose of hard truth to his young son's heart and mind, difficult as it would be to do so.

"You make my heart glad, my son. I am sure that you will be a fine doctor, just like Dr. Agnelli. But one question: How will you pay for it?"

His inquiry startled Berto. As he waited for an answer, Antonio Gallini noticed his beloved Anna standing in the doorway, the woman for whom he would do anything. They had crossed an ocean together. He could refuse her nothing.

Even now, as he looked at the timeworn, rounded face of his wife, he remembered her sunlit smiles in the old country, her auburn hair glowing against the blue Mediterranean sky. He heard once more the voice that had sung the prayers next to him at Mass so long ago.

• • •

December 2, 1899, was bitterly cold in the small village in upper Tuscany, but the young man was sweating in the candlelit room.

"Easy, Pietro, easy! It will be all right."

Pasquale Gallini felt the tension in his son's shoulders and understood. He already had lost one child, and now Maria was having trouble again. The women were busy in the other room doing what women were supposed to do when another woman was ready. It was a mystery to the men—except the *dottores,* and none were here tonight.

"I can't lose her, Papa. You know she almost died when little Pasquale . . .

"Si, figlio mio, I know."

The old man remembered when the child who would have had his name had died quickly after birth. It was a double grief piled on both him and his son: losing the baby so soon after their beloved Antonella had died suddenly.

Pasquale was alone now with his memories of her.

No more, caro Dio, no more!

Both men started reflexively as they heard screams in the back room followed by a deathly stillness that exposed the rasps of their own fearful breathing.

"Dio mio!" Pietro sobbed.

Pasquale held his son, his own heart crying out.

"Antonella, help me!"

Then they heard a second, higher-pitched cry shattering the brief silence, the gasping, angry cry of an infant suddenly ejected from the security of the womb. They stood transfixed as the old wooden door opened and the bent midwife waddled out holding a red-faced, crying baby in her hands.

"You have a son, Pietro!"

Father and grandfather rushed into the birth room followed by the midwife carrying the baby and returning it to the exhausted woman who forever thereafter would be called Mama.

"Maria!" the younger man called out, and the tired young woman turned her face to him.

"We will call him Antonio," she half-whispered.

Pasquale Gallini smiled at the wisdom of his daughter-in-law.

"Come on, Tonio, we're going to the festival."

"No, Sal, my father needs me."

He was the son and grandson of stonemasons. After school he worked side by side with his father and grandfather, cutting, chipping, measuring—whatever was required for the repairs to the great cathedral. From the time he could walk, he had carried the water to wet the stones to keep the dust down, until they had begun to teach him the craft itself.

When they rested, he would sit at his grandfather's knee and ask the old man about the great days when Garibaldi and Mazzini united the country, and how the old man had fought to free the land from foreign influence.

His grandfather would show him the two gold medals for bravery that hung above the straw-filled bed along with the black paper silhouettes of Mazzini and Garibaldi . . . and Antonella.

Antonio first saw Anna at Mass on Easter Sunday. Like the other girls, she wore a white dress and had blossoms in her hair. But there was a difference to her.

He was twelve and he was curious.

He was noticing things he had never noticed before. Her face did not seem like those of the other girls. It lit up the church more than the candles that stood row on row in front of the statues of the Virgin Mary and the Infant Jesus. Her voice was sweeter than the spring birds now trilling the Resurrection of Christ.

After Mass she walked outside and sat in the back of a little donkey cart waiting for her family.

He was twelve and he was bold.

"My name is Antonio Gallini. What's yours?"

"Anna. Anna Abrescia."

He liked the name.

She thought he looked strong for just a boy.

As their childhood romance flowered in the little Tuscan village, another flower was beginning to bloom that soon would stain the earth red.

Pasquale could feel it in the air. The young men were restive, just as they had been almost fifty years before. The blood lust was rising, even in his son, Pietro.

Antonio was now fourteen—almost a man.

Pasquale began to plan.

The town priest knew how to speak and write English, so he called in a favor—the church repairs he had performed but never charged for—and arranged for the priest to teach the boy. He would not permit his grandson to be sucked into the maw of war.

"Tonio, you don't spend time with us anymore. All you do is moon over the carpenter's daughter."

His friends knew him too well.

She would be coming into town today. He would wait for her. It was going to be a busy day. The farmers from the outlying areas would be bringing the cattle to the town for sale. There would be festivities.

He saw her down the street. She was driving the little donkey cart. Then he heard the rumble of hooves, thousands of them: the cattle drive. He saw the cart stop. The girl stood up and looked back in the direction of the noise—she was terrified. He ran, ran, as fast as he could toward her, grabbed the reins from her paralyzed hands and pulled the donkey and cart off the street into a nearby alley just as the cattle thundered through.

He lifted the still-frightened girl out of the cart and then held her for just a moment. He felt strange, like nothing he had ever felt before. Then, as she hugged and kissed him, the strangeness got stronger. She returned to the cart, her face red like the tomatoes in his grandfather's garden.

He felt the burning in his own face and began moving toward her when he heard the clapping of hands and turned to see a watching crowd. Suddenly he was surrounded by his friends who were laughing and dancing, holding fingers to their heads to imitate the horns of a bull.

"Moo! Moo! Moo! Antonio has the horn!"

A few crudely grabbed their crotches.

He realized it was true, and he ran off embarrassed to the shelter of his home.

"Antonio, the other boys are joining the army. Have you done so yet?"

"No, Papa, not yet. I thought you and Grandpapa needed me here."

His father scowled and walked away.

Pasquale emerged from the shadows of the stonecutting room.

"Tonio, I see you with the carpenter's daughter. You love her."

He was embarrassed that it had become so obvious to everyone, but he nodded.

"Listen carefully to me, my son. Yes, I call you my son, because you are more like me than your father ever was. You are a thinker. I will not let you become cannon fodder. Here, boy."

The old man held out a small leather pouch.

"This is for you and your Anna. Take it. It will be enough for you both. Go to Naples, get passage to America. You must leave before the guns start sounding. War is not glory. Many of my friends lie in the ground because of it. Now go, pack your clothes, and say good-bye to your mama. She will understand. Do not be upset by your father."

Antonio took the pouch and could feel the weight of the coins. He hugged the old man and thanked him, knowing they soon would never see each other again. As he left the room, he saw his father standing there, his face darkened with rage.

"Papa, I . . . "

His father turned his back, and the words echoed off the stucco walls.

"Non ho figlio!"

"Mama, I'm leaving for America with Anna. When we get enough money together, we'll send for you and Papa and Grandpapa. It's going to be all right."

Maria looked at her son. She pulled his head to her chest and rocked him as she had done when he was a baby. She was stricken with grief, but she knew Pasquale was right. Her son had to leave in order to live. She turned and took down the small silver crucifix from the mantle and put it in her son's hands.

"It is all I can give you."

"Come, Anna, we'll miss the boat!"

They moved quickly through the crowds at the Naples dock. The great steamship towered over everything as they clutched the two small bags and moved up the gangplank. The steward looked at the young couple, sneered, then pointed toward the steerage section, the cheapest, darkest level of the ship. Crowded and dank, the smell of fear and hope mixed there with incipient seasickness. But it was worth it. They were going to America.

Fourteen days later, they saw the great copper statue rising above the entrance to New York Harbor. It had been a rough voyage, until they finally were allowed to stand on deck.

"No deck chairs for this refuse!" the steward had laughed to his co-workers.

Disembarkation was worse. After the rich passengers streamed leisurely down the gangplanks to the waiting arms of family and friends, the steerage masses were herded off and loaded onto a crowded barge for transport across the harbor to a large, carved-stone and red-brick building. At the entrance, the men were separated from the women and children, and all were grouped into long lines.

Government doctors quickly screened the new arrivals for diseases, passing along those deemed healthy or shaking their heads in rejection when they detected tuberculosis or a severe defect. They sent those not accepted to special holding areas, more like cages, condemned to a return voyage to whatever land they had left.

Then the final line, the ultimate evaluation for the "Non-English."

"Hey, Mike, what do I do with these two dagos?"

The older man turned and saw the two standing there: short, rough-clothed, worn high-top leather shoes, tired.

Children! God help them, just kids.

"Send them over, Tim."

He knew that his partner was always a little too eager to stamp the fatal word UNSUITABLE across the papers of the incoming, but there was something in this couple's eyes, a spirit he rarely saw among the tired line of people.

He looked at the boy: strong, determined, fix-jawed. This one could succeed. The girl holding onto the boy—there was hidden strength there, too.

"What are your names? Do you understand me?"

He hoped they did. It would make his decision much easier, and then he smiled inside as he heard the strongly accented English.

"My name Antonio Gallini."

The man turned to Anna, but Antonio spoke up before he could question her.

"My wife, Anna Abrescia Gallini."

It was a small lie.

The inspector looked at them.

Married? Right, and I'm Charlie Chaplin.

"Okay, son, here's a list of what you need to do. Keep it with you. You look strong. I know a place that needs strong men. What do you do?"

"I am stonemason," Antonio stammered.

He handed the boy a piece of paper.

"Take this card. There's a metal foundry just outside the city. They can use you."

He didn't tell the kid he would receive a commission for sending him, but it was a damn sight better than what his partner would have done.

He offered another card—another commission.

"Here's a cheap place to stay until you get set up. Now give me your papers."

The inspector took them, examined them, and then pulled a fountain pen out of his breast pocket and made a change in the names.

"I'm doing you a favor, kid. In America, your name is your ticket. It's now Galen."

He took a big rubber stamp and marked the papers: ENTRY ALLOWED.

A few minutes later, they walked out of the teeming building and onto the ferry taking them to the place where they would begin their new life.

Dearest Mama,

Anna and I have settled in a place called Newark. It is not far from the great city of New York. I work at the iron foundry. Anna and I are still living in the boardinghouse that a nice officer told us about. As soon as we put enough money aside, we will move to a boardinghouse near work.

Tell Papa that I love him and meant him no disrespect, but Grandpapa is right. The old country is not for us anymore. How is Grandpapa?

Please tell Father Infante that his English lessons have served us well. Anna and I are studying for our citizenship and we both read the questions and recite the answers in English.

I will write again soon.

Your loving son,

Antonio

There was more, much more he wanted to write, but this was his first letter home, and he wasn't sure if it would even reach the little village. It was August 1914, and the war his grandfather had feared was beginning. Besides, he needed to check on Anna. She hadn't been feeling well the past few mornings and could not keep down the food she ate. He did not know why. He wished he understood women better.

The postman left letters on a table in the boardinghouse foyer for the residents to sort out for themselves.

She felt a stirring within her as she descended the five flights of stairs and saw the envelope Antonio had sent away several months before sitting on the table. At first she couldn't understand the words stamped on it: LETTER REFUSED.

Then she realized. Pietro must have seen the return address and handed the letter back to *il postino,* rejecting it as he had his son.

She did not carry it back up the stairs. Instead, she asked the housemistress for an envelope and piece of paper. She stuffed the first letter inside. Carefully she addressed it to Father Infante at Saint Paolo's Church and enclosed a note asking him to give it personally to Maria Gallini.

Quickly, while her Antonio was still at work, she walked to the post office and paid the twelve cents to the man behind the window. She used the pennies she had saved from the laundry and sewing work she did for the housemistress and other boarders. She added a silent prayer to go with the letter. She wanted to hurry back. Antonio did not like her being out at all, now that he knew she was carrying their child.

When she turned to leave the building, the pain hit her, and she collapsed to the floor.

"Mr. Galen, your wife is very sick. I'm afraid the baby came too soon."

He stammered the question he wanted to scream out: "My wife, Anna, will she . . . ?"

"No, she'll be all right. She's a strong woman."

A little while later he walked out of the charity hospital that cared for the poor and the immigrants of the city.

God is punishing us. We should not have gone to City Hall for a marriage license. We should have gotten a priest's blessing—and I should have made things right with Papa.

Why hasn't Mama written?

She sat in the rocking chair on loan from the housemistress. It now had been several months since she had lost the baby. She continued to sew for the lady, and for other boarders who had helped out when she returned home from the hospital. She heard the knock on their door, and then the mistress called out:

"Anna, it's me, Mrs. Flaherty. I have a letter for ye."

Her heart jumped.

"Come in, *Signora* Flaherty, come in."

"Looks important. Got foreign stamps on it, like what my late husband Sean would send me when he went back to Ireland for The Cause. He never returned. Aye, but I've told ye that before, haven't I? Ah me, that man."

Tears filled the woman's eyes, but she shrugged, the universal language of women, and wiped them away.

"Maybe it's from yer folks back home?"

She leaned forward to peek at the envelope as she handed it to Anna, who smiled as she took it and saw the name on the upper left corner: Maria Gallini. She opened it quickly and the older lady held her breath as Anna read to herself.

Dearest Anna,

It has been hard here. Your father and my Pietro joined the army four years ago. We have not heard from them. There is a strange sickness, some call it the Spanish flu, and some call it the Hun's Curse. Please tell Antonio that his grandfather Pasquale caught the sickness. He passed away very quickly. I am not well either. Father Infante is helping me with this.

Go with God, my child.

Another's handwriting was below.

Maria passed away shortly after this was written.
Pray for us all.
Giuseppe Infante

"Bad news, dear?"

"*Si, Signora.* Antonio's mother and grandfather have passed."

"Oh no! Not after all what's happened to ye both. I'll fix something special for when he comes home tonight."

"Thank you, *Signora*."

"Eh, do ye have the sewing ready yet?"

"*Si, Signora*."

The Armistice arrived and none too soon. America started drafting eighteen-year-olds less than two months before the war ended, and by then Antonio had come of age. Military service would have moved up his citizenship, but it would have left Anna alone. As it was, though, the foundry was considered an essential industry, and so he managed to avoid the war from which his grandfather had done so much to protect him.

They had moved nearer to his work after Mrs. Flaherty died from the flu that was now raging throughout their adopted country. So far he and Anna had been lucky. Maybe the fumes from the furnaces kept the devils away.

"It is our curse, Antonio."

His head lay against her chest, his left hand holding hers. Their fourth miscarriage. The loss seared his soul far more than any foundry furnace. Always the bitter taste when you had been so near.

The Roaring Twenties had brought them the hope of minor

prosperity. Anna's scrimping and seamstress work had added enough pennies to their little bit of savings that they had done what their American-born friends had advised them to do: They opened a savings account at the local bank.

Then October 1929 arrived, and their meager nest egg vanished when the bank failed.

Now, for the fourth time, she lay on the hard bed in the hospital charity ward run by an order of nuns. The sisters were thorough, but compassion was a scarce commodity, and she heard them whispering about God's punishment for living in sin.

"Antonio, I spoke with the priest. He is willing to do the Wedding Mass for us. Please, do this for me."

His heart had toughened from the hard times and endless workdays. Fortunately, the foundry had stayed open during the years of the Great Depression, and he had risen to senior foundryman. His identification, stamped into each of the tools he made, was Number 3. He was one of the lucky ones, because he had a job—though the work was killing him, slowly sucking the very air out of his lungs.

He wanted to pound the walls. He wanted to shout at her, even while she lay there under time-yellowed hospital sheets. His mind screamed as he shook his head. How could his wife still believe in the goodness of God? What kind of God would take children—four angels—from a father and mother?

He buried his face in Anna's chest. He could not let her see the tears.

Then he felt the touch of her calloused hands on the roughness of his furnace-burnt face, and his bitterness dissolved. He could refuse her nothing.

"*Si*, if it is your wish, *cara mia*."

Once more the drums of war resonated across Europe.

A voice on the radio announced the news from the Old World that Hitler had annexed the Sudetenland. Austria fell to the charismatic beast without a shot. Soon the world would learn the meaning of the word *Blitzkrieg.*

She could hardly believe it, but she felt it again, that familiar stirring. She went to the free clinic run by Dr. Agnelli.

"Yes, Anna, you are right, but you are thirty-nine years old. We must watch you very carefully."

She nodded, dressed, and walked out of the clinic.

A newsboy in knickers shouted, "Peace in our time, Chamberlain says. Peace in our time!"

"Big breaths, *Signora* Galen. Steady, steady. Nurse, low forceps. Ah, good, the baby's verted."

He spoke the magic doctor words to the nurse. The baby had shifted position inside the womb. It would enter the world headfirst.

"Anna, I need one big breath and push—PUSH!"

He didn't need the forceps. The baby's head was presenting, now the left shoulder, then the right shoulder. He eased the newborn from the womb and the nurse quickly clamped the umbilical cord in two places and cut it.

This one didn't need to be whacked on the bottom to breathe. The red-faced baby boy let out a tremendous howl, and the nurse and doctor laughed.

"Anna, you have a beautiful big baby boy, and from the sound of him he's going to be quite a talker. Nurse, call the father in to the side room."

Antonio had heard the cry, not in his ears, but in his mind and heart. He knew!

He had beaten the nurse to the door, and she was startled to see him already standing there waiting.

"Come in, Mr. Galen. Dr. Agnelli is with your wife . . . and your new son!"

When he was let in to the birthing room, he stood for a moment looking at his wife lying there, weary.

"Antonio, we will call him Roberto, after my father, and Antonio, after you. Here is your son. Roberto Antonio Galen."

With his fire-scarred hands he held the son he had always wanted. He whispered gently:

"You will be strong and smart, *figlio mio,* and I will teach you to be tough against the world."

Their eyes met and father and son bonded.

• • •

Now fifteen, Berto Galen had come to understand he could realize his dreams only through his own hard work. His father had instilled in him the need to drive himself to be the best, and consequently he had made only one friend in high school—and even that one purely by chance.

The school's public-address system vibrated and hummed, as the afternoon announcements began.

"The following after-school activities will be offered this year ..."

Saved by the PA!

He started to sink back into boredom, as he listened to the familiar list of athletic and social activity clubs.

Then he heard it:

"The Radio Club will have its first meeting today in room 215 at 3 p.m."

Something different! Give it a try, at least once.

The 2:50 bell rang.

He grabbed his book bag and headed for the west staircase, the nearest to 215, which as an upper classman he was permitted to use.

He lumbered down the hallway, watching his classmates putting the new freshmen through their ritual hazing: coats reversed, walking backwards, books balanced on heads, and worse—all to welcome the little brothers and sisters to the school.

No one had attempted anything like that with him the previous year. His stony stare had seemed to intimidate even the older kids.

He pushed open the fire door and started up the steps when he saw Thornton about to slam a smaller kid against the wall.

His classmate, Greg Thornton, wasn't the brightest bulb in the pack, but he was the meanest. Freshman Hazing Day was like a high holy day for him. The unofficial rules didn't permit physical abuse, but that never stopped him.

"Cut it out, Thornton!" he shouted, surprising even himself.

"Back off, lard face! I was just explaining to this lowly frosh why this stairway is off-limits."

Thornton raised his arm to strike the younger boy, who was trying to protect himself with his book bag, but then Thornton felt such a tight grip on his arm that he couldn't move. The pain intensified and he fell to his knees.

"For future reference, Greg, leave the freshmen alone. Oh, and by the way, did you know that lard used to be the major ingredient in soap? It's very useful for cleaning up bad situations."

Thornton felt the pressure release on his arm, and he was able to stand again. He glanced at his classmate, glowered at the younger boy, and then walked away.

Galen examined the scrawny youngster, with his crew cut, somewhat cross-eyed look, resembling a deformed, de-furred rabbit.

"What's your name, little brother?"

"Robert Edison," the boy replied, then like a machine gun rattled off, "And I know who you are. You're George Orwell!"

Dear God, he thought, *not another jokester.*

"Okay, I'll take the bait. Why is my name George Orwell?"

"Because you're my big brother! Get it?"

Maybe he should call Thornton back and let him torture the kid, but in a silly way it was funny.

"Okay, I asked for it. Where are you headed?"

"Radio Club meeting and we'd better hurry."

The boy was a quick thinker to assume Galen was going there, too.

"Lead on, Edison."

"Uh, George, what's your real name?"

"Galen, Robert Galen."

They had begun calling each other by their last names, because it became too confusing for both to use Bob.

Appropriately enough, Edison was a whiz at electronics, albeit a bit spastic in his movements. They had agreed they would try for their amateur radio licenses together, so they quizzed each other on theory and practiced Morse code by speaking out the dashes and dots in what sounded like demented baby talk.

They each took their licensing exams and easily passed. They became hams, able to use communications equipment, to understand its theory, and to be able to build and repair it.

Both felt immensely proud, although unlike most of the teenagers of the day, they couched their enthusiasm in subdued tones to conceal the emotion.

"Good job, Edison."

"Likewise, Galen."

Their shared interest made high school much more tolerable. Each knew he was a misfit, not the outgoing sociable type, but each had special knowledge and abilities the kings and queens of the prom lacked.

. . .

It is said that time is a turtle when you wish it to race and a rabbit when you wish it would dawdle. In some ways school couldn't finish fast enough for Galen, and in other ways he never wanted it to end. Soon graduation approached. He had grown to love electronics, but he held tightly to an even greater love. When he wasn't tinkering with Edison or hanging around Dr. Agnelli in his free time, he would visit the town clinics and ask to follow the doctors on their rounds. He knew deep down that being a doctor was a siren call to him. The name *Dottore* Berto still echoed in his mind.

He had won scholarships to attend university, so his father's troublesome question about affording it all had been partly answered, at least for this first big step.

He even expected his father to share his happiness about being able to go to university, but the closer he came to leaving home the quieter his father became, and his mother had no answer when his father summarily rejected all conversation. Then, as graduation day approached, he realized this might be the end of spending time with his only friend.

He knew Edison could take care of himself now. The scared rabbit was gone. The young man had gained the confidence and strength of knowing he could do something really well: electronics.

They promised to stay in touch, a promise they both fully intended to keep.

• • •

A little more than three years later, a much-anticipated letter reached Galen.

He had breezed through his studies, so he could always find time for extra lab work and experimentation. As an undergraduate he had published eight papers, and more kept filtering through his mind, but that all-important letter had dominated his consciousness ever since senior year had begun.

Galen hesitated to open it for fear of what it might not say. Boyle, his roommate, watched him clutching the envelope, not moving, almost not breathing, so he snuck up from behind, snatched the envelope away, but after a second thought and a sheepish grin, he handed it back to the man with those powerful arms.

Boyle had gotten along fine with Galen most of the time, but he had heard what The Bear—as Galen also was known—could do when provoked, and he was not about to tempt fate, not after what Trish had told his girlfriend Mary about her date with the big guy.

Come on, Freiling, finish up. You're not saying anything new.

Galen sat bored witless listening to his physiology professor drone on, repeating the obvious in less-than-understandable terms.

"And so, ladies and gentlemen, just remember that beneath the surface we are what our distant ancestors were. Or, to use a catchy phrase, Ontology recapitulates Phylogeny."

Score another dried-up conundrum for the prune face! Come on! I've got a lot to do before seeing Trish tonight.

"We think ourselves superior to the lower animals, and yet, when we are threatened, we revert. We become that lower order of animal whose prime motivation is survival. Then that wonderful powerhouse, the autonomic nervous system, kicks in and floods the body with stimulants, even rage-producing hormones and other chemicals that precipitate the possible alternative reactions of fight or flight."

. . . or fucking!

"Just remember that when you think you are the rational beings the philosophers say you are. When you are cornered, you are nothing more than a reptile. Have a nice weekend, and don't forget your fifty-page paper is due Monday."

Okay, that's more like it. I finished your stupid paper last week, so no sweat.

He stopped by the dorm, glanced at what he did have to finish, and decided Saturday would be soon enough. Meanwhile, a quick shower and change then off to pick up Trish at her room. What a sharp girl—decent-looking and smart, kind of fun to talk with. He checked his finances. Enough put aside from tutoring the freshmen having difficulty with organic chem to have a nice meal at the Alpine in town then maybe a stroll around the park before the movies.

Let her pick what she wants to see. It can't hurt to build some brownie points for later.

He was feeling good as he did his shave-and-a-haircut-two-bits knock on her dorm door. He could hear giggling on the other side. The female guardian of coed virtue, who looked like Freiling's twin and stared at him as if he were vermin, had to relent on her special Power of No to any boy attempting to trespass the girls' dorm. This was Friday night.

She was standing in the hallway, a few of her dorm mates nearby. He stared at her: saddle shoes, solid-gray poodle skirt, and light-pink sweater that accentuated her, uh, front-to-back dimensions. Her light-brown ponytail topped a strawberry-freckled face.

Oh yes, he was feeling good tonight!

"How's the Alpine sound to you, Trish?"

As he had hoped, it sounded great—burgers, cherry Coke, and something new to the college town: pizza. Not the real stuff like the nanas in the old country would make, but none of his classmates would know the difference.

Satisfied, they headed out for a quick walk around the park, then the Hitchcock movie down the street, then . . . *who knows?*

The old streetlights cast multiple shadows as the couple rounded the monument to Oliver Wendell Holmes. They were about to do the return half-circle when two of the shadows separated from the darkness and stood blocking their way.

"Looka what we got here, a broad and a pig! Maybe we oughta make pork chops and save the broad for dessert!"

The bigger one laughed, his eyes staying focused on Galen and Trish, his hand wrapped around a snub-nose .38.

The shorter one started to laugh as well. "Let's see how much pork the pig has!"

He held a metal pipe and started to wave it around in front of the couple, who stood there staring in shocked silence.

Galen felt strange, almost as if he were standing to the side watching what was happening to him. He felt a flush beginning to burn in his face and a fine trembling in his entire body, as the short mugger kept waving the pipe closer and closer. He suddenly recalled the part of his physiology paper on the flight/fight syndrome:

When you are fighting for your life there is a weird transformation into the limbic-brained beast that resides within all of us. You function ("you" meaning a person, not you specifically) on two levels, almost standing outside of yourself as you descend into the darkness within. You feel the other person's life. The rational ghost denies the truth of the outcome while the limbic beast howls both rage and conquest. Then you physically collapse. The difference between that action and the premeditated action of a trained killer is the overwhelming chemical surge as the sympathetic nervous system floods you with all the rage-producing chemicals it can. Then you lash out at those who seek to kill you and return the favor.

The surge that erupted within him could not be controlled. His left hand shot out, grabbed the shorter man's wrist in an iron grip, and swung the pipe down across the hand of the gunman. His ghost image felt the bones break and heard the agonized scream, as the pipe clattered to the street.

His right arm moved forward, his hand grasping the shorter man's neck and tightening, until he could feel the cartilage start to give way.

The larger mugger picked up the pipe and started to swing it. Galen dropped the other man, blocked the pipe wielder's arm, and twisted it until an audible crack sounded. Again the man let out a guttural scream. Galen started to reach for the screamer's neck.

"Stop, for God's sake stop! You're killing them!"

He suddenly froze at her words. God, it was real! He was living the prophetic words of his own paper!

He leaned against the lamppost, staring down at the two men writhing in pain on the grass-bordered walk.

Then he turned to her and saw her staring at him—not in relieved gratitude but in fear and horror. He saw it in her eyes: To her, he was the beast incarnate, someone capable of killing, even though he probably had saved her life, or at least her honor.

"I'm going home," she said softly then turned and walked away.

"Come on, Galen, fish or cut bait. It's not going to change if you keep staring at it. Let me open it for you. If it's not good, I'll put it down and leave you alone for awhile, okay?"

Galen took a deep breath and handed the envelope over then sat down on the edge of his bed.

Boyle carefully opened the letter, glanced over it, looked up mournfully at his roommate, put the letter on his desk, opened the door, and took a half-step into the hall.

Galen's heart fell, just before Boyle broke into a big grin.

"You got in, you big ape!" he yelled, taking off as fast as he could down the hallway before Galen could grab him.

He went to the desk and picked up the heavy-linen paper with the gold-embossed seal at the top.

Dear Mr. Galen:

It is with great pleasure that we notify you of your acceptance to the Class of 1965 of the university's Medical School. Your exemplary academic record and test scores indicate the potential for a great career in your chosen future field of medicine.

We welcome you. Please submit the enclosed matriculation forms as soon as possible. You have also been granted scholarship status. You will report for introductory orientation session next August 1.

It was signed by the dean.

He ran outside and stood in the middle of the quad, arms outstretched, eyes turned up to heaven.

"I made it!" he shouted, to everyone and no one.

He felt on top of the world as he walked the main corridor of the science building where he had spent most of the last three years. As he passed by one of the labs, he heard his name being called.

"Mr. Galen, may I see you for a moment?"

It was Professor Freiling. Galen had gotten the only A ever granted by the shriveled old man. It must have royally pissed him off, but Freiling couldn't have done anything else. Galen's papers and exams were perfect, and he had even caught a mistake in one of the solutions the professor himself had explicated.

"Yes, Dr. Freiling?"

"Mr. Galen, I hear by the grapevine that you've been accepted to medical school. Is that so?"

"Yes, sir."

"Mr. Galen, I know that you are brilliant, but to be honest, you don't have the personality to be a good doctor. I wouldn't want to be under your care."

Galen knew he was being baited. It was Freiling's style, a last-resort attempt to gain the upper hand.

"Yes, sir, thank you for your confidence in me. Is there anything else?"

Freiling shook his head, frowned, and walked away.

Galen felt as though he had just been shot down by the Red Baron.

He knew Freiling was a bitter man, but even so, he had done well in his class and had hoped that would be all that mattered.

He walked to the pay phone halfway down the hallway and called his parents. It had only been two years ago that they had finally installed a telephone.

He whirled the dial wheel once, and when he heard the operator he gave her the number. A moment later his mother's quiet voice said, "Hello?"

"Mama, it's Berto. Tell Papa when he comes home I got accepted to medical school!"

The phone was quiet for a few seconds, then his mother responded, still strangely subdued.

"Si, Berto, I will tell him. This is wonderful news."

He hung up the phone. He had expected her to be as happy as he was, but he sensed the reserve in her voice. What was wrong?

It was true he and Papa hadn't seen eye to eye on a number of things since he had started college. His father still dealt with him in the old way, never acknowledging his growth as a person or his reaching adulthood. He understood the cultural imperative of the old country, deference to parental authority being the highest level of respect a child could demonstrate.

Yet he had grown tired of the petty arguments over everything, the endless fault-finding and criticism. It seemed as though his father was trying to drive him away.

He would call later when his father had come home from work.

He walked slowly across the campus and sat down on one of the benches outside the main library, which had served as his sanctuary.

"Mr. Galen, are you all right?"

He looked up and saw his favorite professor, Dr. Basily, chairman of the anthropology department and curator of the school museum. His back ramrod straight—the result of a war wound from Korea—

he was never too busy to talk over class points or just about anything else.

Galen wished he could talk to his father the way he did with Basily.

"I just got accepted to medical school, Dr. Basily."

"And this is what gives you the long face? Spill it, Galen."

He told the older man about his encounter with Dr. Freiling and the strangely unenthusiastic response from his mother.

"That old fart Freiling isn't happy unless he's making someone else miserable. Listen, Galen, let me give you some advice that took me twenty years to learn. In your life you will meet two types of people of whom you should be very wary: dream eaters and soul stealers.

"Freiling is a dream eater. He will tell you that what you strive for is not for you, and that you don't have the ability so you shouldn't even try. Dream eaters can be teachers, friends, counselors, or even family. These people, like Freiling, are emotional vampires, manipulators, control freaks. Later, when you become the fine doctor that I know you will be, you will run into the soul stealers. These will be your colleagues, your bosses, collateral individuals who will try to sabotage what you do. They also are emotional vampires who live off your misery. Unfortunately, your worst enemies will be yourself and those closest to you—your family. This is when your guard should be at its highest, and you should resist with all your might."

Basily reached over and ruffled the hair on Galen's head.

"C'mon, let's go to the student union. I'll buy you a soda to celebrate the good news."

"Dr. Basily, would you mind if I asked you a personal question?"

"Shoot."

"Your back must hurt quite a bit. Can anything be done for it?"

"Mr. Galen, it hurts like a sonofabitch. And no, I've been told it's as good as it will ever get. That reminds me of a third point I need to share with you."

"What's that, sir?"

"Shit happens no matter what you do and no matter how hard you try to prevent it."

Galen smiled, the muscles of his own shoulders visibly relaxing—for a short time, anyway.

"Antonio, we have to tell him."

"*Cara mia,* it is not his right to know. It is his duty to obey. I will tell him when he comes home. He will not go away until it is over. He must respect our wishes. That is the way it must be."

• • •

On the day of his graduation, as had been the case in high school, Galen was alone—without family—a disappointment that dampened what could have been a wonderful moment for him. He had achieved *summa cum laude,* and his life was spread out before him, a full plate of promise and opportunity. Dr. Agnelli had invited him to help out at his clinic over the summer, taking Galen under his wing once more. Except now that he had been accepted into medical school, Agnelli treated him as one of the brotherhood and talked frankly about the life Galen would face.

"I'm not sure you know what you've signed on for, Berto. If you're foolish, like me, you'll let it take over your entire life, even to the point of neglecting your wife and children—if you're lucky enough to have any."

He looked at the tired old doctor he had known all of his life—the doctor who had delivered him. Galen felt comfortable talking with him, just as he had with Professor Basily.

"*Dottore,* you know me better than anyone except my parents. You know how much I love what you do, what you represent. I just don't know how to get my father to understand that."

"What's the matter, Berto? Isn't your father proud of you and what you've accomplished?"

"I think he is, but he never says so anymore, and now he wants me to put off going away to school. He won't tell me why. He just says it is my duty to obey his wishes.

"*Dottore,* I'm twenty years old and my father doesn't treat me as an adult with thoughts and goals of my own. I've worked so hard to get to this point in my life. I thought that's what he wanted, what he expected of me. And now . . . "

Agnelli just shook his head. This did not sound like the Antonio he knew. There had to be something wrong. He looked at Galen and gave him the only advice he could.

"Berto, whatever your father says, follow your dreams."

"Anna, I must do it. He must not go, not now."

He looked at his wife, the scars and wrinkles of age and economic hardship dissolving as he remembered the sweetly singing girl he had fallen instantly in love with so many years ago. They had been young, so young back then, with dreams of conquering the world, but as with everyone else the world had fought back and taken its toll. Now he was dying. The foundry soot and flames had given conception to their devil spawn, the thing that grew within his lungs and liver.

Antonio Galen knew he was being eaten from inside, that soon his beloved Anna would be alone. The boy had to stay, at least until after.

She started to ask again: *Why not tell him?* But then she remembered her own father and the men of the village where they were born. It was a loss of face to show weakness, to admit it even to one's children and sometimes even to one's wife.

She knew her husband, and she knew her son. They were so alike. She feared the outcome of the impending contest of wills. The very thought of it worsened the chest tightness she had told no one about.

The women of her village were not so different from the men: They kept their vulnerabilities to themselves.

His bags were packed. It was his last day at home.

"I have to go, Papa."

"A son must respect his father's wishes."

"Papa, you're not listening to me!"

Then he did something he had never done before. He was a man now, stocky, muscular, and full of the electricity of his prime. He reached out and touched the now-shorter, gray-haired man. He meant it as an entreaty, a way of breaking through the wall between them.

For the first time, his father turned and faced him, man to man. The old man's fire-darkened eyes stared at his son for a moment that would haunt the young man forever. He saw his father's jaw muscles tighten and his facial expression harden as he spoke to him for the last time.

"Non ho figlio!"

As Antonio Gallini uttered those words, Pietro Gallini's ghostly laughter echoed in his mind.

CHAPTER 2

Chrysalis

"She's really going to the prom with you!" Edison spoke to himself as he looked in the mirror.

He still couldn't quite believe it—he'd actually asked her to the senior prom and she had accepted. What would Galen have thought?

Galen.

Because of him, Edison had been able to finish high school without too many bruises. For one thing, the rabbity kid had developed the small-animal instinct of running at the slightest hint of danger. For another, the calls of "Let's get Four Eyes" had become a distant memory ever since that chance meeting with Greg Thornton in the stairwell when, miracle of miracles, he'd found a protector and a friend in the schoolmate he had called Big Brother.

Galen was long gone, but the effects of their friendship lived on in the confidence Edison had gained about himself.

Still, he missed the big guy. They had made quite a team in radio club, and life had gone a lot smoother when they'd put their heads together on school projects. They had won the science fair two years in a row, and that last idea of theirs, a device to make people's hearts work better, had become a legend among the high school faculty.

• • •

"Mr. and Mrs. Edison, it's so nice to see you again this year. The boys have done some splendid work again with their project. I just hope the judges will be able to understand it!"

All of the exhibits at the East Coast Science Fair, which their son and his friend Robert Galen had entered, dazzled Ron and Gloria Edison. They shook the hand extended by Concepción High School's principal and nodded thanks.

"Ron, why don't you walk around and check out the competition, while I see how the boys are holding up."

"Sure. Just come get me if anything happens."

Gloria walked back to the boys' exhibit and Ron wandered down the aisles of displays representing the different age groups, from junior high on up. Some of the stuff was routine, but a lot of ingenuity showed as well.

He was proud of his boy, who could beat him hands down with anything mechanical or electrical. Bobby truly was his father's son. He smiled quietly to himself as he remembered how the boy had found that old cathedral-style Philco radio in the attic—the one he himself had rescued from the trash, fixed up, and given to Gloria as a wedding gift back in 1941—and actually restored it to working condition.

How much he had loved those old broadcasts.

"Okay, guys and gals, jivesters and beboppers, this is your old professor, Kay Kaiser, and his Kollege of Musical Knowledge. We're gonna play some special stuff for all our brave men and women in the armed forces overseas. Maestro, let's hear it!"

As Ron's mind drifted, he could hear the strains of "Don't Sit under the Apple Tree with Anyone Else but Me" pouring out of the radio's single speaker. And he could see himself getting up to turn the volume down then going back to sit next to his wife of one month.

• • •

"Honey, I got my notice. We ship out in two days."

Gloria looked at him, the lanky Michigan farm boy she'd fallen for at first sight at the enlisted men's dance, but she didn't say anything. Back then he hadn't known, hadn't seen in her eyes, the secret she carried.

"Will you write to me?"

He hadn't known, as he gazed at his rosy-cheeked Gloria, why the tears had begun to glisten. He had just pulled her to his chest and hugged her, long and tightly.

"Silly, you know I will," she replied.

Then she hugged him back—as though she couldn't let go.

• • •

"Ron, I think the judging is going to start soon."

He snapped out of his flashback and turned around to see her standing behind him.

"Okay, let's head on over."

Just then he noticed a man standing next to a young girl and her exhibit in the junior high school section. He knew that face!

"Wait a minute, Gloria, there's someone here I think I know, but I can't remember from where."

As he started to walk toward the man it hit him.

Ira. It's Ira!

Now he was standing on the deck of the troopship conveying its human cargo of soldiers to the War in Europe, headed toward Naples after Italy had fallen to the Allies.

He could feel the letter in his pocket that he had been carrying with him everywhere.

Dear Ron,

Congratulations, Daddy, you have a son!

I didn't want to tell you that last day. You would have tried to stay and we both know that wouldn't have been possible. Our little Bobby, Robert Aaron Edison, was born on September 18th. Now there are two of us you have to return to.

Be careful. The Red Cross lady said she would get this letter to you.

I love you!

Gloria

He had received it months later, just before he shipped out, but he had read it every day.

• • •

"All hands, commander on deck."

He stood at attention by his bunk.

"At ease, men. The Dewey is transferring a platoon of marines to our ship by special orders. Must be secret stuff for them to transfer troops from the Pacific. I know it's already crowded, but we'll have to double-bunk them. We're only two days from destination, so it won't be for long."

The commander turned and left.

He heard the other men complaining, but with sixteen brothers and sisters back home, it was nothing to him. Double-bunking was a luxury compared to that.

"Edison!"

"Yes sir?"

"Think you can do something about the air in here? You're a machinist's mate, ain't you?"

The chief knew the extra men on board would make it like an oven in the bunks.

He had the fan unit apart in no time. He pulled out the heavy-duty C wrench from the tool kit and began to work. Within minutes the fan was purring again. He hefted the wrench and began to clean off the grease. Beautiful workmanship, he thought, as he read the markings stamped on the handle: NEWARK FOUNDRY 3.

Now he had to endure the gauntlet of backslapping and hair rubbing from the happy men.

They all heard the heavy boots tromping down to their level. The door opened and a gravelly voice boomed out:

"Awright, you jarheads! Git yer gear stowed! The Navy is sharing its luxury accommodations with us, so no fights or crap like that. Anybody steps outta line, you gotta deal with me!"

Tired-looking marines poured into the compartment. One stopped by his bunk, a short, powerfully built, Levantine man, with eyes sunken in chronic sadness.

He stood up and held out his hand.

"Ron Edison, machinist's mate."

The guy looked at him.

"Seligman, Ira Seligman, corpsman. Thanks."

"So who's the foghorn?"

"That's our old man, Gunny Crowley. He's twenty-five if he's a day."

• • •

His mind continued to flip through those past scenes of men under wartime stress, occasionally coming back to the present as he pushed slowly through the crowd. Judges were all around the girl's display now, but the face he thought he'd recognized wasn't there, so he kept heading toward the boys' entry. Then he spotted his son off by himself staring across the room at the red-haired girl.

She's really cute. I just can't believe a girl, and a seventh grade girl at that, could do a project called "Avitaminosis A and Its Effects on Baby Mice." She must be smart. But she's too young for me. I'm sixteen! Uh-oh, Dad's coming over. I'd like to try and talk to her, but I'd better get back with Galen.

As Galen waited for his friend to return, his mind drifted, too.

I wish Papa and Mama could have come. But they probably wouldn't be comfortable here. Besides, Papa has to work.

"Ladies and gentlemen, the judges have made their decisions. Let's start with the younger folks first. For junior high school, best original idea and best in her category: Nancy Seligman."

Applause rang out from the crowd as the principal read each award category.

Edison grew nervous. Someone else won in their category, a kid from Virginia. He hadn't quite heard the name, but it sounded like Crowley.

"Now, the winner of the Grand Prize and the science scholarship. This one's a twofer, folks, in more ways than one. For the second year in a row, our winners are the team of Robert Edison and Robert Galen. Congratulations, boys!"

The project had come out just as they'd planned it, from the design of the circuitry to the demonstration of their device's ability to restart a frog's heart with a time-pulsed direct current. But neither one of them dared tell anyone how they had hatched the idea. Even now Edison had nightmares about it. What if they'd been wrong?

• • •

"Sweet Jesus!"

Edison's words rang out as they watched the '51 maroon Ford veering from one side of the quiet stretch of road to the other before finally ramming into the power pole. The hood sprang open and steam poured out of the ruptured radiator.

As they ran toward the car, Edison's first glimpse of the driver made him stop and spew up his lunch, but Galen kept going.

The guy, who looked old to them, maybe mid-thirties, wasn't going to have any more birthdays. His head stuck halfway out the broken windshield, his body impaled by the steering post.

Automatically, Edison started thinking about the idea of a collapsible steering column and maybe even some type of restraining belt to halt the body's forward momentum. Then the nausea hit again. What remaining bile he had in his stomach ended up on the pavement.

"Hurry up, Edison! There's another guy in here! We need to get him out in case the car goes up."

They both grabbed the passenger door and pulled. It moved slowly and Edison figured it probably yielded more to Galen's strength than his own. The passenger had been thrown forward but hadn't gone through the glass. And there was, of course, no post to skewer him.

Galen was muttering to himself.

"Dr. Agnelli said to always check the airway and neck first—then the mouth, chest movements, heart pulsation."

He was running his hands along the man's spine.

"Keep his head and neck still while I lift him out, Edison. We can put him on the grass."

Slowly, very carefully, they maneuvered the man onto the roadside grass. He was breathing slowly but steadily. Galen put his head against the man's chest and tried to listen.

He looked up at Edison then jumped back in surprise when the man's body started to arch and twitch then lay still. Galen put his head on the chest once more: no heartbeat. He remembered something Agnelli had told him about a way to restart a person's heart by shocking it and pounding on the chest.

"Edison, we need electricity!"

The big kid started hitting the injured man's chest.

Edison was almost tempted to laugh, whether out of astonishment or at the juxtaposition of his name and electricity, or both. Then his mind kicked into overdrive. They couldn't tap the power pole. The only electricity available was from the car battery. He ran to the open hood and saw that the battery had been jarred out of its holder. He yanked with all his strength and it came loose with the wires attached. It was heavy, but he managed to get it over to where Galen was still pounding away.

By then Edison had worked out the procedure.

"I'll hold one wire, you hold the other, and when I say 'go,' we touch the two wires to his chest. Ready? Go!"

The contact from the wires caused the body to convulse suddenly then fall still again.

Galen put his ear to the chest and smiled.

"It's beating!"

They stayed by the man, debating whether one of them should go for help when they saw a car coming up the normally deserted road. They ran toward it, waving their hands. The driver slowed then stopped as he saw what had happened. Edison went up to the car and quickly explained that the guy was still alive.

Twenty minutes later the police ambulance pulled up.

"Don't tell them, Edison," Galen whispered as the ambulance driver and his partner approached. "We'll probably get into trouble if they find out what we did."

"Won't they reward us?"

"That's not the way it works, Little Brother. No good deed goes unpunished."

• • •

Edison stared into the mirror. Taller now, still slender, zits still marking his maturing face, he knew himself better now and what he could do. Time, hormones, and the gym had done their job. He was no longer the scrawny runt he had been. The kid who had once hated PE found he had a natural talent for gymnastics, and he had grown to love it almost as much as he did electronics.

He was about to graduate. No more Mickey Mouse routines for him. Now, headed for Tech, he was finally going to be able to sink his teeth into electronics and radio.

He picked up and admired the little Crosley battery-powered set he had repaired.

"Boy, won't Betty be surprised when I give her this! Bet she'll like it better than some old corsage!"

"Edison, the transmitter is on the fritz again. Want to give it a try?"

The senior in charge of the university's FM radio station had spotted the geeky underclassman awhile back hanging around the broadcast studio, peering at the equipment with curious eyes. When he'd approached the kid, thinking he might have found another aspiring announcer, he was floored to learn he already had his Class A commercial radio license. Not even the technician from the company that maintained the equipment had achieved such an advanced certification.

From then on the transmitter was Edison's baby. He tuned it so well it had never sounded better—and he even did some subbing as an announcer when he set up the first remote broadcasts by the school station.

Edison felt like he was in heaven, but he was also aware that there was nothing eternal about it. He was amazed at how time was speeding by. Before he knew it, he had left undergrad studies for graduate school and his research thesis, then a doctoral dissertation.

His reputation was such that even before he earned his doctorate, various tech firms across the country were pitching job offers. The winner: Ma Bell.

"Edison, your dissertation can't be published."

"What's wrong with it, Dr. Baker? Isn't it good enough?"

Baker didn't respond.

"I can prove every point and substantiate everything. You assigned me the topic, for heaven's sake! Do the other members of the doctoral committee agree with you?"

Baker looked at the strangely intense young man, who suddenly made him feel old and tired of the game. The boy had achieved more in his short time at school than most of his colleagues had in a full career. His only drawback was not understanding how things worked in the real world. This kid should have been born in the Middle Ages, where he could have spent his whole life safely tucked away in some monastery scrawling his manuscripts hoping that someday they would be discovered by future generations.

He was too honest to survive the piranhas out there.

The professor rubbed his bald spot as he thought things through. What he said next probably would determine the boy's entire future.

"Mr. Edison, there's nothing wrong with your dissertation. You've made a persuasive case for a worldwide information and communications system that would link every person and every bit of data available for research. Your encryption programs and algorithms are the most elegant I have ever seen. The committee and I fully agree with your conclusions."

He paused and sighed.

"Don't worry about your degree. Your work has already guaranteed you that. I can, in all honesty, say that you have been the most brilliant student I have ever dealt with."

"What's wrong, then? Why can't it be published?"

Somewhere in Baker's memory the question triggered another time and another young man standing in front of a professor, incredulous at what he was hearing. *Was it that long ago?* He had once been such an altruist, wanting to help humanity with his work.

"Edison, I work here at the university as a full professor of electronics and communications. But I also do consulting work on the side.

With what they pay us here it's been necessary, but it's also an ego builder to know someone out there considers my opinions worthwhile.

"I consult for the government in certain areas, and because of that I am obligated to bring specific types of research to the attention of those involved in national security. Congress passed a law in 1951 called The Invention Secrecy Act that gives the government the right to suppress any invention or research considered dangerous to the national defense. Your paper falls into that category."

Edison laughed at the implication.

"All my paper does is describe a network of individualized communications and exchange of knowledge bases. The programs I've designed protect it from interference. There's nothing seditious in that, is there?"

Such a brilliant young man, Baker thought, *how could he be so naïve?* He looked at the sandy-haired, crew-cut, scarecrow-thin figure standing before him in worn khaki pants and polo shirt and tried one more time to get through.

"Edison, the whole power structure in this country is based on controlling the public's access to information. Can you imagine what would happen if every comment a national leader made could be double-checked for truth and then disseminated instantly countrywide without being filtered through the news media? How about instantaneous access to the stock market? What would happen if it became worldwide?"

"Maybe that would bring about a better world than we have now, Dr. Baker."

Edison scratched his nose and adjusted his glasses. He would have done anything to bring this conversation to a close. He had been raised to seek the truth, to test hypotheses and concepts against reality, but now he was being told that was wrong.

Dear God, an idealist!

Baker shook his head.

"Let me put it another way, Edison. Your government, your country, needs your abilities. There is a department called ARPA, the Advanced Research Projects Agency. The Pentagon runs it. The people there are very interested in your work. They want you to consult for them—part-time. I know you've already agreed to do research work at Bell Labs, but this won't interfere. The only catch is you cannot publish your dissertation and you cannot discuss it with anyone. Officially, your paper title and material will be classified and a replacement will be substituted."

"Dr. Baker, I've never heard of ARPA."

"Well, they've heard of you. That's all you need to know for now—that and the fact that I work for them. Are you interested? Tell me now."

Edison just stood there, not knowing what to say.

"I'll be honest, Edison. You really only have one option. If you don't accept, it will be as though you never attended this university. Everything you've done here will stay here. It won't be my doing, though. Neither one of us has a choice on this."

Edison still didn't speak. After a moment or two, he nodded his head yes then turned and walked out of the office.

Welcome to the real world, boy.

Edison walked aimlessly across the campus, head down, a frown on his face, his mind in turmoil. Until this moment, things had been so black-and-white simple. Something worked or it didn't. If it worked, you used it. If it didn't, you fixed it. The only complexities involved dealing with people. On that score, things had never been easy for him, no matter how hard he had tried to apply the laws of physics to human relationships.

Naïve as he was, he knew immediately that Professor Baker's offer was no offer—it was an ultimatum. As the professor had said, he had no choice. He had to accept. But he didn't have to like it. Besides, sometimes passivity had its own rewards.

Now if he could only get his personal life in order.

His studies took up so much time and his shyness was sometimes so overpowering that he had not had a steady girlfriend all through college. Yet he fantasized about starting a family. He wanted children he could love and teach. He wanted to see them grow and learn to love the things that fascinated him. He also wanted someone to share his feelings, someone to love and to be loved by. Even he knew that you could talk to a piece of equipment only so long before realizing it couldn't sympathize when things went wrong.

He had tried school mixers, clubs, athletic groups, and even cycling competitions. About the only thing he hadn't tried yet was the canoe club.

He had always liked water activities.

Maybe, just maybe, there might be someone there who . . .

He stopped himself.

Face it, Bob Edison, you're lonely.

CHAPTER 3

Butterfly

"Fat, fat, the booboo rat!" "Chubchins!" "Four-eyed fatty!"

They taunted her almost from the first day of school, but she could not understand why the other kids didn't like her. She always did her homework, eagerly answered questions from the teacher, and usually got perfect scores on her tests. She liked math and science, dressed plainly, and loved to debate different subjects. What was wrong with all that?

Why don't the boys like me? Oh, who cares what they think anyway! But why did those girls call me "fire engine?"

Then there were the old women dressed in widows' weeds watching her going into the candy store. She could hear their not-so-subtle whispers about the "Jew girl and her war bride mother." The first time she heard it she ran home crying, but her father held her in his arms, hugged her, and then laughed.

"Nancy, the next time you hear that stuff," he said, "just look right back at those old biddies and tell them your Jew daddy saved their asses from Hitler and Tojo, and then you go up to them and say, 'and my mama saved my daddy's ass.'"

She always giggled when Daddy said things like that. Mama sat in her chair and smiled.

School also had its glories. Every year, beginning at age ten, she would enter the science fair. And every year her project would make the finals—at first just the local school's contest, and then that magic year in seventh grade when she reached the East Coast Science Fair. Her project: The Effects of a Vitamin A-Deficient Diet on Baby Mice.

As usual, the other kids made fun of her at first, calling her the "rat lady," but after she won the regional competition they shut up.

Daddy and Mama accompanied her and helped set up her display, with photos of normal and vitamin A-deficient mice and her commentary. They watched from a distance as she answered all of the judges' questions. Each year many kids would enter projects actually made by their parents, and each year their entries would fall under the weight of the judges' interrogation.

Afterwards she walked around the other exhibits and was impressed by one in particular that involved electrical stimulation of heart muscle in frogs. Then she spied one of the two boys who had done the project.

Beanpole thin. Large Adam's apple. Funny-looking cross-eyed face. Still . . . he's kind of cute. I wonder what he sounds like when he talks.

She was considering whether to approach him when the public address system announced that the winners would soon be named.

Too bad! He might have been interesting, but he looks too old.

She was only thirteen.

"And the winner in the junior high school category: Miss Nancy Seligman!"

She heard her name as if from a distance. Before she knew it, her parents were hugging her and laughing, and a photographer from *Life* magazine wanted to take pictures of her and her project. How could she refuse?

But as in Cinderella, glory lasts only a short time—then the chimney must be swept. Winning science contests and getting all A's didn't cut it with her classmates. Her success gained her no new friends, and as for dates with boys, well . . .

She had watched the other girls going through The Change—losing their baby fat and gaining it in other places. She had seen the boys change, too, and how the boys noticed the girls changing. Through her reading, she had learned the biological reasons for what was happening, but she couldn't understand why even the sensible girls became simpering fools when good-looking guys passed by.

She had to admit, though, that she did appreciate it when she caught them looking at her tresses of golden-orange hair—except now they were even more afraid of her. The cheerleaders were all scatterbrains as far as she was concerned, but they never wanted for dance dates. They never held up the walls in the decorated gyms on prom night, and boys weren't afraid to talk to them. Why were boys always afraid of girls with an ounce of intelligence?

"Nancy Seligman."

"Yes, Miss Bradley?"

"Go to the board and write out the nutritional analysis that you worked on last night."

In so many ways, college was a blessed relief from the way high school had been, and junior high before that—she could display her intelligence freely now, and as she walked to the front of the classroom and began listing the breakdown percentages of the food problem she had been assigned, she began to feel a sense of pride and accomplishment in her studies she never had felt before. She was majoring in nutrition and dietetics, but she also was taking a business and finance course to help when she took over management of the nursing home her parents owned and operated.

"Nancy?"

"Yes, Mama?"

"Can you come home this weekend? We need you to work the desk. Sally called and said she won't be in. She said she is sick."

Her mother's voice still sounded gutturally German after all these years. There was iron behind her words, Nancy knew. She couldn't refuse.

"Yes, Mama."

More likely that little twit Sally has a big date lined up. She knows she'll be too hung over to work. Why do they always think I'll be there to fill in? I have a life, too. Weren't they ever young? What were they like at my age? They never talk about it. I can't even picture what they must have been like.

• • •

"Medic! Medic!"

"Hang on, fella, I'm coming!"

He half crawled and slid across the mud-covered ground, trying to avoid the blood and rain-filled craters. The damn Krauts had caught them in a crossfire. The only thing the men could do was to stay put or die—and a lot had died already.

O God of Abraham, why do you do this to us? Is this some big game to you?

He reached the fallen man. Jacoby! It was Jacoby! He bent over his dying friend and saw the wound. There was nothing he could do. Gently touching the man's face he rocked side to side like he used to do on *Shabbat*. He had no phylacteries, but it didn't matter. He began the Kaddish, the age-old recitation of praise to God in the presence of the dead, remembering the words the rabbi had drilled into his head. Then he closed his friend's eyes.

It was the first death of a friend he had experienced, there in the bloody sand of Omaha Beach—Naples had never been their destination, only a ruse to keep the big mission a secret—but it wouldn't be the last. He would see more of his buddies die, in the hedgerows of France, among the splintered trees of the Ardennes, at the crossing of the Rhine itself. And not just his own countrymen but their enemies as well, men who appeared to grow both younger and older the closer they got to Berlin. Hitler seemed to be sending babies and old men out to die in his desperate effort to stop the invaders and cling to power. Death, destruction, and despair surrounded them.

Ira could only have guessed it at the time, but he and Jacoby were part of the greatest battle ever fought. The men had hit the beaches less than an hour before, along the French coast at Normandy on the sixth of June, 1944. After an eternity of hours, and then days, then weeks, the German defenses slowly gave way as the Allies under the leadership of General Eisenhower pressed forward.

Begging for food by the local civilians increased as they entered Germany in their thrust toward Berlin. The people, ragged, worn out by *Der Führer's* psychotic quest for power, were desperate.

He heard the scratching and scrabbling outside his tent. He got up as silently as he could, and raised the flap. He saw her picking at the remnants of food on the ground where the men had cooked their evening chow. She was young, maybe in her teens. God help him, he realized, he was only twenty-two himself.

"Madchen, was ist ihr name?" Little one, what is your name?

"Ilse."

• • •

Nancy heard the other girls in the class snickering. She knew she looked tired and not at her best. She had stayed up a good portion of the night helping her parents with the elderly patients. She had come to hate the cloying decay of old age. Those poor people had outlived their time, their friends, and their families. Strapped into feeding chairs, they sat staring ahead into inevitable oblivion. The worst ones were confined to bed, thrown back into infant-like dependency on diapers and hand feeding and cleaning, unable to make sense or to talk at all.

Feeding tubes? Bladder catheters? Diapers? Restraints? I'd rather kill myself than wind up like that. I never want to grow old.

She hadn't put her hair up so it hung straight down. Its bright, shimmering color made the others envious, and they took every opportunity they could to insult her. College was turning out no better than high school. She had to escape.

Unbeknownst to her parents, she would be starting as a management trainee at a local bank as soon as graduation was over. She had even scouted out an apartment. She would be out of the house, out of the nursing home for good. She needed to leave the cocoon. She needed a life.

Ilse Seligman wasn't stupid. She knew her daughter was an intelligent young woman and needed her space. But her Ira was stubborn, pigheaded even. She laughed at the thought.

A Jew pigheaded?

That's why she loved him so much. His stubbornness had saved her that night when he stood up against the company commander to get permission to help the starving young girl he had found groveling in the dirt. And he had bucked the rules blocking military personnel from marrying civilians from a combatant country. Somehow, in some miraculous way, he had brought her back to the United States with him.

A war bride, they had called her, and a German war bride to boot!

A Jew marrying a German? Oh, yes, my little one, I know what it is like to be a stranger, an outsider.

He was a good man, her Ira, but he drove his daughter the way he had driven himself. So Ilse prayed that Nancy would find happiness, just as she had that long-ago day.

And then Ilse Seligman's heart leapt with joy. Her daughter stood before her, her face beaming. "Mama, I've met someone!"

"What's he like, girlfriend? C'mon, spill the beans! Is he the strong and silent type, or does he come on hot and heavy? Does he have a big bris stick?"

With that, her best friend Betty giggled, and then they both burst out laughing. But Nancy had little to say about her new boyfriend. Well, maybe "boyfriend" wasn't the right word just yet. "Canoeing partner" might be more appropriate, or even "attentive listener" when she played her violin.

He was kind of cute, in a pet-rabbit sort of way. But could she see herself with him? Golden-orange tresses or not, she knew she wasn't a looker—and at five feet two and one hundred mmmpph pounds? No, she wasn't tall and thin. She thought she might even weigh more than he did, and he was almost six feet.

What does he see in me? Am I wasting time with him? One nice thing about him is he's smart—though he's clueless about dealing with girls—but smart and kind and . . . oh, damn, maybe I am falling for him! Could I have a family with him?

More daydreaming would have to wait. Right now, she had a date to go canoeing.

CHAPTER 4

Sisyphus

"Bill, come on down for dinner. Your father and I are waiting."

He didn't want to go downstairs. All he would get was another recruiting pitch from his retired Marine father. *Be a man! Get tough! Show the world you've got balls, son.*

His father seemed to function on the premise that you had to be the meanest sonofabitch on the block or you would get chewed up.

How did Mom put up with it? For that matter, what could she possibly have seen in him to begin with?

He remembered his mother taking him to church every Sunday when he was little, when his father wasn't around much—too busy saving the world. So, his mother would pray for his father's safety in whatever part of the world he happened to be.

Once, Dad returned home, covered with ribbons, and right away picked him up. The boy had cried, because he hadn't recognized the big man with the rough-skinned face and shaved head. He remembered how Mom had taken him in her arms and tried to explain, but it had not helped. He was different. He didn't want to shoot people. He wanted to help them. And he continued to puzzle over his parents. To him, they were a real-life version of Beauty and the Beast, the gentleness of his mother always overwhelmed by the overbearing crudeness of his old man.

Maybe he was too sensitive. Maybe he really was the wimp his father considered him to be. But what in God's name created a man like his dad, retired Marine Gunnery Sergeant William Crowley?

• • •

Dearest Will,

You can add another stripe to your uniform. You're a Daddy now! Bill Junior looks just like you, right down to the bald spot in the middle of his head! He's going to be a great man, just like his father, I know it.

Will, I pray to God every day to keep you safe. Mom and Dad pass on their hopes for your speedy return. I know you can't tell us where you are or what you're doing. I just know that our love will keep us together.

I love you,

Helene

He was sitting reading the letter, just as he had each day for the past three years, when the captain approached him.

"Gunny."

"Yes, sir?"

"We're ready to take the camp at oh-six-hundred. Get your men together and perform a perimeter search. The Krauts are too quiet tonight. And see if you can find out what that godawful stench is."

"Yes, sir," he said, saluting.

The brass hadn't told him what was so special about this shithole piece of real estate, but it wasn't his job to think.

He approached the dozen dirt-covered soldiers—all that was left under his command—their eyes ranging, never settling in one place, hardened veterans like himself. They had seen it all, and he was proud of them. He would trust his life to any one of these men, and he knew each would do the same for him.

"Listen up, men. We need to do a standard border check—the whole bit. The Krauts can pull some real nasties, but we can do better."

Yes, they could do better. Each and every one of them could gut a foxhole full of Germans before they knew what hit them.

They spread out in pairs, creeping forward almost silently to avoid rousing the camp's guard dogs. Strange, the spotlights weren't scanning the empty ground outside the barbed-wire fencing. So far, so good.

"Holy Mother of God!"

It was Spurling. What the hell was happening? The men knew not to break silence! Holding back in the rear, he crouched down, expecting gunfire from the camp towers, an ambush from a nearby grove of trees—something, but there was nothing. Then he heard the others: Sanchez repeating over and over, *"Madre de Dios!"* Benning crying like a kid and the others moaning. What the hell could it be?

He moved out of concealment toward the men—all of them just standing, staring at a lumpy, silver-gray mound at least eight feet high and several yards wide. In the half moonlight, he could also see the outline of a small bulldozer next to the mound.

That stench! It was getting stronger as he moved closer. He wanted to vomit. He knew that smell, but never so strong, never so awful as this. Not even in the worst battle he had fought. It was death incarnate.

He suddenly realized what he was looking at: It was a mountain of bodies, corpses, maybe thousands, piled like cordwood, compressed into a freestanding mound by the bulldozer.

He stood there with his men, seeing but not really comprehending. He turned his head away. And then the sign over the camp gate caught his eye. He started to laugh. He couldn't stop. He fell to his knees and began to cry. The sign stared back at him in mocking silence.

ARBEIT MACH FREI

Work will free you.

• • •

Bill just couldn't deal with his father right now. He needed to get out of the house. So he slipped quietly down the stairs, trying to ignore the photos along the wall, of his father, his grandfather, even his great grandfather, all in uniform, staring at him in silent disapproval. He was nearing the door when his father yelled out.

"William Crowley, you get your ass in here now or you won't be able to sit on it for a week!"

Bill knew he meant it. He always kept that damned razor strop handy when he wanted to make a point. Will Crowley was a big man, a powerful man. His son, on the other hand, took after his mother in size as well as disposition. Compared to his father's swarthy, six-foot, one-hundred-ninety-pound frame of muscle, he was the proverbial ninety-eight-pound weakling at five feet six, one-fifty. Not a good match.

Head hanging, he walked slowly into the dining room, taking his place at the table. His father glared at him. His mother, trying to relieve the tension, announced, "Bill wanted to surprise you, Will. He's just been accepted at the university!"

"Well, why didn't you say so, son? Have you signed up for ROTC?"

"No, Dad, I'm going to register for a double major in divinity studies and biology."

His father started to spew out his usual cluster of coarse profanity. One of the few words Bill could make out in the torrent was "pansy."

"Please excuse me, Mother."

He got up from the table and quietly walked to the front door, opened it and left.

"Will, he's still a boy. He doesn't know what's out there yet."

"Ellie, how can I make him understand? He needs to be tough!"

"You had the dream again, didn't you? Have you told Billy about it?"

She put her arms around him as he shook his head as the tears came.

Bill climbed into his jalopy and drove into the countryside, just as he had so many times. And before that he had worn the tires off his bicycle doing the same thing.

It was getting dark as he motored along the country road. His mind, still knotted up by the ongoing conflict with his father, failed to notice the figure moving along the road's shoulder. He felt and then heard a strange bump. He pulled over and, in the remaining light, barely made out a body-sized shape lying on the pavement about a dozen yards back.

He raced over and saw a shabbily dressed man lying there, blood streaming from his nose and mouth. Maybe he had been drunk and stumbled into the path of Bill's car.

He crouched down and tried to pull the man to the side of the road when he felt the man's whole body suddenly shudder and then emit a long gasp of air from his mouth. Bill knew: The man was dead.

He ran back to the car and drove as fast as he could to the nearest pay phone, dialed the operator, and asked to be connected to the local police. He heard the desk sergeant answer then blurted out the location of an injured man on the road. He hung up before the officer could ask his name. He leaned against the wooden phone booth door and began sobbing uncontrollably.

He had killed someone.

. . .

"Bill, I'm so proud of you, a college graduate now, and going to medical school. I wish your father were here to see it."

"Thanks, Mom. I couldn't have done it without your help . . . and Dad's."

He half-swallowed those last two words. His father had died suddenly of a brain aneurysm a year back, but he still couldn't escape the double nightmare of his father's memory and the dead man on the road. His sleep would never be normal again, always haunted by the twin specters of disapproval and damnation.

"Mr. Crowley, may I speak with you?"

Professor Hardison, chairman of the Philosophy and Religion Studies department, had acted as a steady mentor for him these past four years. He could talk with him about anything—or almost anything, with the exception of that eternal black mark on his soul.

"Bill, I know it's been rough for you since your father died. But you've continued to produce remarkable work. The entire department would love to have you stay on in the graduate program and get your Doctor of Divinity here. If you are what we think, you might even become chairman one day!"

He couldn't bring himself to tell Hardison that he had received a similar offer from Dr. Blankenship, head of the biology department.

He also couldn't tell anyone that he had secretly been relieved when his father died. As he thought about it again, he felt the usual overwhelming guilt crushing him. How could God accept him as a purveyor of His word when he was patricidal in his heart and a murderer in reality?

"I'm honored that you hold me in such high regard, Dr. Hardison. And someday, I hope to live up to your expectations. But I've given considerable thought to this. I'd like to be a medical missionary someday, so I think medical school should be my next stop."

Hardison put his hand on Bill's shoulder, as Blankenship had done, and wished him well. Both men knew that Bill Crowley would become a fine doctor. But they also sensed a darkness hanging over him. And both prayed that the darkness would someday lift.

CHAPTER 5

Non Ho Figlio!

I have no son!

The sting of those words still haunted him three months later as Galen accompanied his medical school roommate to his parents' farm in Spout Springs, Virginia. Only a four-hour drive from Richmond, it might as well have been in another world. He had seen a farm only once before, and the quiet expanse of the tree-surrounded pastures seemed foreign to the city kid—agreeably foreign. He imagined the spaces filled with soot-scalded, decaying buildings and shuddered.

He sat with Dave and his father under a large maple tree. Both men, bean-pole thin—one with a craggy, lined face and arthritis-knobbed hands, the other still smooth-skinned and supple-limbed—chewed on grass-seed stalks and stared off into the distance, seeing things he could not fathom.

Twins, Galen thought, *not father and son.* He wondered what it would have been like if his own father and he could have just sat together like that, saying nothing. But that wasn't the cultural imperative in his home, and he envied his friend for having it.

When he first met Dave just a couple of months before, he had wondered what devils had driven him to leave the peacefulness of his country home and dive into the helter-skelter study of medicine.

If our roles were reversed, I would have stayed here, surrounded by the trees, the plants, the birds—even the insects!

Their early probing into each other's backgrounds hadn't unearthed the motivation behind Dave's career choice. His father and mother had come from pre-Revolutionary War pioneer stock. Both sides of the family had been farmers back in the old country, and they had become farmers here. The major difference was that here they enjoyed the fruits of their labor.

Earlier, inside the house, Dave had shown him the handmade furniture, some going as far back as his great-great grandfather, whose shaving kit Dave kept almost like a shrine on his small bedroom clothes chest. The hand-thrown pottery jugs and dishes his ancestors had made so carefully still bore the baked-in fingerprints of those long-dead men and women. The farm boy held them as gently as he would any relics of the saints.

Sitting under the tree and taking in the landscape, Galen tried desperately to think of something to say. As he noticed the cattle grazing, he found his opening.

"Those bulls look pretty fierce, Mr. Nash."

His roommate doubled over and burst out laughing. His father, barely containing himself, looked at Galen.

"Shee-it, boy, bulls ain't got teats!"

The city boy stared as father and son laughed uncontrollably, holding each other. He felt tears welling up but couldn't stop them. Then he felt the older man's arm around him and heard the words he so much wanted someone else to say:

"I'm sorry, son. I didn't mean to hurt you."

On the way back from the farm, Galen finally asked Dave why he had chosen a career in medicine. The answer surprised him, because it was the same reason that had driven him.

The farm boy talked of seeing for the first time the doctor who had ranged through the community's valleys in his beat-up ancient black Ford. He seemed like some 19th-century Methodist circuit rider, going from place to place checking the families and their children for everything from low-iodine-induced thyroid goiters, so common before iodized salt, to the dreaded childhood disease, polio.

Young David had watched as the doctor clucked like a mother hen at Big David's healing arm wound, sustained from an errant sharp scythe. He stared wide-eyed as the portly sawbones reached into his big black leather bag, filled with who knows what mysteries, and took out a small glass syringe. Carefully twisting on a stainless steel needle he had removed from a jar filled with red liquid, the doctor took another bottle, smaller and milky-colored, stuck the needle into its rubber stopper, and pulled up some of the liquid into the syringe.

His father became wide-eyed as well.

"Y'all really need ta do that, Doc?" his father asked in a shaky voice.

The gray-haired doctor looked his father right in the eye.

"Big Dave, you don't want to die like Rufus's pigs, the ones that got the tetanus, do you? What would Mary and little David do without you? Now, this stuff's called tetanus antitoxin and it's made from horse serum. You ain't sick with horses, are you?"

Before his father could reply, the doctor wiped his shoulder with some of the red liquid, stuck the needle into the skin, and pushed the plunger of the syringe until it was empty. The patient hadn't even had a chance to complain.

"And that," Dave said, "was when I knew I wanted to be a doctor."

A strange Mutt-and-Jeff relationship had developed between the city boy and the country boy.

Galen remembered the day they met, two days before medical school classes began. He had just settled into his assigned dorm room and started out for a walk around campus. Like a restless animal, he needed to stake out his territory.

He had stepped into the hallway and was headed toward the door when he heard the noise of suitcases being dropped. He turned and saw a scarecrow-tall kid, surrounded by luggage, getting ready to use the water fountain. Not a good idea, as he had found out earlier when he had turned the knob and just barely avoided damaging an eye from the powerful flow shooting up to the ceiling.

"Wouldn't do that if I were you," he called out.

"Who are you?" a soft, nasal Southern accent came back.

"I'm your guardian angel."

He approached the thin kid and held out his hand.

"I'm Bob Galen, room 103."

"David Allen Nash," came the reply, "and it looks like we're gonna be roommates."

It had become routine. Whenever they had that rare free day-and-a-half weekend, they would drive to Dave's farm. The country boy's clunker of a Volkswagen bug froze their butts in cold weather and cooked them in the heat, but it ate up the miles of highway between Richmond and Lynchburg like a magic carpet.

It was worth it to get away once in a while from the never-ending grind of pounding large amounts of facts into their heads. They spent their first two years as bookworms, poring over the dense small-print texts in their monastic cinderblock-walled room, so Dave's VW bug always seemed like a deluxe escape vehicle.

From the start they had sounded each other out, trying to comprehend the vast differences in their prior lives. They talked hour after hour about life, career goals, girls, family, girls, and girls, especially on the long drives to their country getaway.

When they arrived at the farm that November afternoon of freshman year, it was a Halloween day. The air was crisp and clean, and the leaves were turning kaleidoscopic from the effects of waning sunlight and dropping temperatures. The yearly cycle of death and resurrection had brought out the underlying russets, scarlets, and yellows hidden behind the now-dead chlorophyll-green cells, all part of nature's mystical fall magic show.

Mary, Dave's mother, was busy in the kitchen fixing piles of homegrown fresh food for "her boys," now including Galen. Big Dave was whittling a piece of tree limb, occasionally stopping to rub what he called "the rheumatism" from his hands in front of the antique cast-iron wood-burning stove.

"Ever meet a conjer lady, Bob?"

Uh-oh, Galen thought. *Roommate's got that glint in his eyes, the one that appears just before he tries to play a joke. Okay, I'll take the bait.*

"What the hell's a conjer lady?"

"Come on, we've got some time before Mom's ready with dinner. City Boy, you're in for a treat! You're gonna meet Aunt Hattie!"

Galen felt the tension of the unknown as he and Dave trudged down the dirt road about a mile and came upon a weather-beaten clapboard shack, no bigger than a one-car garage, with an aluminum stovepipe sticking out the side. A small outhouse sat about twenty feet away.

"Aunt Hattie is the local witch lady, Bob. All the women come to her for potions, herbs, and women's advice. She's really nobody's aunt and she's been here so long no one even remembers when she came or how old she is. Even Doc Stevens gives her her due. But whatever happens, whatever she says to you, don't treat it as a joke."

Dave knocked on the short, time-warped door. The voice from inside was high-pitched but strong.

"Come in, young David Allen. Bring yer friend in, too."

How did she do that? There are no windows on this shack.

He felt as Hansel and Gretel must have, but this decaying hovel wasn't made of gingerbread. They stooped down to enter the dark room lit only by a single kerosene lamp sitting on a small, handmade table and light seeping through cracks in the walls. Galen could make out various smells but couldn't place what they were. He saw sheaves of different plants, tied together, hanging from the low ceiling rafters. *Must be the herbs she uses,* he thought. Then he heard the raspy breathing and turned.

The old woman was ebony black. Spikes of white hair radiated from her scalp in a static electricity free-form sculpture. Her skin, drawn tight over swollen arthritic bones, glistened like black marble. Two eyes, catlike, shone above the surrounding room light. Yellow-white piano-key teeth stood at attention. She sat there in a makeshift rocker and seemed to be mumbling softly to herself.

Is that a corncob pipe on the table? I didn't think they were real, just something people wrote about in books!

"How yer folks, young David? Big David and Mary fit?"

"Yes, Aunt Hattie. This is my friend Bob, from school."

She eyed Galen, and he suddenly felt naked and exposed as she motioned him to draw closer to her.

"Come heah, chile. Let me git a good look at ye."

As he approached she took hold of both his hands and stared harder. In the closeness of the small room Galen felt chilled as she spoke, slowly, each word, each sentence a penetrating arrow.

"I bin waitin' fer ye, boy . . . Bone Man be comin' fer me soon . . . you 'n' him'll ha' some mighty fierce fights . . . you gon' win some, but you gon' get bit, too, speshully when you done try ta do gud."

She paused a little longer.

"Thas when it hurt da mos'."

Galen pulled his hands away taking an involuntary step backward as Dave stepped forward.

"Aunt Hattie, what about me? You told me I would be a doctor when I was just a little boy."

He looked at her as she turned toward him, her brow creased in sorrow.

"Bone Man ha' plans fer ye . . . Jes' remember, not e'en da Bone Man'll separate ye from yer friend."

Another sharp chill climbed up Galen's spine. He lived in a world of concrete reality and felt annoyed at both himself and the old lady for the irrational fear she had elicited in him. He turned impatiently to his friend.

"Come on, Dave, its getting late. I think your mom will have dinner ready by now."

He turned to leave when the wind sighed through the chinks in the ramshackle shanty—and he could swear he heard the woman say to him in a low voice:

"Yo' papa, boy. He wan' ye to fo'give him."

The telegram with his name on it was sticking in the door when they arrived back at the dorm that Sunday evening. It was the first of two he would get that year summoning him home to say a final good-bye to each of his parents.

• • •

Sophomore year was pathology year, and it was also the year when familiarity led to meeting and talking with the distaff side of the class. There were fewer girls than boys, but a number of his classmates were already married or spoken for, so the field had some grazing room.

Galen and Dave tried to be eclectic in using what spare time they had for dating, but it soon became apparent that Dave was smitten with Connie Matricardi. Connie had arrived from Florida after spending some post-college time teaching elementary school. That was fine with

Dave. As he put it, "A good farm boy is always willing to learn, so who better than a teacher?"

"City Boy, I seen you staring at that Ross girl. What's the mystery with her?"

Galen blushed. He didn't know the answer, but he knew he was fascinated by the girl from upper New York State, with her aquiline nose, lean face framed by auburn hair, and what his roommate—country boy that he was—called a racehorse figure. He wasn't sure how to approach her or even if he should try. He thought that, maybe, sitting next to her in the cafeteria would be a good opening gambit. Then it hit him.

Good lord, I'm acting like a high school kid. Is it that bad?

Just as Boyle had opened that acceptance letter for him, back in college, Dave solved this problem when he picked up the food tray that Galen had just loaded up and paid for and walked over to the girl still standing in line. The scarecrow loudly announced that the gentleman sitting over at the table wanted to buy her lunch. Galen was mortified as half the cafeteria turned to look at him. Then Dave, grinning from ear to ear, escorted her to his table.

"Ah, Bob, I think Connie is waiting for me over there. I'll just leave the two of you here."

He made a fast exit as Galen rose, not knowing whether to go strangle his roommate or pull out a chair for the girl standing there. He chose the latter.

"I'm sorry about that," he mumbled, "but I certainly would like you to enjoy that meal."

"By any chance is your name Miles Standish?"

Her long eyelashes flashed as they reflected the ceiling fluorescent lights. Her smile outshone them.

They both laughed as he looked at her directly and said, "No, but I know a certain guy role-playing John Alden who's going to get scalped when we get back to our room later."

They stared at each other both blushing like kids.

"Bob Galen."

"June Ross. Are you the one who keeps breaking the class grading curve?"

"I don't know. I don't pay any attention to that stuff. It's hard enough to keep cramming our brains without having to worry about class rank. But I bet you're no slouch with the grades, either. I've heard your presentations and they're darned good."

He hoped that hadn't come off too corny. He was starting to sound like Dave, his New Jersey accent now softened by the beginnings of a Virginia twang.

"As are yours."

She smiled at him and the lights became even dimmer.

Strange how things get started. If Dave hadn't pulled that stunt, he probably never would have gathered enough courage to approach June. And if that hadn't happened, Dave and he probably never would have moved out of the dorm into their own apartment.

At the end of their second year, the city boy and the country boy moved to a townhouse on Church Hill. It was in a poor, totally black area of the city and was all the two could afford. The money each earned by tutoring freshmen and doing scut work on the wards only went so far. Neither man had wealthy parents to pick up the tab.

June and Connie also had moved, but their finances were much better, so they had found a nice apartment in one of the old antebellum brownstones in the better section of town called The Fan. Boys being boys, the roommates spent time there as well.

Then the pair of girls became a trio, and June and Connie's other roommate, Peggy Dalton, had latched onto someone she kept calling Babyface.

"He's the sweetest thing you could evah imagine. He's a real S'uthern gentleman," she would repeat over and over in her North Carolina accent.

They knew immediately who she was talking about. It had to be Bill, Bill Crowley. Stocky, maybe five feet seven on a good day, he really was a gentleman. And with his rounded visage and hair that tended to either stick straight up or come out in a cowlick—a definite babyface.

"Hey," Dave asked one day, "if he's Babyface, then what do you call me and City Boy?"

The three girls giggled, looked at each other, and giggled again.

"Scarecrow and The Bear!" they shouted in unison.

June looked at the two guys, who blushed.

"And what do you gentlemen call us ladies?"

June arched her perfectly formed eyebrows and other parts of her anatomy at the roommates in catlike grace.

Galen looked at Dave. The farm boy knew what side of the nest he was on. Turnaround was fair play. They had to take up the defense, even though Bill wasn't there to join in. And knowing Bill, he probably wouldn't have said a word anyway.

Dave looked at Connie.

"I'll be darned if you ain't The Teacher. Sure enough, you are. And you," he said, looking at Peggy, "well, you gotta be The Southern Belle. Ain't that so?"

Galen had been holding back, but he finally looked at June. Without blinking, he said, "And you, dear lady, are The Model."

At that, both guys ran behind the couch to escape the onslaught they knew was coming. Except that they weren't very good at escaping—and they really didn't want to be.

• • •

It made life easier that third and all-important year for each to know that he or she had five other friends, with one even more special. Now they wore whites, with the guys in trousers and either long- or short-sleeve shirts depending on the rotation they were in, while the girls nicely filled out their skirts and blouses. It was only on surgical floors that the difference in the sexes became blurred, as they all wore the shapeless blue scrub pants and tops, their heads covered in hair-confining caps, their faces concealed by the ever-necessary masks.

Galen had just begun his first rotation, a six-week stint on general medicine. Here patients from the emergency room who had been admitted for further evaluation and treatment were assigned to the newly minted third-year students.

"Mr. Galen, you have a patient. Please do the initial workup and be prepared to present the case to Dr. Stottler."

The resident tossed him the admissions file, grinned, and walked away.

Whoa, hey, wait a minute! What the hell do I do now?

This was not like in the books and pictures. He saw the nurses watching him, so he kept a straight face. He picked up his little black bag, the one that all of the students had received their freshman year and had longed to carry for real.

He began reading the file.

Room 506. Patient's name is Johnny Mangold. What did the ER intern write?

"Twenty-year-old white male, history of metastatic bone cancer of the jaw, admitted for stabilization. Possible brain involvement now. Probable etiology: chewing snuff."

Dear Lord, twenty years old, younger than I am.

He walked into the semi-private room now occupied by one patient. The lights weren't bright and it was already 10 p.m.

Great, I'm supposed to work in the dark.

He moved to the window-side bed and started the spiel he and his classmates had practiced since day one.

"Hi, I'm Dr. Galen. May I sit and talk with you? We need to get a bit more information and take a quick look at things before letting you sleep."

God, what a damned liar he had become. For one thing, he wasn't a doctor yet. For another, it would probably take him at least an hour to do the student physical, which required every tiny bit of information and a full-body examination.

The biggest lie of all was the bit about sleep.

Yeah, right, with noises, footsteps, and all the other background sounds that made hospitals so inhospitable. Wake up and take this pill so you can sleep. Real restful!

He sat next to the bed. His patient was no more than a boy, but he was dying. They talked about his condition—the tumor found growing in the bone at the back of his nose and jaw. Galen went through all the memorized questions he had to ask and then said, "Johnny, I need to look at you. Is that okay?"

The boy smiled and Galen heard something from out in the hallway near the door.

He looked up to see some of the nurses seeming to stand around a medication cart but peering into the room. They quickly moved away when they saw him looking.

"Doc, hold on a second, I just need to remove this," Johnny said.

While Galen watched, the boy reached up to his face. Galen heard the snick-snick of latches as the boy removed the entire left side of his face and skull. It was a prosthetic, a synthetic replacement covering the surgically removed cancerous bone and tissue cut away in an attempt to save Johnny Mangold's life.

He stared at the boy, now half-human, half-skeleton.

"That's a very nice piece of prosthetic work, Johnny."

He couldn't think of anything else to say. He picked up his light and began to examine the boy. Exposed blood vessels pulsated in time with his heartbeats. From the corner of his eye, Galen saw the nurses furtively watching him again.

Now he understood.

Okay, ladies, did I pass your test?

He finished, thanked his patient for the time spent and began to put his equipment back in his bag. But something wasn't right. In the shadow-filled room he sensed a palpable darkness hanging over the boy's bed.

It was 3 a.m. by the time he had written up the extensive paperwork he had been warned Dr. Stottler would expect. He had heard through the grapevine that Stottler was a tough taskmaster. He dozed sitting up, his head propped on his medical textbook. Next thing he knew, his managing intern was shaking him.

"Come on, that kid in 506 is going sour!"

He awoke with a start. He had just been talking with Johnny. They ran down the corridor. The nurses had lined up the crash carts filled with medications to use in an emergency. The resident was already there, pounding on the boy's chest as the floor nurse attempted to increase oxygen flow through a nasal cannula in the remnant of the boy's face. Student and intern stood by, watching the final struggle.

The resident, two years post graduation, stopped, looked at the nurse, and shook his head.

"Time of death: oh-four-thirty," he called out, and the nurse recorded it on the chart.

CHAPTER 6

Bittersweet

"Annie, who do we have to baby-sit tonight?"

The emergency room floor nurse picked up the assignment sheet, which listed the fourth-year medical students rotating on ER service. She handed it to the nursing supervisor, who quickly scanned the names under the day's date.

"We got Babyface and The Bear. Should be okay."

"Yeah, compassion and competence, a good pairing."

"Hi, I'm Bill Crowley."

He held his hand out to the heavyset character leaning against the wall. The room was crowded with all his future classmates trying to introduce themselves to one another. This one was different.

"I'm Bob Galen."

Definitely not from the South by the sound of his voice. New York?

"Where you from, Bob?" The soft, lilting sway of a Virginia gentleman came through.

"I'm a carpetbagger, Bill. Just got in from New Jersey."

"Didn't we beat you guys at Appomattox?" He waited to see the Yankee's response.

"Sure, and Jeff Davis is president."

They took an instant liking to each other, and Bill thought he knew why. There was something melancholic about the big guy—something he could relate to—only he knew it couldn't be worse than his own burden.

"Damn, it's the Benadryl Lady again!"

"Who's that, Bob?" Crowley saw the frustration in his partner's face as the elderly African-American woman walked through the ER doors.

"She's a waste of time. You know the routine. She comes in complaining of being 'short of wind.' She's had every asthma and heart workup we've got—but there's nothing wrong with her. All she wants is a shot of Benadryl!"

"How about I take a crack at her?"

"Yeah, fine. There's a DOA coming in. I'll take that one while you go nuts with our frequent visitor."

As Galen skulked away, Crowley sat down next to the doll-sized figure sitting in the emergency room waiting area. She was dressed in a petite yellow housedress with a checkered apron-like front. Her hands kept twisting and untwisting a pale-pink cloth handkerchief.

"What's the trouble, ma'am?"

He reached over and held her mahogany-colored hands in his own pale white fingers. He could feel the arthritis and the tension in her.

"Can't breathe. Mah wind's short agin."

"Please tell me more." He studied her body language, the words not spoken.

"Ah was sittin' theah in mah livin' room an' it come on me."

"Was anyone with you?"

He felt her fingers tighten and her body begin to tremble.

"Mah son dun come in fra' work."

"Then what happened? Did he try to help you?"

"No, suh. He wer havin' de shakes."

Now it made sense.

"Ma'am, did your son have the shakes the last time you lost your wind?"

Her tension increased. "Yassuh."

"I think I can help you. Excuse me for a moment."

He got up and went to the nursing station.

"Annie, could we get Social Services down here? I think the Benadryl Lady's real problem is an alcoholic son."

"Yes, Dr. Crowley," she replied, watching him walk away.

Strange to find compassion in such a young man.

Dr. Crowley!

Not yet, he thought, but it sounded so good! And coming from a nurse with more experience than most of the doctors working the ER, it was a real compliment.

The night proceeded with the usual knife, gun, and club injuries, plus chest pains, earaches, and stomach cramps. Galen and Crowley worked well together, and soon the full waiting room was emptied.

"Let's take a quick break, Bill. That was a good call with the Benadryl Lady."

"Thanks. I think there's a coupla sodas in the fridge."

They sat in the back lounge, and Galen recounted his experience with the person who was brought in dead.

"You know, Bill, I remember getting that man as one of my admissions last year. He'd come in to the ER with chest pains, and they sent him up to rule out a heart problem. That, to me, was a dump job from someone here who didn't want to spend the time evaluating him.

"Anyway, here I am, it's 2 a.m., and I'm talking to this poor guy who's scared out of his mind that he's going to die. Seems every male member of his family died at age forty-five. He had just had his forty-fourth birthday and was starting to get chest pains even lying down. I did the million-dollar third-year student exam on him, and guess what? Nothing, absolutely nothing! The only positive bit of information I had was that damn family history—every male on his father's side gone at forty-five.

"So, Stottler walks in at 6:30 for rounds and I give him my workup. He tosses it on the table and we all follow him like a royal entourage to the guy's bed. Stottler stares at the guy, listens for about ten seconds with his scope then turns to us.

"Pompous jackass that he is—and you've suffered with him, too—he doesn't even bother to lead us out of the room. He stands there in front of this terrified guy and starts berating him for being a hysterical personality with conversion-reaction symptoms. In short, he was calling the guy a fake, a malingerer. He points at the resident and orders him to discharge the guy. When the resident starts to ask for at least a day for more testing, Stottler gives him that drop-dead stare of his, and the resident backs down. The guy goes home, and I felt so sorry for him it surprised me."

Bill looked at his friend and nodded. "There's still hope for you Northerners."

Galen laughed then caught himself and continued.

"Well, tonight they wheel in the Go-to-Jesus cart from the ambulance, I pull back the covers, and there's my man. His forty-fifth birthday was a month ago! Right now, I would love to have Stottler here. I'd shove his conceited mug right against that poor dead guy's face and ask him how hysteria and conversion reactions did that. If nothing else, I'm going to make sure Stottler is the star performer at pathology rounds when they do the postmortem on him. And I'm going to be damned sure to emphasize that family history."

The siren of an arriving ambulance dispelled the hope of any further rest as it pulled into the ER driveway. It could be anything from a heart attack or trauma injury on down, so they waited, feeling the usual tension build in anticipation of what would come next.

"Take it easy, guys. This one's easy," the ambulance driver said as he jockeyed the rescue cart through the doors, the patient covered from head to toe with a sheet—another Go-to-Jesus case. DOA. Dead on arrival. All they had to do was make sure the vital signs weren't there, sign the release papers, and send the corpse to the pathology department morgue.

"Whose turn is it to do the pronouncing?" the floor nurse asked.

Bill looked at Galen and reluctantly nodded.

"You did the last one. This one's mine."

"Dr. Galen, we've got a kid in sickbay 3."

"Call me if you need anything, Bill."

As Galen left, Crowley walked to the back holding area, where the dead were routinely wheeled to avoid upsetting the living. He unhooked the stethoscope from around his neck, reached down, and pulled the cover sheet back.

My God! My God!

The derelict stared back up at him, unseeing eyes open to eternity. Crowley fell to his knees and began to rock back and forth. His moaning got louder and louder until the crescendo ended in a wail.

"Come on, Bill."

Galen had his arms around the shaken Crowley. He gently shifted him over to a folding chair then turned to the cluster of ER personnel staring at them.

"It was someone he knew as a boy, someone who worked for his father."

He hoped that excuse was good enough. Quickly he signed the papers, handed them to the nearest nurse, and asked one of the attendants to take the body to the morgue.

"I'd better stay with him for a while. Can you get the intern to take my patient?"

The floor nurse nodded, and the crowd left them alone.

"Tell me what happened, Bill."

"I killed a man. I'm a murderer! God's punishing me!"

He was trying to curl up into a ball. Galen held his breath then said something he was not used to saying.

"Tell me about it. Let me help you."

The story poured out between gasps and muffled sobs. Galen finally understood the underlying sadness of his friend. He looked within himself and realized he had found the meaning of the word empathy.

"Dr. Galen, we got another one for you," the floor nurse whispered. "It's a little girl. Bad asthma. The family was just driving through on their way up north."

He heard a voice loudly calling for someone to help his granddaughter. It sounded familiar, but he couldn't place it, and he didn't have the time. The girl, about seven years old, was in *status asthmaticus*, the worst form of asthma, usually controllable only if you were lucky.

He set up the IV drips to hydrate her as the nurse put the moisturized oxygen mask on her face. She was gasping, fish-mouthed in a desperate attempt to breathe. Her face was pale, her eyes closed. She didn't even move when Galen inserted the large-bore needle into her tiny vein.

He tried the standard approach first: adrenalin in 0.5 milliliter doses subcutaneously. No luck—she still struggled to breathe.

Next, he started an IV drip of aminophylline. He hated that drug. Therapeutic dose and toxic dose rode side by side.

He felt for an arterial pulse, found it weak and thready, then jabbed the special needle into the artery and pulled back on the plunger, drawing her blood. When he had collected enough, he pulled out the needle, threw the sample into an ice bucket, and handed it to the nurse, who took off down the hall to the lab.

Five minutes later she returned with the numbers: still no change in arterial oxygen.

He was growing desperate.

"Nurse, would you get me an ampoule of IV Solu-Cortef?"

"Dr. Galen, only the attendings are allowed to use that!"

He looked at her, then at the girl who was still using all the chest-wall muscles she could just to breathe, then back at the nurse without saying a word.

She unlocked the special cabinet and handed the small container to him. She was going to stay and watch. It was a CYA maneuver on her part. She could always say he had forced her to do it, but she also had heard that The Bear often pulled rabbits out of his hat in critical medical situations.

What's he doing? She had never seen a contraption like the one he was assembling. He was hooking up another glass IV bottle with Ringer's lactate and injecting the whole vial of Solu-Cortef into it. Then he piggybacked the second bottle onto the first through a side fluid port in the plastic tube and opened up the flow. The girl was now getting both aminophylline and Solu-Cortef.

Young doctor and veteran nurse stood side by side, watching.

The trick, Galen knew, was to medicate without overloading her with fluids. She could die just as quickly from that as from her asthma. Children were not just small adults, and adult drugs often caused unexpected effects in them.

Galen kept his fingers crossed. He wished he had access to some of the experimental drugs that he knew were now only in early development—beta-agonists, the pharmacology boys called them. But he had to use what was available.

Slowly, the girl's chest wall stopped its heaving. Her neck and rib muscles no longer distorted her face and torso with tightening. She began breathing more easily. Even her face was pinking up.

Galen exhaled for the first time in what seemed like several minutes.

"She'll need to be admitted at least overnight for monitoring. Better let the on-call peds interns know they have a close one to watch."

The floor nurse left him with the little girl. He looked down at her. *Maybe someday you'll be famous, or you'll do something good for humanity. Or maybe best of all, you'll have a little girl of your own. Uh-oh, I'm getting maudlin!*

The gurney attendant arrived, followed by the pediatric admitting intern.

"Good job, Galen. We'll take her from here."

He started to walk to the nursing station. As he approached, he heard the nurse.

"She's out of the woods now. Would you like to talk with the doctor?"

As he pushed open the swinging door, the nurse spoke again.

"Oh, here he is now. Professor Freiling, this is the doctor who took care of your granddaughter. This is Dr. Galen."

CHAPTER 7

Crescendo

Galen sat alone at the desk. All of the detox unit patients had lined up and gotten their 11 p.m. medications. Now, he hoped, they were sound asleep and not causing any problems.

Just a few more nights and I'll be able to get that ring.

He smiled at the thought.

You're getting soft, old bear. Can girls really do this to guys?

He took out his notepad. Time for another letter to Dr. Basily. Actually, past time, he realized. Had things moved so quickly?

The last note he had written was to pass along the name of the Hospital for Special Surgery, the only facility in the country experimenting in new back-surgery techniques that might help his old professor. That had been in January. Now it was April. Strange, the man hadn't replied.

Well, here goes:

Dear Dr. Basily,

I hope things are going well with you. Have you looked into that new back procedure yet? So much has been happening since we last wrote. Graduation is coming up in less than a month and, oh yes, I'm buying a ring. Yeah, I told you about June. I think I'll wait until May to propose, just before graduation. Never thought I would do that, did you? Now, if I can only survive doing extra shifts and ward work to pay for it!

He paused, thinking of his lovely June. Hard to believe he was dating such an intelligent, good-looking, personable girl—or rather, that she was dating someone like him! He hoped she understood why he had been so busy lately. He hadn't told her about the ring, but he was sure she wouldn't be upset. She was so compassionate, so loving, so . . .

Okay, hotshot, focus on the letter!

People never cease to amaze me with what they say and do. Remember that first year when I told you about my trip down here?

His mind drifted back to that six-hour train trip from New Jersey. He was still smarting from the final argument with his father, so he didn't react much when the conductor walked through the coach car calling out in good humor, "Ladies and gentlemen, we've just crossed the Mason-Dixon Line. All you Yankees be on your best behavior, now, ya heah? Y'all now in the South!"

He had gotten off the train at the Broad Street Station of the Richmond, Fredericksburg, and Potomac Railroad, the old RF&P, and sought out a bus headed for the medical school. As he boarded, he saw a seat two-thirds of the way back and headed for it. Suddenly he heard this voice yelling at him from the front. It was the bus driver. And what was he saying?

"Boy, get yo' ass back up heah! Now you listen up, boy. Ah knows you ain't from aroun' heah. But you stand right theah behin' me."

What was going on? The whole bus was laughing at him! Then it hit him. The bus was an open Oreo cookie: front half white, back black! He knew about the various demonstrations building up in the South. But he also knew the rest of the country had its share of the same problem. The race riots in Boston, the riots and lynchings in 1920s Oklahoma, Knoxville, Detroit.

He remembered taking the train into Manhattan when he was a child and wondering why some of the cars were filled with whites, while others were exclusively black. Pennsylvania Station had separate waiting rooms, bathrooms, water fountains, and snack stands for whites and "colored."

But the buses, well, seats were supposed to be catch as catch can, no matter who or what you were.

This was different.

Now, four years later, he could laugh at his former ignorance and relative innocence.

Well, Dr. B., this next bit ought to top that little story. As you know, the junior and senior medical students here are the first lines of care for patients in the hospital. We get to do almost everything. My roommate Dave (aka Country Boy, aka Scarecrow) and I were assigned to the same ward, so we got to know each other's patients. I was assigned an old gentleman who just happened to be the chief of one of the local Virginia Indian tribes. The chief had come in with what's called unstable angina, heart pain not controlled by his nitroglycerin tablets. Dave was assigned to the chief's roommate, Bobby Lee Withers, who had shut his kidneys down drinking moonshine whiskey.

It turns out that Bobby Lee is a dyed-in-the-wool Southerner who hates everyone from blacks to Catholics to 'furreners,' and is a full-fledged member of the Ku Klux Klan. My roommate is a good ol' boy, so he knows how to talk the lingo with Bobby Lee. We would sit there and listen as Bobby told us about the meetings and the secret passwords and handshakes.

Did you know that when a Klansman meets another man but isn't sure if he is also Klan, he offers the secret handshake and says 'AYAK?' Are you a Klansman? And if the other guy is Klan, he answers 'AKIA.' A Klansman I am.

It just so happened that Bobby knew of a KKK meeting coming up and Dave, devil that he is, dared me to go with him and see if we could sneak in. The passwords worked, although I got strange looks from the Klan guard at the tent entrance. The stuff we heard wouldn't have made sense to a third grader, but all of those men were cheering and chanting.

Then we got lucky, because I spotted one of our professors there, so we high-tailed it out before he saw us. (Note how I am picking up the lingo here. And I've been told I no longer sound like I'm from "Joisey.")

Bobby Lee didn't make it through the kidney failure.

My Indian chief, who reminded me of you whenever we talked about philosophy and other stuff, also didn't make it. I miss him.

You know that Dave and I are living in an apartment on Church Hill. I don't think I told you about our neighbors and the time we were almost lynched. After seeing the difficulty the kids in the neighborhood were having getting medical care, we decided to set up a clinic in our apartment. Yes, I know, it really isn't legal but Dr. B. I have seen kids die from simple ear infections that spread to their brains because their parents didn't have or wouldn't spend the fifty cents for the pills that would have cured them. So Dave and I and our friends Bill, Peggy, June, and Connie decided to see the kids in the evening when we were there. We had some friends in the pharmacy department who saved us the antibiotics and other general stuff that was nearing expiration date but was still good. They normally just pitch it in the trash, so we thought it could be put to better use. We didn't want or take any of the pain pills like codeine, because that really would have gotten us into hot water.

When Dave and I weren't there, usually two of the others would cover, keeping our free clinic running, and we really did some good. Kids were no longer being carried into the medical school clinic dying from preventable stuff. Moreover, we got to know our neighbors. We were the only white people living there, and from what I've told you before you can understand that we were watched from a distance.

One evening, the neighbor living in the apartment next door came to the door with her little boy who it turned out had a simple viral cold. We gave her some of the cold prep stuff we had and she started to talk. Turns out she is a lady of the night, if you catch my drift, who runs her business out of her apartment. She wanted to know if we could treat haircuts. Dr. B., "haircut" is slang here for syphilis. We had some injectable penicillin, and that took care of her little problem.

The next night the neighbor from the other side of us came over with his wife, who was complaining of chest pain. We don't have an electrocardiogram machine—that's only for rich docs already in practice—but from what we could tell, her condition fit more with an inflammation of the cartilage in her breastbone called costochondritis, which is handled easily with aspirin. That seemed to make both of them happy.

Her husband told me that he had been to Korea, like you. He said that at one point they thought he was dead, missing in action, and shipped his trunk and kit home. Then they found him alive! The funny part was, in his trunk was a fully equipped machine gun with lots of ammo. When he gets drunk or it's a holiday, he goes out and shoots it off. Scared the hell out of us the first time it happened.

So, you ask, what's all this leading up to?

Since you asked, I'll tell you. Our particular housing area became friendly with us. But like in other parts of the country, some residents living a little farther away didn't take to our being in "their neighborhood." Luckily, it was just Dave and me, or rather I, who were there that night when the crowd came to get us and string us up.

They would have done it, too, except our lady of the night neighbor stepped outside and started calling out men's names, telling them to leave or they wouldn't get any more poontang. I'll let you guess what that means.

Then our other neighbor walked out with his machine gun, fired off a burst, and that was it. The crowd lit out, we haven't been bothered since, and we're now getting kids from those other areas.

It's hard to believe how close I am to graduating. There won't be anyone there to see me except Dave's parents, but that's all right. They've become surrogate family for me. So wish me luck with the ring.

More later,
Bob Galen

"Ruby, who's covering tonight?"

The round-faced African-American woman who worked as unit secretary on the fifth floor, general medical wing, looked up and grinned at the gray-haired floor nurse.

"We got us a six-pack of the good stuff tonight, Gina. Five West is The Teacher, The Model, and The Southern Belle. Five east is Babyface, Scarecrow, and The Bear." She started to giggle. "Good thing they're workin' on separate wings. Lawd only knows what those six would be up to if they were all on one side!"

Gina started to laugh, too. "I'll bet that ol' farm boy knows how to handle the chickens! And if he doesn't, I'll bet The Teacher learns him real fast!"

Both ladies started to cackle. Ruby, in between the laughs, added, "And Southern Belle has got Babyface all diapered up. Wonder if he's bottle-fed or . . . "

The older nurse cut her off by clucking disapproval then changed the subject. "Somebody needs to take The Bear aside and give him some advice on how to deal with the ladies. He works all the time when he should be spending more time with The Model. I got a feeling about those two."

June, will you marry me?

He had worked night shifts as a clerk in the detox unit to earn the ring money. Night after night, 11 p.m. to 7 a.m., and then on to his own senior clerk rotation at the hospital. It had taken over seven months, and he hadn't told her why he was working so hard.

In his mind he had outlined the way he wanted it to go: Graduation, the wedding, and then both would head to their residency programs in New Jersey. He had been accepted both in Virginia and there, but June wanted that OB-GYN spot up north. And her friend Peggy was headed there, too.

Unless he had missed his guess, he expected Bill would propose to Peggy soon. And Dave, that old beanpole, had latched on to Connie like an octopus! Maybe it could be a three-way wedding, each of them acting as best man and groom at the same time!

He actually felt happy. That didn't happen too often for him. He would pick June up at her place. That's when he'd propose. If it went as planned, he would head back with her to his and Dave's apartment.

He still had the bookcase he had rescued from a dumpster in the back seat of his beat-up old car. The car was a gift to himself from the remainder of the money he had earned—he would need it for his residency. The bookcase would be a good surprise for Bill, who had stacks of books piled up on the floor of his own place. The three guys would meet their dates on Church Hill. Peggy and Connie were going to meet them for burgers and fries. He would be alone with June, and who knew what the free afternoon would bring?

He headed down Franklin Street toward the Fan District. The old Civil War-era houses stood like aged doyennes, quietly watching each new generation come and go in Richmond. As he parked in front of her apartment house, he touched the ring box in his pocket one more time just to reassure himself. It was a talisman for his new life to be.

"June, will you marry me?"

He knew immediately what her answer was—he didn't need to hear it spoken. His crooked smile poorly masked his feelings. He tried to make a joke to let her know that he understood.

"Hey, City Boy. Is June in the car?"

Bill saw it first. "Bob, are you okay?"

"Yeah, fine. Tell you what, guys, why don't you check the back seat of my car. There's a surprise there for you, Bill. I've had a long week. I think maybe I should just catch up on some rest today."

Dave looked at Bill, nodded, then the two headed outside.

Galen headed upstairs to his bedroom and closed the door.

"She turned him down, Dave. I knew he was building up to proposing. You know how close Peggy and June are. Peggy told me June didn't know how to tell him when it happened. If I had only known I might have buffered it. I didn't realize it would be today."

"That's why he was busting his ass with the extra work. I'll bet he even bought a ring. Maybe it's for the best. Maybe he'll latch on to someone later. But it sure sucks now. Come on, Bill, let's call the girls and put this off for today."

Bill nodded agreement, but deep down he knew it would be years before Galen would share his soul with another woman.

The sounds of Elgar's "Pomp and Circumstance March No. 1" echoed through the auditorium as the graduating class of the School of Medicine walked double file to the front and split into right and left lines as they found their seats. They remained standing until the completion of the music then sat down and waited.

"Ladies and gentlemen, honored professors, members of the School of Medicine, Class of 1965, we welcome you to this most joyful ceremony. Let me state that, according to your program, we will begin announcing the names of this year's Doctors of Medicine. Each in turn will come up to the stage to receive his or her diploma. Then, when all are seated again, these doctors of the future will recite the Oath of Hippocrates, that pledge of service taken by new doctors for centuries.

"There are now two versions, the ancient and the modern. As many of you may know, the ancient version evokes the names of the Greek pantheon of gods who represented health and well-being.

"Today, however, we are honored to present to you the modern version, just written by Dr. Louis Lasagna, Dean of Tufts University Medical School. We are honored to be among the first institutions to attempt to bring modern-day relevance to this sacred oath. For the purists in the audience, though, I will take the liberty of reciting the first part of the ancient version before the actual recitation.

"We will now begin the awarding of the degree of Doctor of Medicine. Dr. John Adams . . . "

He heard the names being called off alphabetically. As each name was announced and family and friends in the audience applauded, whistled, and yelled out, Galen knew his name would be met with silence.

"Dr. William Crowley."

He clapped loudly, knowing that Bill only had his mother there.

"Dr. Robert Galen."

Nothing, but then he heard clapping, faint at first, then increasing.

Must be Dave's folks. Thanks for that!

He crossed the stage and accepted his diploma from the dean. He shook the man's hand, then the chancellor of the university's, and walked offstage to his seat.

After the full roster had been called, the dean again approached the microphone stand.

"I will now read to you the first part of the ancient Oath of Hippocrates. It is truly a work of poetry: 'I swear by Apollo physician . . .'"

He listened as the dean named the ancient gods.

Are they still around watching us from Mount Olympus?

The dean stopped and looked out at his audience.

"Ladies and gentlemen, I now ask the Class of 1965 to stand and recite after me the modern-day version of this historic oath."

The entire class stood, recited their oath in unison with the dean, then let out a cheer and as tradition dictated moved the green tassels on their mortar-board caps from right to left. It was now official. They had made it. The lights brightened in the large auditorium as the new doctors and their families moved out.

Galen stayed where he was. His friends would best be left with their families for the moment. He turned to put his diploma on one of the folding seats and it fell forward onto the floor.

"Dr. Galen, I believe you dropped this."

He turned around to see a man bent over picking up his diploma. When he straightened up, he recognized his old professor.

"Dr. Basily! What are you doing here?"

Before the man could answer, he heard another voice.

"Young Dr. Galen, it would be more correct to ask what *we* are doing here."

He turned again to see a second familiar face.

"Dr. Freiling!"

"We couldn't let you go through this alone, Bob. And this prune-faced old weasel told me what you did for his granddaughter. By the way, do you notice anything different?"

"Your range of motion is normal, Dr. Basily. You've had the surgery."

"Score one for the medical profession," Freiling replied. "And I think now is the time when you should be calling us Harry and Jack, Dr. Galen. You are now one of us, with all the curses and disadvantages accrued."

"Yeah, prune face gave me a C back in 1946 when I deserved at least a B in his class, so take what you can get from him, Bob."

Freiling shot Basily a mocking glare, then said dryly, "You got exactly what you deserved and earned. In any event, Dr. Galen, our families are here, including a young girl who wants to thank you for being able to breathe. And we'd like to take you out for dinner, assuming that you understand our teaching salaries are still minuscule compared to what you are going to earn someday."

Basily laughed. "What cheapskate is saying is, don't order anything expensive."

"By the way, Bob, where is that young lady you were telling me about?"

The two older men saw the response in his eyes and said no more.

CHAPTER 8

Pavane

He was covered with her blood.

He sat in the middle of their living room crying.

He couldn't stop.

Ten minutes ago she got up from the table.

She said she had a surprise for him but had left it in the car.

He followed her to the door, but she told him to wait, it wouldn't take long.

He watched her cross the street and open the driver's side door.

The car came careening down the street, weaving from side to side.

He saw the impact before the sound hit his ears.

The car door screamed as it was torn off its hinges.

She made no sound.

He knew before he reached her.

He held her.

He heard her last words: *I love you, Tony.*

The stuffed toy dog lay in the road.

The little card tied around its neck lay open.

The words written on it would pierce his heart forever.

Tony, guess who's going to be a daddy?

He couldn't stop ruminating, twisting and turning his soul with memories. He was an attending physician, one of the big boys now. He had completed his residency and had started working in the Real World. The buck stopped with him. He was now the guy the students, interns, and residents came to when the fit hit the shan, and he loved it! This was what he had worked, groveled, and sweated to achieve for so long. But he also knew something was missing.

He had gotten burned once. He was a fast learner. After June had left for her residency in obstetrics, he had taken himself out of the ritual dating/mating game. In all other things he hadn't hesitated to put his hand back in the fire, but personal relationships hit too close to home. He hadn't even managed to understand his parents, and now they were dead and gone, so he had left the fun-and-games stuff to his friends.

Dave and Connie and Bill and Peggy had tied the knot, and he had served as best man for both of his friends. But, as Bill had surmised, The Bear wasn't going to let his toes get burned again.

Not for a long time. Maybe never.

Once in a while, even from a distance, his friends would try to set him up. Dave would call from Florida, mentioning an eligible lady doctor who would be in his neighborhood for a conference. Bill, ever more subtle, had talked to him about his own life with Peggy, how she had filled a large void in it and how he now felt at peace with himself.

But Galen had become gun-shy. He had horrified the girl whose life he had saved back in college and then killed himself physically to buy a suitable ring for June, only to get shot down.

Nope, not now. Maybe not ever.

• • •

He had been run off his feet that long-ago day, what with patients in the office, patients in the clinic and nursing home, and finally hospital rounds. Thank God he was just about finished, except for the inescapable paperwork of writing on the patient charts.

He entered the nursing station and was about to sit down when one of the nurses approached him with a clipboard.

"Dr. Galen, would you do us a favor? One of the medical students had to certify a patient as dead, but we need an attending's signature on the chart."

"Okay," he replied, "but I need to check for myself. Where's the morgue cart?"

"It's over by the wall, Dr. G."

He picked up his scope, hooked it around his neck, and started toward the special domed cart used to transport the newly dead without upsetting other patients. He was about to open the upper end when he heard giggling.

Oh crap! I smell a rat.

He braced himself for another practical joke. He knew the staff thought he was a bit uptight and enjoyed seeing him startled. He was never nasty or disrespectful, far from it, but they considered him aloof, avoiding all of the gossip and scandalmongering that goes on in any organization.

He opened the cart lid and looked in.

She was petite, a Dresden doll with a Jackie Kennedy hairdo. Her skin lacked the mottled-ivory, blue-gray, and red coloration of the recently deceased.

Suddenly her eyes opened and looked directly at him.

They were lavender eyes. He'd heard that Elizabeth Taylor had lavender eyes, but he had never seen eyes like this. They seemed to twist his insides and bring on that flutter that only June had ignited in him.

He stared at her, steeling himself against the unwanted vibrations within then turned to the crowd of nurses and attendants who were peering at him from behind the corridor wall.

"Yep, she's a deader, no question about it! Must have died of terminal ugliness. Was it a man or a woman?"

"Help me up, you big idiot!"

"So, the dead can talk, can they?" he laughed as he easily helped her off the cart and set her upright on the floor. As he did so he felt the electricity, a tingling of self-awareness shoot through him. He watched closely as she smoothed out her nursing uniform, the pressure of her hands revealing her well-proportioned chest and hips, and read her name tag: LENNY.

He pointed at it, still fixed on those amazing eyes.

"Lenny is a boy's name and you sure don't look like a boy. What's your real name?"

"Elena. Elena Jensen."

"May I have your tag for a second?"

She stared at the husky young man with the wavy brown hair and fair skin, who stood at least a head taller than her five feet four inches. He had sparkling eyes, not the muddy shade of most brown-eyed people she had known. There was something of the feral in his face, with a bit of pathos. Someone must have dealt him a blow in the past, she mused. And yet she felt gentleness in the way he had carefully picked her up out of the cart.

He was strong, too.

She detached the tag and handed it to him. He took it over to the unit secretary's desk and grabbed a thick black marker pen. He crossed out LENNY and printed LENI in big letters then handed it back to her.

She looked at him and slowly pinned the tag back on her uniform. She felt the rising flush in her face and was surprised to see the deepening blush in his.

The unit secretary let out a laugh.

"Sisters, we got us a forest fire in here!"

• • •

He sat a long time in the darkened room after her funeral. He had turned over his work to colleagues. He wasn't sure he could go back or even that he wanted to.

They had made so many plans, testing each other's feelings to be sure that each detail would work for both. He hadn't wanted to leave anything to chance. He remembered that disastrous past proposal.

They had picked out a nice townhouse apartment near the hospital. His old place was just a bachelor pad more reminiscent of medical school digs than appropriate for someone rising in his field. He had tried to straighten and clear out the place, getting rid of accumulated grunge and airing out the rooms despite the brutally cold winter weather.

He went over the words a third time and then called her.

"It's me."

"Hi, me," she giggled.

Even on the other end of the phone, he felt the heat of embarrassment.

"I . . . uh . . . would you like to have dinner tonight?"

"Sure! Your place or mine?"

Oh, geez, this is moving too fast for me!

He couldn't think of a way to backpedal out of the corner he had painted himself into.

"Uh . . . well . . . "

Damn! Why was he so tongue-tied? He wasn't a kid anymore.

"Well, how about I pick you up and we try that little Chinese restaurant near the hospital. You like Chinese? I mean, if you don't we can go somewhere else, if that's not okay."

"That's fine. See you at seven."

She hung up and looked in the mirror. She felt shivery. She stared at the pictures of her parents and brother stuck in the upper corner of the vanity mirror. She was the only one to survive the auto accident ten years ago and had lived alone throughout her schooling.

Mama, Papa, Glen, I think I love him. I hope that's all right with you.

The old saying was true: An hour after you eat Chinese food, you feel hungry again. But this wasn't the hunger of an empty belly. She had invited him back to her place, another efficiency like his—but much better kept. They sat on her small lilac-colored couch and awkwardly talked about their families and their past lives. He called her Leni and she, demanding equal time, wanted a name for him.

"Not Bob," she said. "We need something special, just for us. What's your middle name?"

"Anthony," he replied, a little embarrassed.

"No," she said, "it's Tony." And she leaned over kissed him. His left arm, already around her shoulder, tightened its hold. The evening was still young, and so were they.

They moved into their new home the same day they went to the courthouse for their marriage license. Neither one was big on ceremony. There was no family left to eat rubber-chicken reception dinners, and they hadn't told their friends. He bought her a ring. He didn't want to jinx things by using the one he already had. No, that was for memory, to remind him not to be such an uptight asshole.

Their hospital associates didn't know either, though they noticed the difference in the two, especially when they were on the same floor.

"Elena, I thought you hated green. Where'd you get that sweater?"

The nursing supervisor had worked there thirty years and knew all of her girls. She guessed what was going on when the young woman just smiled back.

"Dr. G., we're having a going-away party for Mary and we're taking up a collection."

Normally he would just have pitched in a dollar, so he flabbergasted her when he took out a ten-dollar bill and stuffed it into the box she held.

That early spring morning she felt queasy but didn't tell him. She went to the hospital lab with a urine sample and asked her friend to run an HCG level—human chorionic gonadatropin—the gold standard for pregnancy.

The rest of the day she floated through her rounds, trying to think of a fun way of telling him. She signed out and headed down the stairs, exiting at the waiting room area. She walked over to the little gift shop and peered in the window looking for inspiration. Staring back at her was the stuffed toy beagle dog, its overlong nose and ears and sad-sack eyes calling out to her, *Take me home with you.*

She sat in her car and carefully wrote out what she wanted to say on the little gift card hanging from the toy dog's neck.

Oh, my, he's going to be in shock!

And this was going to be the happiest night of her life.

Over and over he played it: "Pavane pour une infante défunte."

Ravel had it right, he thought, as he stared at the wall. He got up to replay it when the voice echoed in his head.

Tony, you have to go back. I'll always be with you.

He turned off the record player and started to clean up the room.

Philosophers have said that time heals all wounds. But wounds don't heal as normal tissue. They form scars. You don't bleed anymore, but the tissue is no longer the same.

He returned to his schedule, putting in more time than ever before. He needed to work. He had to work. Time alone meant thinking, ruminating. But, inexorably, time did pass.

He grew older, getting involved in the medical side of government as well as his practice. He worked thirty hours a day, eight days a week—patients in the office, patients at the free clinic, plus rounds at the hospital, nursing homes, and certain unnamed government facilities.

And he grew older alone.

• • •

He found himself walking the ninth floor corridor.

Finished! No more tonight.

He turned the corner quickly heading to the stairway and collided with someone. He looked down and saw one of the floor nurses lying flat on her back. He was so tired he almost laughed at the wordplay: floor nurse floored.

He didn't recognize her. Must be new, he thought, as he reached down to pull her upright. She brushed off her uniform and glared at him. Not bad-looking, probably in her late thirties or, like him, early forties. Her face relaxed into a smile as he stared at her. He started to apologize and looked into her eyes, those same lavender eyes. He looked at her name tag: CATHY. He stood there dumbfounded as she stared back.

In his mind he heard the voice saying, *Yes, Tony.*

He looked at her. She hadn't said anything.

"Do . . . you need any help?" he stuttered.

Cathy Welton had no family. She had been orphaned at age five and her foster parents were long gone. She had put herself through nursing school by work and scholarship and found that her true forte was oncology. She had the rare ability to combine compassion and competence in a field where emotional burnouts were common.

Optimism can carry you only so far when you are surrounded by inevitability, but she had cared for her patients tirelessly for more than sixteen years, dealing with the classic Kübler-Ross confrontational stages against the Fates no matter how they presented. Her colleagues often said she did her patients and their families more good than any preacher. And for each one, she was there when the thread of life was severed.

Each saw in the other the same theme of intertwining grief and loss, and they were drawn together because of it. No need for soul searching. They both knew the signs. It wasn't long before she asked him what he wanted her to call him. She also wanted something other than Bob, something close and personal. He was reluctant to tell her, maybe for fear of the same outcome, but in the end he relented.

"Call me Tony."

It was déjà vu all over again, as Yogi Berra used to say. They planned, and planned together. He couldn't bear living in the apartment with its crushing memories, so he bought two homes side by side. He lived and worked in the one house while he fixed up the other for the two of them. She decided to quit her hospital job and work with him full time in the office.

"Tony, did that dinner bother you in any way?"

It had been a hectic day for the both of them and they had ordered takeout to give themselves more time to rest. They also wanted to go over their dream of adopting needy children.

"What's the matter, honey?"

"My stomach hurts, I feel nauseated, and I want to throw up. If I didn't know better, I'd think I was pregnant."

She had undergone a hysterectomy for severely bleeding fibroids five years before. But pregnancy didn't cause penetrating, drilling pain from front to back anyway, and other conditions such as an ulcer also didn't fit.

Galen called a friend in the radiology department and they headed over to the unit that evening for magnetic resonance imaging. The hammering noise of the rotating MRI unit vibrated through him as he and the radiologist stared at the screen. The computer program was piecing together cross sections into composite images as it electronically sectioned off portions of Cathy's abdomen. The micro-universe of proton spins painted its picture of inevitability.

"There, Bob."

The radiologist pointed to a swelling in the C-shaped pancreatic head. He looked at Galen, who had gone pale. The shadow doctor remembered his friend's past experience.

Galen turned without speaking and went to help Cathy out of the scanner.

He took Cathy to the best oncologists he knew. The answer was the same: pancreatic cancer already metastasized. They both knew what that meant. They also knew the treatment protocols were devastating by themselves.

"Tony, I just don't want to prolong it. I know what happens. I worked the oncology wing for sixteen years. Promise me you won't let me suffer."

He couldn't say anything. He held her and nodded his head.

He couldn't control her vomiting. He had tried decadron IVs to reduce the swelling in her brain. She wore a wig now. They had tried an experimental drug that seemed to give some respite, but the effect was only temporary. The morphine oral suspension controlled the pain, but it made her act confused as well.

He sat by her bed and stroked her hand. Her face was drawn, pale. Her weight was less than it had been in her early teens. Sunken eyes looked up at him.

"Tony, you look so serious."

She was drifting in and out of consciousness. The skull was upon her.

"Let me worry about that, Cathy. You just rest up. I'm going to try something different for the nausea. There's some new experimental anti-nausea stuff I've gotten for you."

"No one could ask for a better doctor than you, Tony."

She tried to sit up, but he held her back.

"Let me raise the bed for you."

He kissed her forehead.

"No, Tony, don't stop me. Leni wants me to come with her."

• • •

He sat in the darkened room.

Ravel's "Pavane" played over and over.

He got up, turned it off, and walked outside.

They both loved flowers, Leni and Cathy.

This would be their memorial, the flowers he would plant year after year.

It was late spring now, the season of resurrection. It was time for him to get ready for the summer flowers. He walked through his garden, planning where each floral pattern would go.

Two butterflies, lavender-hued, flew side by side with him.

CHAPTER 9

What If?

"Come on, Bob, be serious!"

"So what's wrong with Murgatroyd or Theofilos if it's a boy?"

She had felt the nausea and first thought it was the flu. Then the early-morning vomiting began. Her cycle was two weeks past due. Her mother smiled when she complained about the queasiness, then she placed her hands on Nancy's abdomen and floored her when she spoke in her heavy German accent.

"Meine Tochter, sie tragen neues leben."

My daughter, you are carrying new life.

That evening, when Edison had arrived home from his job in New York City, she waited until after dinner, sitting next to him as he sprawled on the couch to unwind.

"Bob, let's repaint the spare bedroom. We're going to have a guest pretty soon."

"Great, just what I don't need right now. Which side of the family is going to drive us nuts this time?"

"Neither."

"Well, who is it?"

"I don't know the name yet."

"What do you mean, you don't . . . ?"

He stopped.

"Yes, Daddy," she had said, smiling with a face as rosy as her shimmering hair.

And she remembered him falling back on the couch, his mind obviously racing. Robert Edison, able to map out complex circuitry in his head and design unheard-of stuff from scratch, didn't have the slightest idea what to do about a baby—his and Nancy's baby.

What do you feed it, cheese and crackers?

Where do you go to get a crib?

Nancy, like all women, possessed an ability exclusive to her sex: She could read his thoughts. At least that's how it seemed to him, as she stroked the back of his neck and whispered:

"Don't worry, honey, we'll work it all out."

They had been trying for five years and it finally had happened. They had talked many times about adoption, fertility studies—the works. But even on two salaries, and good ones at that, the costs were beyond their means. So they had kept on waiting for those telltale signs.

She didn't mind the extra weight—not yet—as she found herself staring daily at the window displays of the baby shop as she walked from her car to her job at the bank. She kept thinking: pink or blue? And she daydreamed about times when, as the baby grew, she would sit at home after work and bow on her violin the old German folk songs her mother had sung to her as a child.

She was pleased but not surprised when Bob became ever more solicitous of her health, reminding her of what she should eat, drink, and do. But she had to draw the line when he suggested that he wanted her to stop working

"Bob, I'm only three months along!"

But quickly it became eight months, and she began to feel as conspicuous as she looked.

"Bob, I think I need to see Dr. Ross today. I don't feel right."

She grew lightheaded as she stood up and started to go into the kitchen. Then she felt the sudden wetness and panicked.

It can't be my water yet!

She went into the bathroom and examined herself and saw the red liquid running down her thighs.

"Bob!" she cried out as she found herself swaying and falling.

"Mr. Edison, we have to operate on Nancy right away."

June Ross was a skilled obstetrician, and she knew she had to convey the urgency of the situation without panicking the young man standing in front of her. But even she felt panic, that haunting fear all doctors face when confronted by the possibility of inescapable loss.

"The baby's placenta is separating from where it attaches to Nancy's womb. I'm sure you already know that the placenta is the blood, food, and oxygen connection for the baby. Normally it connects along a particular part of the uterine wall. But sometimes it's too low, and as the baby grows it causes a pulling along the cord. When this happens it tears blood vessels and causes the bleeding your wife saw today. We have to get in there to help the baby. I know it's early, but it's imperative. We need to do an emergency Caesarean section to get the baby out."

She couldn't tell him there was a high chance he would lose both his wife and child, and that if Nancy survived she wouldn't be able to have any more children. Some day, if the research she had been following produced its intended results, doctors would be able to spot such problems much earlier. The new ultrasound techniques were just coming into use. For now, she could only give him hope.

That was all she had as well.

"Okay, Jack, go slow on the induction," June told the anesthesiologist. "Her pressure is already low. Increase colloid fluid input. She's already had two units of whole and four units of packed cells."

As the gowned and masked and capped team stood over her, Nancy felt increasingly detached—almost floating. It was just like that one time she had taken a couple of drinks in college. And her mind drifted away as the room darkened around her.

"She's under," the anesthesiologist said.

June prayed as she made the first incision.

• • •

"Nancy, I, uh, well, uh . . . "

He's going to do it. I was right! Mother didn't think so, but I knew it!

He was shaking like a tuning fork and his eyes were clouding up.

Oh, please, don't cry, Bob, don't cry!

"Nancy . . . "

He paused to steady himself, putting his hands on those long red tresses of hers that always held him spellbound. He swallowed.

"Nancy, will you marry me?"

He stood there like an expectant puppy, too afraid to ask anything more for fear of being swatted. His mind raced.

I'll just jump in the lake and drown myself if she says no.

"Well, yeah, I guess so, okay," she heard herself saying, almost like an observer standing apart.

She saw his eyes widen as he tried to take in her response.

Dear God, tell me I didn't say it that way!

It hit her: She was just as flustered as he was.

Think, girl! You can do better than that! Try again! He really loves you!

She looked up at this almost six foot tall scrawny man/boy, put her arms around him and started over.

"Yes, Bob Edison, I'll marry you!"

She had uttered those words nearly two years after their first apparently inauspicious meeting. She had planned a nice day on the lake canoeing with her old college roommate who had just arrived in town.

She spotted the geeky kid, looking like a muscle-less Popeye, approaching the canoe she and Betty had planned to share. Slender, acne scars, glasses—just what she didn't need today.

Wait a minute, he looks familiar. Where have I seen him before?

She tried to shoo him away, gently at first then more insistently. But he was clueless! The more aggressive she got, the more he persisted. The club had assigned him to this canoe for the race, he kept repeating.

She apologized to her friend and, almost snarling, climbed into the canoe as Geekface joined her quickly.

I think I'll teach him a little lesson in canoeing.

She forked her paddle into the water and began a rapid and powerful stroking action that threatened to unbalance the vessel. But surprise! They were moving swiftly, faster and faster, ahead of the others as the unexpected annoyance proved to be as adept as she was.

Maybe it won't be so bad after all. I just wish he would stop staring at my hair.

So it began.

There were more canoe trips, more competitions they won as a team. And slowly he began to talk! Yes, he was one of those odd people who played with gadgets and never stopped taking things apart and putting them back together. He was a technical engineer for Ma Bell and lived and breathed electronics. But slowly his shell was cracking, and he turned out to be a really nice guy.

They began to meet for meals and she soon realized that this one-hundred-twenty-pound beanpole could eat more than six normal people. He was bottomless!

There was that day at the bank where she worked as a teller when she saw and then heard a florist's messenger bound into the lobby carrying a huge bouquet of red flowers and, horror of horrors, begin to call out her name!

Customers and coworkers started to laugh as the messenger spotted her scarlet-red face and immediately headed toward her, and then they clapped as he completed his delivery.

Then came the clincher—that July day in 1965 when he asked her if she would like to accompany him on a trip to the Great Lakes. They would drive up through New York, cross into Canada at Buffalo, head northwest across Ontario, skirting the lakes then drop back down through Michigan's Upper Peninsula to Mackinac Island. He had picked out a bed and breakfast there where they could enjoy the simultaneous beauty of Lake Michigan and Lake Huron.

That unforgettable day, when she heard him speak those fateful words, they had been sitting together holding hands watching the sunset.

"Nancy, will you marry me?"

The words still echoed in her head, because it was the beginning of forever for them.

Nancy stared out into the early dawn light from their room at the B&B. She normally didn't get up this early—especially after last night! She grinned at the thought. But something was nudging her, making her awaken from that wonderfully comfortable bed before sunrise.

"Bob," she called out, "are they having any reenactment ceremonies at the fort this morning?"

She looked over at her husband-to-be, pajamas drawn up and scrawny bare legs sticking out of the blankets.

Edison shook his head sleepily. He wasn't a morning person, barely moving from his spoon-shaped position, facing her pillow and holding it like a favorite stuffed toy.

"I don't know," he mumbled. "Lets ask when we go down for breakfast . . . later."

She continued to stare out the window. A soldier stood on the lawn—Civil-War-era uniform with sergeant's stripes on the shoulders, handlebar mustache, and grizzled red-gray beard—and seemed to be staring right back at her.

Nancy watched as he slowly raised his left arm and waved, not in greeting, but as a call to follow. Then he turned and headed down one of the forest paths.

"I think I'll take an early breakfast, Bob."

She heard only snoring in reply.

Good, she thought. Sandy's on duty for the breakfast shift. The young college boy had come down from Nova Scotia to earn school money and was the best and most friendly of the hotel staff.

"Good morning, Sandy."

"Good morning, Mrs. Edison."

She flushed.

Not quite yet, but it does have a nice sound to it.

"Does the fort have a reenactment ceremony today?"

"No, ma'am, why do you ask?"

"I saw a soldier out in the courtyard this morning. He was dressed in a Civil-War uniform and he waved at me before heading down one of the paths."

The boy looked at her intensely.

"Did he have a beard and were there sergeant's stripes on his uniform, ma'am?"

"Yes, do you know him?"

"Ah! You saw old Angus, Angus Urquhart of the clan Urquhart, as he would say."

"So, he's an actor working at the fort?"

"No, ma'am, he's a ghost."

"Bob, Bob, get up, now!"

She was shaking his exposed right shoulder. No luck. So she started to tickle the bottoms of his size-twelve feet and called his name with her face right at his ear. His whole body jerked and he sat upright on the edge of the bed, his eyes still closed.

"Okay, no need to shout. What's the problem?"

"No problem, just . . . well, I saw a ghost this morning."

Edison opened one eye. He knew she didn't drink.

"Remember when I told you about the soldier outside?"

"No."

She sighed and shook her head. He still wasn't wide awake.

"All right, tell me about it," he said as he stretched back out on the bed, pointy-toed feet shivering without the comfort of the warm blankets.

"I was looking out the window at dawn and saw him standing out there. He waved his arm as if he wanted me to follow him. I asked Sandy, the waiter at breakfast, about him. He said it was old Angus, the Fort Mackinac ghost!"

Edison processed the thought.

"Are you sure the boy wasn't just kidding you?"

"No, Bob, he was serious. He said others have seen the ghost over the past seventy years, including Mark Twain when he stayed at the Grand Hotel in 1905."

He was becoming more and more awake.

"If old Sam Clemens had seen him, then maybe . . ."

"Sandy said that Angus, Angus Urquhart of the clan Urquhart, was one of the last soldiers stationed here at the fort before they were shipped elsewhere in 1895. He was a Scotsman who had immigrated to the U.S. and made the army his home. He had no family, just the army, and had risen to the rank of sergeant. By all accounts he was a good soldier. The only trouble he caused was with some of the remaining Indians. He apparently liked to take his bagpipes and march around playing them in an area they considered their spirit ground. They were furious at his apparent desecration of their sacred area."

Now Edison was getting hungry, a powerful incentive for him to get up and dressed.

"So how come he's a ghost? I mean, sure, if he was at least middle aged in 1895, he wouldn't be around now in 1965."

"Sandy said that a few months before leaving for the mainland, his company was sent on bivouac in the forest. When they returned, Angus wasn't with them. They searched for him but never found any traces. There was no reason for him to desert, and no way could he have done so without being noticed. He just disappeared. He's still listed on the rolls as missing in action."

"So what can we do about it?"

Nancy grinned.

"I think a nice romantic walk in the woods would be a good idea!"

Edison munched on some extra biscuits he had snatched up after hurriedly scoffing down part of what he had hoped would be an immense breakfast. Nancy was leading him toward the path where she had last seen the soldier.

"Do you know where we're supposed to be going?" he muttered.

"I saw him go down this way. I bet we'll know shortly if he's a real ghost!" she replied.

But they continued for almost an hour without result. Though the foliage was thick at this time of year, enough sunlight penetrated to make them build up a sweat. Fortunately the competing lake breezes served to moderate the effect.

Suddenly Nancy caught a glimpse of something moving off the path to the left.

"There he is! That's him!"

She tugged at Bob who followed her off the path into the deeper woods.

Then she saw him, her ghost soldier. He was standing by a tall Michigan Pawpaw tree. He looked at her with a piercing stare then smiled and disappeared.

She grabbed Edison and pulled him along in pursuit.

"Bob, did you see that?"

"I see a big Pawpaw tree that we're going to crash into if you don't slow down."

"He's here! I mean it must be where his remains are. Help me check the ground."

Both got down on their knees and used branches and hands to push away the forest surface cover of decaying leaves and twigs. They kept at it until Bob cried out, "What's that?"

Nancy reached over and pulled an object from the dirt. It was old, a corroded metal button. Could it be from Angus's uniform?

"Bob, go get the park rangers, quick! I think we found him!"

She waited in the forest stillness while he ran back toward the park offices.

Good thing he's so thin. He'll get through the woods fast.

The forest noises suddenly ceased and she looked up from where she was sitting. The apparition stood before her, smiling again.

In her mind she heard him.

God bless ye, lassie! Ah've lain here al' this time and nay un has helped. Ye mus' do a thing fer me so ah can rest easy. Do ye ken?

Nancy nodded.

Tell me what to do, Angus.

He pointed at the ground in front of her with his right hand.

Ye mus' remove tha' which hols me here.

He now pointed to the left side of his chest.

She didn't quite know what to make of those words, but she dug with her hands in the soft forest loam and suddenly felt something. She scooped more dirt away and the outline of a skeletal rib cage appeared. Gently she moved the soft soil away from it and saw the spear point lodged between the fourth and fifth ribs.

She looked up at Angus. He appeared pleased, nodding his spectral head up and down. Slowly she reached in and tugged and twisted until the point dislodged from the remains.

She heard heavy running footsteps approaching. Bob appeared first, followed by two park rangers. She was standing by the Pawpaw tree, humming to herself.

"Nancy, are you okay?" Bob asked, regarding her with a worried gaze.

"I'm fine and so is Angus," she replied.

The two park rangers looked at her smiling face, then at each other.

"Ma'am, the mister here says you found something important."

"Yes, very important," she heard herself say. "A lost soldier has been found."

They stood and watched while the remains of Angus Urquhart of the clan Urquhart, Sergeant U.S. Army, were buried with full military honors on the grounds of Fort Mackinac. As the rifles fired off, she heard that familiar voice once more.

Lassie, I kenna leave less ah warn ye. Ye and yer laddie mus' go now! Ye have stirred up pow'rful forces, the same uns thet held me here.

"But Nancy, we have two more days here."

He didn't want to go back to work.

She couldn't give him the real reason, but she knew they had to leave.

"Bob, I'm worried about my mother. She wasn't feeling well before we left."

She crossed her fingers behind her back, so it wasn't a lie.

"Okay, today's last ferry leaves in three hours. That should give us enough time to pack and check out.

She knew he was upset, so she added the sugar coating.

"By the way, the State Park Authorities have picked up our tab because of what happened. Isn't that great, Bob? We can put the money toward the wedding!"

It was a while before their embrace ended. He smiled at her, looked at the big four-poster bed and whispered, "We still have three hours."

They boarded the ferry and settled down. The peaceful voyage to the island was now replaced by wind-chopped water, roiling the boat back and forth.

They reached the mainland dock and returned to their car just as the sky darkened with storm clouds.

"Strange, I checked the 2 Meter Net and there was no storm indicator."

Even here he can't be without his ham radio.

"Good thing we left when we did," she replied.

She turned on the car radio and listened to the local station newsman proclaim sunny good weather for the next two days just as the heavy storm-driven rain began to ricochet off the windshield.

They headed north and then east, Nancy encouraging Bob to travel as quickly as possible. She knew there was something out of the ordinary about the change in the weather. The radio continued guaranteeing fair weather as the winds picked up in intensity. Then she saw the funnel . . . no, funnels! Tornadoes! Here and at this time of year!

They raced along the highway, finally crossing back into the United States at Buffalo. As they did so the weather seemed to break, the clouds thinning out to admit the sunlight once more.

Ye made it, lassie. God be wit' ye and yer laddie. Sa'day Ah'll pipe fer ye.

• • •

They were still peering down at her, those people in the masks and gowns. Where was she?

Then she saw him, in their midst. He was wearing his kilts and holding his bagpipes over his left shoulder.

Angus, are you here to pipe for me?

Nay, lassie, ah play fer the wee-un.

"She's coming out of it. Get her over to Recovery. I'll go talk to her husband."

"June, let me help. I'll talk to him."

She looked at her old classmate from medical school.

"Thanks, Bill."

CHAPTER 10

Middle Ground

Time is a one-way street. We are born in a scream of life, not realizing that birth is the overture of death. Meanwhile Fate permits us the conceit that we have some sort of control over our brief existence then laughs as our best intentions go south, tragedy strikes out of a clear blue sky, and our most foolish endeavors produce wonderment.

Galen was older now. He had begun cutting back on the more strenuous activities in his career—less hospital work, no more traveling to present papers to colleagues. He even found himself entertaining thoughts of what had seemed an anathema to him in the past: retirement.

As usual, he rose at 4 a.m. and took his morning walk before the first rays of the sun appeared in the east. He completed his two-mile jaunt, returned home, and examined the appointment book. A light schedule so far, he thought, as he glanced out the window.

The fourth crescent of summer began brilliantly that day. Azure blue skies lit by a poached-egg sun raised the thought of flying. Maybe, just maybe, he could get out to the airport for the afternoon.

Flying always seemed to bring him closer to Leni and Cathy, just as gardening did. Air and dirt, sky and earth, they were the only activities he truly enjoyed.

He ate his usual light breakfast of blueberries covered with wheat germ in a bowl of milk.

Yes, maybe some time in the Piper.

He washed down breakfast with a cup of bi lo chun tea. Savoring its flower-bud aroma, he carried the cup into the waiting room and turned on the radio to WBJC, Baltimore's classical station, as he scanned the morning papers. Then, as always, he paid homage to the gods of continuing medical education by spending two nice solid hours reading through the research journals.

Mirabile dictu, no early calls. In retirement, every morning could be like this.

Just before 8, right on schedule, he heard Virginia, his secretary, pull into the parking lot behind the modest suburban home that also served as his office. She had become a fixture there, beginning part-time over twenty years ago after her husband died of cancer. She also was something of a fixture in the D.C. area, where she had lived and worked since before World War II. Many times she talked about the days when the city still was a sleepy town, when you could walk up to a president who was strolling boldly down the city's sidewalks and shake his hand. And she remembered when many of the landmarks were erected, including National Airport and the Pentagon on the Potomac's marshes.

"You ought to take the day off," she said as she efficiently began rearranging the stack of leftover papers on her desk.

"Why, do you want a day off, too?" he laughed.

"It would do you some good to get out of here more often. You're not getting any younger."

Ouch!

She didn't speak her unspoken thought.

You ought to start planning for retirement.

But he felt it, nevertheless, that arrow sting of truth. Maybe he should cut back on his government consulting and just do aviation medicine. What would it be like to have free time, to work only when he wanted and not worry about the rest?

By 9, he already had seen three scheduled patients plus three walk-ins when another came running up the walk, shouting as he entered:

"An airplane's hit the World Trade Center!"

Galen noticed the music had stopped on the radio. He turned it off and turned on the small television in the waiting room. Every channel was showing the same image: New York City's World Trade Center North Tower wrapped in flames and smoke. And then he gasped as the TV cameras showed another plane smash into the South Tower.

Before anyone could even begin to fathom the magnitude of the event that was unfolding, the news arrived that a third aircraft apparently had crashed into the Pentagon.

By then, the Federal Aviation Administration had ordered every aircraft flying over U.S. airspace to land, and thousands of air-traffic controllers across the land watched nervously as one by one the blips on their radar screens disappeared. For the first time in many decades, America's skies were empty.

The group in his waiting room stood in stunned silence, unable to speak or move, their eyes glued to the small screen.

In apparent slow motion they saw the South Tower of the Trade Center collapse, followed soon by the North Tower, each disgorging a giant plume of smoke and dust that forced its way through the narrow corridors between the buildings of Lower Manhattan, as bystanders on the ground fled for their lives.

They all could feel the skin-crawling fear rise within, and Galen realized that the country had just entered a new and uncertain phase of its existence, one that had not been experienced even at Pearl Harbor. The homeland itself had been attacked. Maybe tens of thousands had just died. The United States was at war.

He looked out his front window and could see the smoke cloud rising in the southeast in the direction of the Pentagon.

No, no flying today. And suddenly retirement again seemed like a faraway dream.

"Bob, am I starting to look older?"

He watched admiringly as she stood in front of the bedroom mirror running her fingers through her still-gorgeous long red hair.

What do I say? If I agree, it'll upset her. If I disagree, she'll know I'm lying.

He looked at her again, the woman who meant so much to him: wife, lover . . . no, something more . . . best friend! And that thought prompted the solution Edison desperately needed.

"Honey, you've never looked more beautiful to me."

What a smoothie! Nancy thought, as she put her arms around him and they stood there embracing.

Sometimes he knows just what I need to hear!

The young desperately seek to grow up quickly and gain the freedom they envy of adults. They put on makeup, dress provocatively, take amino-acid protein shakes to bulk up, constantly stare at themselves in the mirror, and incessantly ask: Are we there yet?

The old look at their younger counterparts as reminders of bygone times while they suffer the realization of their encroaching mortality. They also look in the mirror, but with trepidation instead of admiration, and they seek out plastic surgeons, age-reversing nostrums, and exercise programs, all in an attempt to return to the temple of youth that will no longer grant them admittance.

Then, there is the middle.

Middle age, that is, or Middle Earth, that flat-footed, more-hair-on-the-ears-than-scalp, Hobbit-infested stage between youth and senility. It means the onset of backaches, headaches, and reflux, a time when most human beings enter a phase of consolidation and nesting. Those who have moved well into their careers, marriages or equivalents as a result are held captive by the palpable chains of responsibility.

For some, it is a time of achievement and satisfaction. But for most, it is the breeding ground for second guesses and thoughts about what they have not accomplished so far, for worrying about the ever-shortening future, and for calculating the amount of work time left and the amount of money needed for retirement. The gremlins of age go merrily about their vanity-robbing work: thinning the hair, widening the waist, and rendering the eyesight no longer eagle-keen. Erectile dysfunction emerges big time in men and menopause begins to erase the essences of womanhood.

Time marches and Fate watches.

"Nancy, I'm going to be away again. The company wants me to take charge of the Olympic Torch Bearer Run sponsorship. The participants will go from New York to Washington on their way to Atlanta."

"Why you, Bob? You're not a PR man. You're their top R&D guy. What does that have to do with the Olympics?"

"Seems they think my reputation will carry some weight."

He sat down wearily on the couch in their New Jersey suburban home. Yes, he was tired, tired of the daily commute to New York, tired of putting his life at risk every day on Route 22, tired of arguing with science-ignorant managers who wouldn't recognize an electrical circuit if it bit them, and tired of non-stop, non-productive meetings that repeated the obvious day after day—and now this.

Why him? Probably because nobody in marketing wanted to handle it, and so they called on one of the nerds.

At least he could demand first-class travel arrangements.

"Dr. Galen, here are your phone messages."

The list his secretary handed him ran five pages, on which most of the items were non-urgent, but he would answer them all as was his habit. And he would perform two house calls—for two of the sickest.

He sat down and, number by number, called and spoke with and crossed off the names, until he had finished. Then he picked up his bag and headed out to his twenty-year-old Jeep in the parking lot. First stop, Rosie's place, then Mrs. Falcon's.

Rosie Washington was the daughter of slaves. She and her extended family lived on a fifteen-acre farm just outside town. It fronted a highway now on two sides, but the old split-log house, without electricity or inside plumbing, had served Rosie and her late husband, Abraham, for more than seventy years. She was one hundred five now, waiting to meet her Creator and be reunited with Abraham, who had died some twenty years before.

Galen always enjoyed seeing her when she had come to his office. Mahogany skin glistening, the four-foot-eight-inch Rosie would tell riveting stories about the days when she and Abraham had first married and started to farm in the upper reaches of the old South.

Now she was dying. She knew it and her family knew it. But it was, strangely enough, a celebration of life's passage rather than an anticipated time of grief. She had done so much in her century-plus-five of living, and now all she wanted was heavenly rest with her mate. Her family cared for her better than any hospital could, as her tired heart muscle slowly failed. Galen had anticipated her passing at any time, but he hoped for one last visit with her.

He parked the old Jeep on the side of the highway and began the half-mile walk up to the house. There was no driveway, no road, just the fading marks of wagon wheels from a time when Rosie and Abraham took their produce to market in the city by horse-drawn cart. Now, any vehicle would have trouble making it up that path. Finally he arrived at the open farmhouse door and saw Rosie's great-great-granddaughter standing there.

"C'mon in, Doctor. I think she knows you're here."

He entered the spotless small bedroom where Rosie, the family matriarch, lay propped up on hand-made, down-filled pillows. He could see her shortness of breath, only partly relieved by the medications he had provided. A small oxygen tank ran its trickle through her nosepiece as she opened her eyes and smiled at him.

"Goin' ta see Abe t'day, docta," she gasped. "He tol' me las' night he'd be a-comin' fer me."

Galen knelt down by the old four-poster bed and held the hand of a living legend. He felt the thready, irregular pulse and, using his stethoscope, listened to the labored breathing. He looked up at the old sepia-tinted photograph mounted on tin and framed on the wall showing two serious but smiling young people holding hands, dressed in their Sunday best. He knew it was the wedding picture of Abe and Rosie, taken long ago by some itinerant tinker/peddler traveling through the farm area by wagon.

As he continued his examination, he thought of himself, no longer the altruistic young doctor, older now but still learning from his patients. Then he was struck by what he did not see: The Darkness. He had sensed it so many times over the deathbeds of his patients, but not here.

He heard sounds and turned to see members of Rosie's family crowding into the small room—from sons and daughters in their eighties all the way to small children. Then he noticed a tall man, youngish with mahogany skin, moving toward the other side of Rosie's bed.

He saw Rosie's eyes open, taking in the sight of her family, her immortality. She smiled, and when she saw the young man standing beside her, she smiled even more broadly.

Galen rose from his kneeling position and stared, first at the man, and then at the old photo.

No, it couldn't be! It must be a great-grandson.

Then he heard what was no longer there. Rosie had stopped breathing. He felt for her pulse, listened again with his stethoscope, and turned toward the family, but they already knew and began singing, not mournfully but joyously.

Galen repacked his medical bag and walked through the house. He looked around for the young man but couldn't find him.

As he made his way slowly down the hillside back to the Jeep and climbed in, he wondered: ghost or coincidence?

He shrugged to himself.

Can't take any more time. Still have to visit the Falcon home.

The young maitre d' of the swank D.C. hotel almost bowed and scraped as he pored over the courses of the banquet meal Edison had specified for his Olympics-bound torchbearers. It was going to be one big publicity show with him as the centerpiece representing the company. He couldn't afford for anything to go wrong—not this night. He already had called Nancy twice just to hear her voice, to know that she was still there for him.

Back in town, Galen drove through a series of neighborhoods, each one more elaborate than the last, until he reached the suburban castles of The Neighborhood. That's how the rest of the area referred to the enclave of mansions along the Potomac River. Here lived the richest and most influential powerbrokers to the nation and the world.

Marilyn Falcon was a self-effacing country girl at heart who still had not understood the trappings of power that surrounded her. She lived with her daughter and son-in-law and had enjoyed all of the perks he could provide. But nothing could prevent the inner destruction, the eating away by the cancer that was killing her.

Galen drove past the gate and up the long driveway to the coach-style turnaround in front of the Georgian mansion. The maid already had opened the door to let him in and Anne Creding, the dying woman's daughter, stood waiting for him in the large antiques-filled anteroom.

"Mother seems to be deteriorating very quickly today, Doctor."

He detected no sign of grief from the daughter, just a flat voice and flatter expression, as though she was describing a pet that had to be put down. But then, pet owners tended to show their sorrow at the impending loss of a beloved animal, and Anne Creding displayed no such emotion.

He nodded and followed her to the mother's bedroom, where silk blankets and pillowcases adorned the bed and special pillows helped prop up the old woman.

He moved to her side. Marilyn Falcon was comatose now. The cancer drugs no longer held sway. Maybe it was for the best that she could not perceive her surroundings or feel any pain. He turned to Anne, who stood by looking like some cigar-store Indian princess staring ahead blankly.

"She's going now, Mrs. Creding. Is there anything I can do for you?

Anne just shook her head coldly—no verbalization, no sense of loss.

Maybe she's in shock, too upset to react in any human way.

At least, that's what he hoped was happening. But in his years as their doctor, he never had seen an overt sign of affection or concern by the daughter for her mother. Anne Falcon Creding had tried to ignore what she considered her mother's lower-class background when she married the wealthy and powerful Branson Creding, a Boston Brahmin who now held a Cabinet-level position. But her mother's very existence exposed Anne's ill-fitting social roots, no matter how hard she tried to conceal them.

So perhaps, Galen thought, *Anne considers Marilyn's dying a favor.*

He turned to the old woman who now exhibited the irregular gasping of the dying. Yes, The Darkness was there this time, very strong, and soon Mrs. Falcon was no more.

Galen signed the form certifying time of death. As he prepared to leave he heard the startling words:

"Help me with her."

Well, well. Maybe Anne is feeling the loss after all.

Maybe she wanted to arrange her mother in a dignified pose. But his skin crawled and he shuddered involuntarily as he saw the look of grim determination on the face of the dead woman's daughter then noticed her hands. They were holding a small hammer and chisel, and she grimaced as she stared back and said something that made him pick up his bag wide-eyed and walk out:

"I need you to hold her mouth open. I'm not going to bury all that gold in her teeth."

"Dr. Edison, is something wrong?"

The hotel manager felt sudden panic as he heard the troubled voice on the other end of the telephone line.

"Yes, we're all sick. We need a doctor for the whole team, including me!"

Edison hung up just as the latest overwhelming wave of nausea hit him. He had suffered through food poisoning before, but this was different. His skin was turning beet red, and he felt like millions of worms and bugs were crawling across his flesh. He was the last to be hit, after he had received calls from several of the torchbearers complaining of the same symptoms.

The hotel doctor arrived at his room and examined him.

"Damnedest thing! I've never seen food poisoning do this. Dr. Edison, I'd like to call a friend of mine. He's local and often consults at the White House. May I use your phone?"

By then Edison didn't care if the quack called the Pope. He had never felt so physically miserable. Saliva poured from his mouth, his skin burned and itched, and his intestines felt more like fire hoses. Now he was starting to wheeze, and he felt numb around his mouth.

Galen had arrived back at his office still shocked at that last turn of events. He had left the deathbed of Rosie with a sense of . . . what? Elation? Proof of something intangible? But then there was Marilyn Falcon. What did that poor dead woman ever do to deserve such malignancy on the part of her daughter? He sat down and seriously contemplated quitting. He felt the same inner torment as he did when Leni and Cathy had been taken from him.

Then the phone rang.

Naturally! What if it's that Creding woman again?

"Bob, this is Jack Stevens. Yeah, I'm still doing hotel medicine. Beats working for a living. I got a strange one here. Can I tap your brain?"

Galen felt weary, but he would help his old friend.

"It's like food poisoning but not like any food poisoning I've ever seen," Jack told him. "They're all beet red, vomiting, salivating, and crapping up the place. They're wheezing, and they're ready to tear their skin off."

"What did they eat for dinner?"

Galen felt that old itch in his head as he scoured his little gray cells and came up with an idea even before Jack's next words confirmed his suspicions.

"Salmon," he said. "The chef said it was freshly caught and brought in down at the E Street wharf."

"Don't believe him," Galen replied. "This is scombroidosis. Get them all on steroids and diphenhydramine, stat! They're getting whacked by histamine release."

He hung up the phone, shaking his head.

Scombroidosis! He hadn't seen a case since med school. Bad stuff. Chemicals released by salt water fish when their skin starts to rot and break down.

Can trigger one helluva allergic reaction!

After the hotel quack had given him two injections, Edison began to feel human again. In a little while he would call Nancy to let her know he was okay.

"You were right, Bob, that seafood dinner was bad news," Jack told Galen after the emergency had passed. "We had the lab run tests on it. I think that chef, and maybe the food supplier, need some closer scrutiny."

"Glad to hear it, Jack."

"Nancy, how soon can we retire?"

She heard the plaintive tone of his voice on the phone. He was still in D.C., the Olympic affair had ended, and the effects of the illness had passed, but the powers that be had told him not to come back just yet. They needed him to take a short hop to South Carolina to check on a government security lab that was having some trouble.

Not even an extra day to recuperate from his banquet fiasco! Even worse, he couldn't find a direct flight to the small southern town where the lab was located.

Another one of Uncle Sam's damn hidden facilities!

The only way he could get there by tomorrow was to rent a car and drive or hire a puddle jumper, but he surely didn't feel well enough to drive that far.

Why does this have to be done on a Saturday, anyway?

"Take it easy, Bob. I'll spend the weekend analyzing our finances. You just get this last thing done, and if they try to make you do more, tell them to go lump it!"

She hung up the phone and sighed to herself.

Things were getting worse at the bank, too. She was manager now—actually manager of the whole state—but upper management had no clue about the training deficiencies of the new employees they were hiring and no understanding of the need for increased security with the new computer systems. She felt like a voice crying in the wilderness. But she also knew that if anything did go wrong, she would take the blame. This was no way to live.

She carefully laid out all of their assets and liabilities on a spreadsheet. They certainly couldn't afford to stay in the New York-New Jersey area. The taxes on the house and the utility bills alone would eat up their savings within several years. They would have to move.

She had heard that Bob's company was considering changing the retirement and pension plans to something far less satisfactory. And, if Bob was right about the rumors he had heard, the company was trying to get rid of its higher salaried employees—like him. Her mathematical mind did some quick calculations and she smiled.

Gee, it actually would be better if he did retire, but only if they offer him a buy-out and allow him to keep his old pension plan.

She had watched her own retirement plan at the bank very carefully. They wouldn't get away with anything while she had anything to say about it.

Maybe it was just the day, or maybe it was because he was away, but Nancy suddenly started feeling blue. Up popped the memory of that long-ago day when the hope of having children of their own was lost, followed by more memories of the denials by the adoption agencies. It overwhelmed her. She put her head down wishing Bob was there to hold her.

She sat up again.

Snap out of it! Bob needs me to be logical now! Could we really do it—retire, escape the rat race, and move away? Could I see myself not working?

Then she smiled as she remembered something her mother had told her when she was first married:

"A woman never really quits work–she just stops getting paid for it!" The grimness of Friday's death watches gave way to a Saturday lit with sunshine. Galen took advantage of the lovely morning, walking through the yard before the first patients arrived and thinking once again that maybe he could get in some flight time later in the day.

It'd be great—doing a little cross-country hop in the aviation club's Piper.

He walked back in to the office, called the club scheduler and discovered he had lucked out. He had called early enough to be the first one requesting use of the plane.

Okay, today I get in some sky time!

He became wistful as the usual companion thought crossed his mind: He'd feel closer to Leni and Cathy up there.

"I'm sorry, Dr. Edison, we only have a Cherokee available. That'll get you to where you want to go in South Carolina. Hell, if the parking lot of the company is long enough, old Sam can even land you right where you want to be!"

"Old Sam?" Great! My pilot is going to be a World War I ace!

It was VFR all the way, that perfect, clear kind of day when you could almost see forever. Galen had gone through his preflight check carefully, filed a cross-country route south toward the Carolinas, made sure his fuel was topped off, and checked the aviation weather forecast: no storm fronts anywhere along the Southeast coast.

He shook his head in wonder. Was it five years ago when one of his agency friends had cajoled him into taking flying lessons? How he had resisted at first. Now, other than his peaceful forays in the garden and the daily numbing routine of his patients—though he needed that numbness to keep the demon of memory from sending him into depression tailspins—he squeezed every spare moment into the air.

He was certified for IFR, instrument flying, but there are times when seat-of-the-pants sky blue is the most enjoyable. As he taxied down the runway, he could make out the air traffic controller in the tower giving him a wave. He knew them all.

"Piper 2874J you are cleared for takeoff."

"Roger, tower. Keep 'em in the air, Joe!"

He noticed the Cherokee, a small charter plane, taxiing up behind in queue.

Not a bad plane to fly. Maybe the club will get one someday.

He held the brake in check as the engine RPMs built up and he could feel the tug of the prop as the plane wanted to roll.

Off we go!

No matter how many times he had done this, he always felt exhilaration as the plane began accelerating and the nose lifted off the runway. Quickly he and the little Piper were airborne. He banked left and headed south-by-southeast toward the coast. This was the scenic route—and one of the purest forms of solitude he could have.

The growl of the single engine, the forward thrust pressing against him—yes, this was the escape he needed. He had dedicated his life to his patients, spent entire days listening and talking, but especially listening. He didn't wear clerical robes, but what his patients told him . . . no . . . *needed* to tell him, included bits of personal information no less sacrosanct than those spoken in the confessional. There came a time when he simply wanted to hear no more.

An hour into the flight he noticed the Cherokee again on a similar heading. It was faster than the Piper, with more range.

Must be going farther south, but by all rights, it should have been well ahead by now. What's going on?

Then he spotted it: a stall out! Was this an instructor teaching a student about stalls?

"Cherokee 29371K, Cherokee 29371K, this is Piper 2874J. Everything okay, guys?"

The voice of the other pilot quavered as it came on.

"74J, I think we're out of fuel! The forward gauge is reading empty. We must have had a leak."

"71K, check your fuel tank switch. Switch to auxiliary now!"

Silence, then he saw the prop turn over and the plane begin to pull out of the stall. Then he heard the pilot's voice again, sounding sheepish.

"74J, this is 71K. Thanks, man! I plumb forgot about the auxiliary. I owe you one!"

"Roger, 71K, do you have enough for destination?"

"More than enough. Over and out."

Galen frowned. He would have to check up on the pilot later. That type of dangerous mistake never should have happened.

Wonder who did his last flight physical?

Back over the airfield, Galen circled and made a smooth all-point landing, taxiing to the hanger with no waiting. All in all, it was a nice day and a productive flight. But what would tomorrow bring? What would it be like not having to worry about tomorrows?

He could almost hear the Fates laughing.

"It's got to be some kind of an omen, Nancy. First the food then that idiot in the plane. I thought my guts were going to go through the windshield when we went into freefall. Good thing that other pilot saw us and knew what to do. Now I know for sure. I want out!"

She sat in the bank's corporate headquarters contemplating Bob's words and staring at an enormous panoramic painting of an ocean scene on the wall.

Probably not even real, just a print—though that thick piled rug and cherrywood wall panels sure do look real.

The secretary to the CEO sat impassively staring at her monitor screen, periodically pressing the answer button on the switchboard and speaking softly in monotone into her telephone headset microphone. It made her look like some weird insect with abnormal mouth parts on one side only.

What am I doing here? Dollars to donuts it's something I warned them about and they ignored, and now it's come back to bite them on the ass! Fools!

She hoped it was true, but then changed her mind, because she remembered that in any corporate structure the scapegoat becomes the person who *issued* the warning, not the one who ignored it.

The human insect spoke.

"Mr. Frederickson will see you now, Mrs. Edison."

Nancy rose slowly, took a deep breath to steel herself against the impending idiocy, and walked toward the heavy paneled door. She pushed it open and found herself in the CEO's suite.

I could fit most of our house in here!

She walked across the thick-pile rug to the pedestal that elevated the CEO's desk above the height of mere mortals.

He was watching her, hoping, she thought, for any sign of fear or weakness.

Well, Bucky, not this little girl! Let's get it on!

He rose from his imperial-looking leather swivel chair and moved to shake her hand.

"Hello, Mrs. Edison. Good to see you. I trust that your trip into New York wasn't problematic?"

"No, Mr. Frederickson, it was a pleasant drive."

Right, and I slit my wrists for fun, too.

"Please sit down. We need your input on a sudden and rather serious problem at the bank."

He pointed to a heavily stuffed high-back leather chair that, when she settled into it, made her feel as though she was a one year old sitting in her highchair.

Bet it's computer security. That's the last one they ignored.

"Mrs. Edison, the bank has just received a ransom note."

Before she could react, he continued.

"Yes, a ransom note. No one is being held hostage—or, I should say, all of our customers using our credit cards are being held hostage. Computer hackers have broken into our system, and now they're threatening to release all of the credit-card numbers and their PINs across Europe unless we pay their price."

He rambled on, but she had heard enough already.

Just the scenario I raised with them two years ago!

Now that the horse was out of the barn, what did they expect her to do? She had told them about the inadequacies, the downright criminal laxity of the bank's computer security, and the entire board had laughed at her as though she was carrying a raging case of paranoia. Now, they actually wanted her to come up with a solution, fail miserably, and then be used as their incompetent little scapegoat.

No way!

"So, Mrs. Edison, what would you recommend that we do? The board has decided to set up a committee on computer security, and all of the members think you should chair it."

Not this time, Buster! Not me. I've played your game too long not to recognize a setup.

She smiled at him like someone about to lay down a winning hand.

"Mr. Frederickson, the first thing I would recommend is that any unusual credit-card activity be noted and the card holder called about it. I doubt if these hackers are going to wait for the bank to agree. I would put as many employees as possible to work on it. You can tell the card holders that the inquiry is routine to monitor unusual purchases and that the bank is always working to protect their security."

She had to restrain herself from bursting into a guffaw at that comment.

"For those who note something wrong, cancel the cards and issue new ones. Those that don't can be watched carefully. The alternative is to cancel all of the cards and replace them on the pretext of 'improving service.' Either way, the old numbers are no longer valid. The bank may have to eat some loss, but it will be worth it to avoid the bad publicity. Oh, and be sure not to try to blame the customer. That will backfire on the bank."

"I can see that the board made the right decision in selecting you as security-committee chairperson, Mrs. Edison."

"No, sir, I'm afraid that they didn't. You see, my husband and I are planning to retire very soon, and I would not be able to give the time such an important committee would require."

Gotcha!

She saw his face drop as he realized that the intended goat had refused to enter the slaughterhouse gate.

"Dr. Galen, your bank is on line one."

Your bank is on line one? Why do these calls always seem to happen on Mondays?

The way the day was going, the news didn't surprise him. The waiting room already was full, the call-back list was at four pages, and it was only 11 a.m. But there shouldn't be any overdrafts.

What's going on?

"Dr. Galen, this is Mr. Stevenson from the credit-card security department. Periodically we do checks on purchases to protect our customers and we noticed some purchases that don't quite fit your profile. May we confirm these with you?"

Profile?

He should have expected that. Everyone knows everything about everyone. Well, not quite everything.

"Go ahead, Mr. Stevenson."

"Thank you, Dr. Galen. We see a purchase from a company called Herrenhaus. Did you make a purchase from them?"

"Herrenhaus? That sounds German, and the name doesn't ring a bell. I know that name translates to 'Men's House.' What was I supposed to have bought?"

There was a long pause conveying the embarrassment of the caller.

"Uh, sex toys and videotapes, Doctor."

Galen started to laugh out loud. Should he be upset because his profile didn't consider him to be into that sort of thing, or should he be upset at someone using his card to buy such stuff? He decided that the latter was worse.

"No, you're right, Mr. Stevenson, that definitely isn't me. How did this happen?"

As he listened to the explanation, he realized that the bank representative was reciting a big pre-scripted lie.

"Most of this happens when our customers are careless in throwing out receipts or making telephone purchases, Dr. Galen."

Galen felt his temper rising. He was very careful about receipts.

"Mr. Stevenson, that is impossible with me. I will do some checking on my own. In the meantime, cancel the card, issue me another one, and I will check back with you in 24 hours. You do realize that I expect no charges or penalties because of this."

The bank representative's voice hesitated as he agreed. Galen hung up.

The rest of the morning offered the usual chest pains, fatigue, earaches, bladder infections, and one soon-to-rupture aortic aneurysm that he quickly ordered to the hospital for emergency surgery.

Then he made some calls. It was still good to have certain contacts. One of them confirmed what he had suspected: Eastern European computer hackers had broken into the bank's security system and stolen tens of thousands of credit-card numbers and PIN verification data.

Interesting how the bank was trying to blame the victims.

The next day he called Stevenson. Even with the card canceled, charges of over $37,000 had been attempted all across Europe. The bank security man repeated the big lie about customer failure, but Galen erupted.

"Mr. Stevenson, maybe even you don't know the real story, but I do. Your bank security was breached by hackers who stole the numbers from your computer. It will be a matter of hours before this news reaches the media. Do you really want to continue with this lie?

Several days later, he read about the resignation of the bank's CEO "for health reasons."

Nancy did a quick scan of the financial section of the paper before leaving for work. Soon, she thought, this would end. And then she saw the notice:

"J.T. Frederickson, longtime bank CEO, retires for health reasons."

She smiled and uttered aloud, "B-a-a-a-a!"

Edison walked into the breakfast nook and saw her grinning. She didn't say anything until she put the finance section in front of him. Then she repeated, "b-a-a-a-a-a-a-a," and they both burst out laughing. No scapegoats here!

"Bob, we can do it!" She looked at him collapsed on the sofa. He'd had a rough week, saddled as he was with two communications-center revampings down in the Washington area, one at the Pentagon, the other across the Potomac at the CIA. Massive constructs like modern-day pyramids to man's technical skills, they required the complex cohesiveness of an advanced communications system. And that was his baby.

"Six straight days away at this. Now they want me to do a review of the cell network at the World Trade Center, that mess they're trying to reconstruct. I'm ready to call it quits."

"I told you, we can do it. Look at the spreadsheet. We'll have enough and more. The only question is where we should go. How about somewhere in the mountains?"

"Nancy, the only affordable mountains around here are in Pennsylvania."

"Okay, when you get back from Lower Manhattan, we'll head off to see the mountains!"

Galen always had liked trains. And it had been a long time since he had made that trip down across the Mason-Dixon Line. Now he was heading back up to present a paper on genetic linkages to death rates. He just wished it wasn't in New York.

Maybe do a bit of sightseeing. Haven't seen Ground Zero yet. Too bad they had to knock down all those surplus electronics stores we liked to haunt when we were kids. Sweet God, how long has it been since I went with Edison . . . now why did I just remember that name . . . on the train into New York to get parts for our experiments? Wonder what he's doing?

The steady rocking of the car and clickety-clack of wheels on rails lulled him to sleep.

Edison stood looking through the chain-link fence that had been erected to keep visitors from falling into the ten-story-deep hole in the ground where once had stood two of the world's tallest buildings. Now, the heavy equipment and the army of workers had succeeded in removing all but a tiny pile of rubble from the site.

God, what people are capable of doing to one another!

He remained with other silent onlookers, trying to take in the scene, trying to imagine what it would have been like to be here on that horrible day. Then, for some reason, he experienced a sudden flashback to his less-burdened days as a high school student.

How many times had Galen and I . . . ?

He caught himself.

How many years has it been since I've seen the big kid? He must be getting old.

He turned and walked away the same way he had arrived—in silence.

Galen walked past Virginia's desk headed to the office kitchen to make a cup of tea. When he returned she held out a slip of paper.

"Here are some more calls, Dr. Galen, but two of them don't make any sense."

Virginia was a very straightforward and commonsense woman, and she usually could elicit enough information from even the most reticent caller that he could prepare himself for the conversation. Working thirty-seven years for a federal agency, she so often put it, "if you don't learn to deal with idiots in the government, then you can't work there." But now she seemed truly frustrated at being unable to tell him what the phone calls were about.

"What did they say?"

For the first time he could recall, he saw exasperation in her face. She shook her silver-coiffed head.

"Still doesn't make sense," she half-muttered. "One called himself Babyface and the other one Scarecrow. Said they knew you and not to worry about calling back until later in the day. Both left phone numbers, out of state by the looks of them. Sounds like a scam to me."

Galen started to laugh out loud at the improbability. It was the first time Virginia had seen him laugh, much less smile. She stared at him, hoping that he hadn't finally snapped from dealing with what he did on a daily basis.

He quieted down and looked directly at her.

"Don't even try to understand," he said. "It's just two old friends from school. I haven't heard from them, I guess, since Cathy . . . "

Then he stopped and returned to his office. She knew enough not to pursue the matter.

He sat at his desk, staring at the names and their corresponding numbers.

Dave, Connie, Bill, Peggy—the four of them had visited him only twice, the first for Leni and the second for Cathy. It had helped to have them here both times, the four of them sitting and talking, carefully trying to distract his mind from the brooding darkness that had overwhelmed him.

He hoped it wasn't an emergency for either of the couples, but then, he thought, they wouldn't have called in that manner if something bad had happened. He tapped the phone buttons for the first number. It rang four times before he heard the pickup click and the all-too-familiar Virginia nasal-twanged voice: "This is Dr Nash. Who's calling?"

Galen couldn't resist a joke. He muffled his voice and spoke in deeply ominous tones.

"Your time has come, young David! Time to visit Aunt Hattie!"

"City Boy! Good to hear your voice, even if you are a terrible actor!"

"What's up, Dave? You've got my secretary's bloomers tied in a knot. She couldn't figure out what was going on."

"Haven't you talked to Bill yet?"

"No."

"Okay, here's the scoop. Peggy and Connie got to talking on the phone a while back. Bill's set up a real medical missionary practice in South Carolina and Connie thought it would be fun to get the 'A Team' together again and give him a hand this weekend. The practice is inundated with refugees from Florida and the coastal areas. They expect an onslaught this weekend with the influx of migrant farm workers. Think you're still up to it, City Boy? Haven't you gotten lazy with all those rich government types you see?"

Galen was speechless. How many years since the team had worked the wards and the ER, triaging, treating, and emptying beds at unheard-of speeds? It had provided a thrill of the hunt, deciding who was sickest and who could wait and then tackling them. He and Dave and Bill could deal with up to twenty an hour. The girls could do almost the same. He shook his head as he remembered the time he and June . . .

He snapped out of the reverie.

That was a long time ago. A lot of (stuff) has happened since then.

"Dave, does Bill really want us to come down? He's always prided himself on being able to handle things, just he and Peggy."

His old friend heard the uncertainty in his voice. Dave wasn't stupid. He knew Galen was indirectly asking whether June would be there.

"Hey, Bob, it's just the four of us and you. And the beaches are pretty this time of year. You might just find a mermaid to take back to D.C. with you."

"Don't you dare pull any stunts, Country Boy! I'm older and meaner now, and I'll spot a setup! I'll call Bill and confirm the weekend. But remember, no tricks!"

"Scout's honor."

"You never were a Boy Scout, Dave."

"Don't you know it, Bob!"

He hung up the phone then punched out the next set of numbers. Two rings.

"This is Dr. Crowley, how may I help you?"

Same voice, same offer of help to anyone who needed it.

"Bill, I think we need to change your nickname to Preacher."

"Bob! Good to hear from you! Did Dave pass on the message?"

"Yes, in his inimitable way. I just wanted to be sure it's just you guys and me?"

Bill also understood the unasked question. He and Peggy had thought about June, but for better or worse, she was tied up in some heavy-duty work for the next several months, so he could answer no honestly. He also didn't mention that she was married.

"Okay, it's set then. I'll either drive down or fly. I think there's a small airport near you, Bill. I'll have to check weather patterns first, but in any event look for me Saturday. We'll whip those patients of yours in line before you can do your fishes-and-loaves trick."

They both laughed, and Galen felt the surge of renewed vigor. Maybe he had been getting stale.

No, it isn't all dull and routine. Their hairs would stand on end at some of the stuff I've been privy to, even if it has been sheer luck and proximity to the capital and its sundry agencies. They don't know how lucky they are to be where they are, doing what they do, and knowing only what the local newspapers and radio and TV stations tell them. It's a whole different kettle of fish up here.

Galen called the local aviation-weather hotline. Not a good idea to risk flying a single engine this weekend. A tropical depression was forming off the Bahamas. It could go either way: staying a nuisance storm or spiraling, picking up speed, and turning into a full-blown hurricane. Better that he drive down at night to get there in time.

He called a local colleague to cover his patients over the weekend then began packing. Tomorrow was Friday. He would work his usual day then rest for several hours before leaving at midnight.

Ought to give me plenty of time to get to the mission for the 9 a.m. patient calls.

Now it was 4 a.m. He never needed an alarm. He just knew. He always could wake up when he needed to. Sunrise wasn't for another hour and a half. He got out of bed, slipped on his walking shoes and began his daily exercise circuit. No jogging! That was for the masochists who enjoyed the worn-out knee cartilage and unstable ankles and hip degeneration brought on by all the accumulated pounding. No, a brisk walk allowed for thinking, motion, and care in not falling on uneven pavement.

He walked rapidly down the driveway and even in the dark realized that he needed to cut the grass before it was suitable for safari hunting. He'd do that after sunrise. The next-door neighbor was away so he didn't have to wait until 7:30.

He missed the hundred-year-old maple and oak trees the highway department had removed to widen the road in the name of progress. His yard was now shorter by half from his contribution to the new road. He remembered the original yard size and the time it took to cut it. Then he remembered who was on his schedule this morning: Joe Rosario.

• • •

"Hey, mister, I can show you how to start that mower. Want me to try?"

Galen was new to the suburbs and never had cut grass. Only weeds grew in the cracked concrete and old split-slate paving stones in his childhood neighborhood. Grass? That was for parks and the rich people's homes on the other side of town. What did he know about grass or cutting it? But this was his first house, his first yard, and he was damned if he wasn't going to be a responsible homeowner.

His move into the neighborhood and the strange sound of his name were enough to create suspicion among the white-bread natives who had been born in the town. So he bought his first gasoline-powered lawn mower from the local Southern States store, read the directions, convinced himself that any idiot could put it together, and then ran into one small problem: It wouldn't start.

He quickly learned the routine suffered by all who venture too closely to small gasoline engines. He pulled the starter cord and cursed then pulled it again and again while swearing by all the powers that be that he wouldn't let the machine beat him. But of course it did.

He felt like he'd entered one of those Robert Benchley short-subject films that used to play before the movie started when he was a kid and could scrounge up the nickel to go see one. Man versus machine. Guess who wins?

"Mister, sure you don't want me to try it?"

He looked at the boy, thin, just about five feet tall, sun-tanning adding an extra glow to what must have been Mediterranean ancestry.

"Okay, kid, it's all yours."

He stepped away from the possessed machine.

"What's your name?"

"Joe, Joe Rosario. What's yours?"

"Galen, Bob Galen."

"You the new doc?"

"Yeah. How'd you know?"

"Everybody knows everything about everybody in this town."

The boy squatted down, checked the gas tank for fuel, looked at the oil dipstick, and then took off a rectangular metal gadget on the side of the engine. He looked up at Galen.

"Mister, you pull the starter while I cover the air intake."

"Won't you hurt yourself?"

"Nah, go on, try to start it now."

Galen didn't want the kid to lose his hand. That would be a great start for his career. He looked down at the boy.

"Tell you what. Let me put my hand over the opening. You show me how, and you pull the starter cord. You strong enough to do that?"

"Course I am," he snorted.

Galen covered the opening. The boy took one quick pull of the starter, and the demonic contraption broke into its loud single-cylinder growl.

"Here, Mister, watch how I put the air filter back on."

And Galen did, learning his first steps in being a homeowner from a thirteen year old.

"Mister, I think I'd better show you how to cut grass, too."

The kid began walking steadily up and down in overlapping rows, creating a velvet green blanket where wilderness had been. When he finished, he pushed the mower over to Galen, looked up at him, and said: "Think you can do that now?"

Galen grinned, nodded, and reached into his pocket to pay the boy when the kid half-snarled.

"You're probably going to do like the others and flip a dime at me, aren't you?"

Uh-oh, some deep water here.

He reached into his pocket for his wallet and took out a five-dollar bill.

"Here, Joe, that's for the lawn and the lesson."

The boy's face registered a mixture of astonishment and suspicion. He stared at the adult standing there and then muttered: "I suppose you expect me to cut the grass for the rest of the summer for that."

"No, Joe, that was for today. I learned a long time ago that you pay a man what he's worth. And you certainly earned it."

The kid's frown melted into a grin. He started to walk away, holding the money tightly in his right hand.

"See ya, Mister."

That was the start of many visits, sudden, unexpected, usually when Galen was working in his garden. Joe would watch as Galen installed his annual bedding plants then stop and sit under the old maple tree facing the backyard parking lot. Cathy was there then, and she would bring out pitchers of water and shake her head as Galen and the boy would get into animated philosophical discussions on everything from teachers to girls.

The boy grew in size, age, and perspective, taking on deeper and deeper thoughts. Finally he left for college, and Galen continued their talks by letter, encouraging, warning, advising him.

And then Cathy was gone.

• • •

So why was Joe coming to the office today, Galen wondered, as he finished his walking circuit and got out the now-much-older mower. Joe had done Marine reserve duty then completed a master's degree and now consulted on Capitol Hill. He had the world by the tail. Six feet tall, muscular, still tanned from outdoor hunting and fishing, he was the picture of health.

Joe Rosario showed up promptly at 8:30. The older man had seen him happy, angry, frustrated, but never worried. And Joe looked worried. Though he obviously was trying to maintain his usual level of what he called rational behavior, the worry seeped through the chinks in his defensive armor.

"Doc, I'm losing feeling in parts of my hands. It's like I'm wearing rubber gloves. And there are times when I don't see things right, like there are holes in my vision."

Galen cringed internally. He had heard and seen this before. He quickly ran through the tests he could do in the office then sat down and faced the young man straight on. He had never lied or joked with Joe when things were serious, and this was one of those times.

"Joe, I want two other doctors to see you. One is a neurologist, the other an ophthalmologist. The neurologist will conduct certain nerve-function tests that I can't do here. The eye specialist will do what's called Visual Fields testing.

"What do you think it is, Doc?"

Galen sighed.

"Joe, my gut feeling is that you have MS—multiple sclerosis. It's a condition that affects certain parts of the brain called white matter and the sheathing around the nerve fibers called the myelin. When all that gets affected, it interferes with the brain's ability to sense, feel, and see. But I could be wrong, so I want those two consultants to see you. Will you let me set up the appointments?"

The younger man nodded then raised his head and stared at Galen.

"Is there any treatment for it, I mean, if you're right?"

Galen pulled his lips together then put his hand on Joe's shoulder.

"You'll get through this, Joe"

He quickly made the arrangements for the further testing then proceeded with the rest of his schedule.

What a time for something like this to come up!

Now he had doubts about making the weekend trip, feeling the pull of conflicting obligations. But he slogged through the usual run of rashes, colds, muscle pulls, and chest pains, and ended the day on an upbeat note.

"Trish, what's up?"

The young woman sat with her husband of one year, looking somewhat green around the gills.

"She's been getting real sick in the morning for the past couple of days, Doc. Think it could be food poisoning?"

Gary Grambling had met Trish Knowlton at a local church function and it was love at first sight. Both were deeply committed to their religious faith, and both had done missionary work in Africa. Now, after a year of marriage, the normally exceptionally healthy young woman was ill.

Galen asked several questions then took a blood sample. He asked the two young people to give him about ten minutes to run the test, retreated into his lab for that long, and then returned to the examining room, where he sat down facing the couple, smiling.

"What do you two want to name your case of food poisoning?"

Gary caught on first.

"You mean she's pregnant?"

The realization of it made him stand then sit down again abruptly, as Galen nodded his head.

Then Trish made the remark that Galen would remember for decades and never let the young woman forget she had said:

"Doc, how did this happen?"

After the office day was over, he walked through his back yard, going from plant to plant, letting himself unwind. The setting sun was still casting its orange-and-crimson light across the evening sky. Actually it had been a typical day, with the beginning of a new life easing the impact of the possible crashing of another. How often had he experienced those two outcomes?

He approached the section of the garden he had set aside in memory of Leni and Cathy. The special *hemerocallis* lilies were not yet ready to bloom. Two young house sparrows landed on the still-unopened bud scapes and began their evening song.

Time to go!

He sat up in bed. It was 11:30 p.m. He had packed the Jeep earlier. Carefully he closed up his red-shingled home/office, left a message with the covering doctor's answering service, then set out. What was he in for? Was this whole trip just the equivalent of male menopause—or andropause, if you wanted to be technically correct? Was he really trying to recapture those long-ago memories? Did he still have the necessary skills? He would know in ten hours.

"The Bear came over the mountain, the Bear came over the mountain, the Bear came over the mountain—to see what he could see!"

He heard the singing through the Jeep's open window.

The two women stood in the doorway, as he pulled into the parking lot of the concrete-block medical clinic/mission with its big red cross and open-hands logo. He quickly stepped out of his now-dusty vehicle and hugged them both.

"Teacher! Southern Belle! How come the two of you don't seem to get any older?"

"Didn't you know, Bob, all women cast magic spells so their men can't see what they really look like?" Peggy laughed.

Connie nodded in agreement then added, "And we put special potions in your food to confuse you even more."

"Well, that explains how you two hooked such outstanding members of the male brotherhood!"

He was laughing, too, as he picked up his duffle bag and followed his two friends into the house attached to the clinic.

"Speaking of which," he continued, "where are the other two illustrious members of the A Team?"

"Bill's getting some of the stuff set up in the clinic. Today we'll probably need to vaccinate at least a hundred kids who belong to the migrant worker families. We're the only place they're willing to go to, so the state provides us with the vaccines and we try to do at least that for them. I can't imagine how these families survive, let alone the kids."

Peggy had taken on her serious look, and Galen knew she truly was concerned about the people she and Bill looked after.

Connie sat down next to him.

"We brought the two boys, you know, Tommy and Andy, and Bill told Dave where the nearest beach was. They should be back any minute now."

Just then, they heard another car pull in and Connie stood up to look out the window.

"That's them," she called out as she headed to the door. Galen followed her. In the open doorway he saw the tall-but-not-as-thin friend and roommate from school, now sporting a mustache and being pulled by two very active little boys. The older had Connie's eyes and facial structure, while the younger was his father's miniature twin.

"Hey, Country Boy, you ain't no Scarecrow no more. When did you decide to grow a lip duster and get pregnant?"

"Better watch out, City Boy, I might just sic my rug rats on you!"

The two still-damp munchkins ran up to their mother.

"Mommy, Mommy, we got to swim at the beach here and there were jellyfish and Daddy had to help this man and lady who were bitten by them and Andy and me put one in a pail but Daddy made us throw it back in the water so we just put seashells and . . . "

At that point the boy ran out of breath.

"Slow down, Tommy, slow down. What did Daddy do to save the man and lady?"

"It wasn't much of anything, just typical Man of War stings. I guess you don't see that stuff up in D.C., do you, Bob?"

"No, Dave, we have worse critters called politicians. There's no cure or treatment for 'em. But go ahead and tell me about it. Teach me, Country Boy!"

"Well, it was pretty obvious these two were Yankees like you. Probably the only water they ever saw was rain going down gutters. The boys and I were sitting there on the blanket drying off and here they come barefooted, running in and out of the surf like a couple of newlyweds, when the guy says, 'Hey, Nancy, take a look at this!' Then he reaches down into the water and, damned if he didn't try to pick up the jellyfish. Next thing I know, he's screaming at the top of his lungs, and his wife is pulling him out of the water and trying to settle him down by telling him 'Easy, Bob, easy, Bob.' Funny—even had your name. So the boys and I run over. I never go anywhere without my kit, and in Florida you gotta be prepared for stuff like this. I yell at her to stop, just as she was about to put wet cold sand on his hand."

"Okay, Dave, I know about jellyfish nematocysts that sting and release poisons and that stuff. Cut to the chase!"

"Still the impatient one, O Bear Who Talks? In any event, I stop her from triggering more poison release and tell the boys to fill their sand buckets with hot water from the rinse-off tap. We pour the hot water to inactivate the poison, then I used some of the vinegar I carry in the emergency kit to neutralize the toxin even more. You do know the stuff is heat labile, right?"

"Right, so you're the greatest healer in the world."

"Glad you admit it, City Boy! It's kinda funny. The guy couldn't stop thanking me. His poor wife was standing there just shaking her head at him. He looked like a scared, cross-eyed rabbit holding its paw out. All he could keep saying was that he would never retire down here. Kept muttering about hurricanes and now jellyfish. Come to think of it, I think their car had a New Jersey license plate. Had a familiar name, too, but I can't remember it right now."

"Hey, slackers, time to get to work!"

Bill had entered the room and walked over to Galen, arms extended to hug his old friend. Babyface had yielded somewhat to a beard and his scalp hair was a defeated army against the onslaught of male hormones. But he was still the same Bill, open and extending himself. Galen looked at his old friend and saw that he was at peace. He truly had found a double calling in his work.

"Come on, guys, let me show you how I've set things up. Peggy, can we get one of the helpers to look after the kids?"

Three adults left the room to enter the clinic side while Peggy took the two boys to the housekeeper. Tommy kept nudging Andy, teasing the younger boy, until Andy whacked him and he yelled, "Just for that I won't tell you what the man's name was."

Andy sniffled.

"I know who the man is. We learned about him in school. He invented the light bulb. That was Mr. Edison."

"You have quite a setup here, Bill. How can you afford to run it? You must have, what, ten, twelve exam rooms, an operatory, even X-ray. How can you afford to do this?"

Galen was impressed by the scope of his friend's setup, but he also knew Bill and Peggy weren't getting rich here. This was all *pro bono,* as the lawyers would say.

"I managed to get some state and federal grants. At first neither wanted to have anything to do with me, until they realized no one else would handle these people, and if I stopped it would cost them ten times more. Peggy and I don't need much and we saved every penny when we first started. We were also not lucky enough to have kids, so . . . ," and he paused, "so here we are!"

Loud, unmuffled car and truck engines caused the three to turn and look out the windows.

"The local farmers are bringing in our first load of patients. There're some extra lab coats in the closet there. Peggy and I can show you where to find anything you need. A Team, start your engines!"

They worked steadily through the late morning, vaccinating crying children and babies, their ochre-brown faces glistening from the tears. Then they cared for the adults: the pregnant young wives who had received no prenatal care until today and the macho men with their gaping wounds from farm accidents and internecine knife fights.

They saw malnutrition, parasites, and fear, but none of the wealthy suburban high-fat degenerative diseases of heart and bone. Heart attacks and arthritis were the least of these folks' worries.

The five worked the assembly line, just like in the old days, until 6 p.m. No breaks, no stopping except for the bathroom as their energy reverberated throughout the clinic. But even the best intentions cannot sustain the flagging energies that affect the middle-aged. By 7 they had dealt with the last stragglers and the very-weary-but-still-animated friends sat around the table in the main examining room comparing notes.

"I don't think we need to go jogging tonight, Bill, do you?" Peggy asked.

The other four laughed, and Dave added, "Tell me again, when did I enlist in the Marines?"

"Is it like this every day, Bill?" Galen asked.

"No, guys, today was busy because of the migrant workers. We have quiet spells, too."

"Outside of stuff like this, do you have any other big problems with the practice? Down where we live in Florida, sometimes the gangs try to hold up small businesses."

Dave was getting that wistful look, Galen noted.

I'll bet he's thinking he'd like to stay on here. Come to think of it, I probably would, too.

Bill shrugged.

"We haven't had any break-ins or gangs yet, but I'm sure it's only a matter of time until civilization reaches us. We're not that far off the main highway, so anyone can come by."

Almost on cue, they heard heavy engine noise pull into the lot. Bill peered out.

"I don't recognize that car. Must be strangers. I'll go see what's up. You folks just rest. We've got another busy day tomorrow."

"On Sunday?" Connie asked.

Peggy told her about the Sunday services Bill convened for the migrants before opening the clinic for abbreviated hours.

Then the four heard loud noises coming from the entrance. The next thing they saw was Bill being frog-walked into the exam area, a knife held at his throat by a stocky Amerasian-looking man while his companion, a taller African American, .38 in hand, followed.

"Wallets and jewelry, now! Where's the drug cabinet? Hurry up or he's dog food!"

Galen knew that look: flat, dull eyed, very dangerous. The made men in his old neighborhood showed similar looks, but these two were more animated. They were druggies, probable stone killers if crossed. They weren't going to take and leave without having some fun. He looked at the black man, calculating odds, weighing some of the old maneuvers from when he was a kid.

Let's try the insult route. Maybe rile the gun-holder into a rash action.

If he was right, he might just pull them all out of trouble. But if he was wrong, Bill would die.

"Su Madre!"

He half shouted it out, and time seemed to stand still. Everyone looked at him, the women horrified, the men almost questioning, and then the two men faced him.

"What did you say, Honkie?"

He moved closer to Galen but kept the gun close to his chest.

Still no leverage.

If he remembered both his later training and his growing-up lessons, he had to get the aggressor both angry and distracted.

"Su Madre."

Even with the walnut skin coloring, Galen could see the flush rising in his adversary's face as he drew closer.

"Go ahead, Honkie, say that one more time!"

"Su Madre," he repeated, almost snarling.

That was enough. The man reflexively brought his arm forward aiming the gun at Galen's head. But Galen was prepared. Using the extended arm as a lever, his own arms shot out, twisting then bending back the other man's gun hand. The revolver discharged, sending a bullet into the floor and at the same time distracting the knife-holder, who relaxed his arm momentarily.

Dave pushed Bill aside and grabbed the knife-wielder's arm, also bringing it backward, but the Asian-looking man was slippery as an eel and managed to stab Dave along his left shoulder. Blood appeared on his shirt but he continued twisting the man's arm until he heard an audible snap, followed by a loud scream as the assailant fell to the floor.

Galen twisted harder on the other felon, and a second shot rang out. The two men stood there, locked in combat until the dark man slid to the floor, blood pouring from his chest.

"Back to your roots, eh, City Boy?" Dave gasped then started to fall forward. Galen caught his friend, held him up, and carried him to the nearest examining table.

Dear God, no, not Dave! If you really exist, don't take him now. No more losses, please!

He tried to stay calm and professional. He knew his friends were in a state of shock.

"Peggy, call the police! Connie, you and Bill get me a wound suture set. I've gotta put Scarecrow back together."

Bill was bending over the bullet-wounded attacker. No breathing, sphincters loosened—he was dead. Then he examined the other man still writhing on the floor from the rotational fracture. This thug would live. He knelt back down over the dead man, gently closed his eyes, then prayed for the forgiveness of his soul.

Galen had cut off Dave's shirt to examine the wound.

Soft tissue penetration only. No retained debris.

"Dave, I'm going to numb this up with lidocaine and irrigate it then we'll close you up good as new."

His friend's vital signs looked good. The fainting was just from the shock of being wounded. As the local anesthetic took hold, Galen examined the wound, decided on layered closure, irrigated it with saline then began the patchwork of closing it. Connie stood by on Dave's right side, holding his hand.

Galen suddenly felt the silence, his peripheral vision catching the side stares and eye contacts among his friends. He knew immediately what was wrong, and why he now stood alone in the crowded room.

"Hey, Dave, did I ever tell you about the first person I ever sewed up?"

"At least ten times, Bob. Just get it over with so I can get up and punch your lights out for scaring us half to death."

"What, you didn't like my movie-hero role?"

Yeah, they're reacting the same way Trish did.

Connie shook her head and spoke up.

"You took an awful chance, Bob."

"She's right," Bill added as Peggy walked back in, heard what was being said, then agreed with the others.

They really don't understand. They've never had to fight for their lives or watch their friends get killed. I can't blame them, but damn it hurts when my closest friends look at me like I'm some wild berserker.

"Listen, guys, I grew up with people like this. I know what they do, how they behave. They wouldn't have left here with just money and drugs. They would have laughed as they killed Bill, you, and me, then raped and killed the women. They probably would have killed the kids and housekeeper as well."

He paused to finish working on Dave.

"There, that closes you up. Want me to work on the mouth next?"

His friends stared at him, not sure whether they should accept his assessment of the situation or not. Medical professionals and hospital veterans all, but none of them had ever been confronted by anything like this, and they just didn't know what to do or say. They also had never seen Galen when he was truly angry. There is a natural guilt feeling among those who have never taken a life, even in self-defense. The limbic beast protects and shames all too well.

Loud knocking at the door broke the silence. Bill went to open it, coming back with two highway patrol officers.

"What happened, Doc?" the older one asked, as the younger officer knelt down to look at the dead and injured assailants. Bill started to explain, when the young officer let out an exclamation:

"Jesus, Sarge! These are the Interstate Killers!"

Galen looked at his suddenly wide-eyed friends then quietly asked, "What do you mean, Corporal?"

The older officer cut in.

"These two have been going up and down the interstate, finding small businesses open late. Their usual MO is either to break in if the place is unoccupied or, if the owner's unlucky enough to be there, rob, torture, and kill him and whoever else is there. You folks are lucky they fouled up."

The sergeant looked at them, silently counting out five people, then shook his head. "If those two had succeeded, this would have been a massacre."

"Corporal, forgive me for asking," Bill interjected, "but how can you be so sure these are the two men you say they are?"

"Doc, one of the places they entered had a security camera. To my dying day, I will never forget the spattering of blood and the vicious raping that camera recorded."

An ambulance under police escort had carted away the wounded assailant, and the coroner's truck picked up the dead man. Quiet descended once again on the clinic. Galen had taken off his bloodstained lab coat and was walking outside in the parking lot, looking up at the quarter moon. He felt someone's hand fall on his shoulder and turned to see Dave, left arm in sling, standing next to him. Bill, Peggy, and Connie were just behind him. He looked at his friend and old roommate. What could he say? Then Dave said it for the four of them.

"Hey, Bob, those were some mighty fierce-looking bulls you took out."

The other three had heard the story many times before about his visit to Dave's home, but there was now something tender in the way Dave said it.

Galen looked at his four classmates, hesitated for just a second, and then in his best imitation of Dave's father's voice, yelled out, "Sheeeeit, Boy! Bulls ain't got teats!"

Sunday passed quickly. The neighbors had heard by the grapevine, and the migrant workers crowded into Bill's Sunday services in unheard-of numbers, just to be sure that Padre Bill and his friends were all right. The five worked the clinic to mid-afternoon then rested before splitting up to return home.

"I wish you three could stay on. We'd have one hell of an operation here," Bill said.

"Did I just hear you cuss, Babyface?"

Dave and Connie had rounded up the two boys and were standing next to their car.

"Hey, City Boy—or maybe it should be City Bear—did you just teach Bill some of your New Jersey words and manners?"

Galen shook his head and laughed.

"No, Dave, I think Bill just grew up a little."

He looked at his friend's shoulder one last time.

"Be sure you find a good doc back in Florida to follow up on that. Connie, do you accept perverse wounded farm boys as patients?"

"What do you think I've been doing since school?"

"Teacher has taught me more than you know, Bob," Dave replied with a wink and then a wince as Connie hit him on the right shoulder.

"Peggy, keep an eye on Bill. I'm afraid that Dave and I have warped him permanently now," Galen added as he climbed into the Jeep.

He headed out first, watching his friends in the rear view mirror as he headed back north. Must be a trick of the light, he thought, as he saw the shadow over Dave's head.

"Bob, this is perfect!"

Nancy gazed down from the top of the mountain, the half-completed house sitting there like a giant rook.

"We can do it," he agreed, and put his arm around her.

They stood there, looking at their future, and both of them felt that mixture of trepidation, relief, and completion. They were about to begin a new and exciting phase in their lives.

CHAPTER 11

Slippery Slope

One morning he opened his morning paper and did something he swore he would never do: He turned to the obituary page.

Half jokingly, he sometimes told his patients that every morning he scanned the names in the obituaries and, if his wasn't there, he would proceed as usual with the day.

Some of his patients joked back that even if he did discover his name there, he still probably would come upstairs and go about his usual duties. Now, looking through the obituaries, Galen began to wonder if that might not be true.

The great philosophers have written volumes about youth and old age, and modern-day analysts meander over the middle. But there is a fourth niche, one of resignation and loss. It begins inserting its ugly head into that narrow notch of birthdays between the middle and the end. Some call it late middle age. Others cautiously label it "perigeriatric," as if dancing around it in a tarantella of denial will forestall its onset. It is the time when children are grown, careers are winding down, retirement is truly imminent, and the genetic scythe starts thinning the human wheat field.

Friends, acquaintances, neighbors, family members become sick and die. That, by itself, is the human condition. Until the genetic mages can prevent the progressive shortening of the telomeres, which leads to cell death, and at the same time block the terrible cell immortality of cancer, those inevitable entropies will claim us all.

Earlier that morning, Galen had stared at a street scene before him when the disruption of dawn had not yet broken the stillness of night. He already had begun his morning walk in a decidedly somber and contemplative mood, thinking about colleagues dying of sudden heart attacks or piecemeal from cancer, and of patients getting older and showing the wear of time. Was this already happening to him? Would it happen to him? He mentally shrugged. Of course it would. He wasn't from Krypton.

And then he saw her, the woman dancing on the sidewalk. She was elderly, doll-like, and ninety-percent undressed. He watched her pirouette, extend her arms, and bow gracefully in different directions, a grotesque ballet macabre. He continued to stare until he realized that he knew her: It was Lucille, Lucille Desmond.

"Dr. Galen, my friends recommended me to you. Will you accept me as a patient?"

The dignified woman sat in his examining room in a tailored dark dress suit, expensively cut, and with refined manners. She was a retired university dean, holder of several doctoral degrees in education and the arts. Now she had moved into a townhouse just across the street from his office to be near "her family." She was, she said, perfectly healthy, went to the local athletic center daily, read at least one new book per day, and could converse at length on just about any subject. To Galen's eye, this was what growing older should be.

That was before he heard the silent laughter of the Fates, the whisper of "watch what We are going to do to her."

And They did.

For a while, things went smoothly. No untoward events, not even colds. But the family she had hoped to enjoy was nowhere to be seen. Things always came up to prevent the holiday get-togethers. Grandchildren were too busy for Grandma.

Galen noted gradual changes: recent memory failures, forgotten names, an inability to articulate as well as she once so admirably had done. She knew it, too, and waved her long artist's fingers in a diagram of despair as she mentioned increasing forgetfulness.

"Lucille, let me run some tests on you, call it preventive maintenance."

All of the tests—blood, vitamin B12 levels, diabetes, thyroid, and other areas that could affect a person's mental status—were normal . . . except for the brain imaging, which showed some suspicious activity. Coupled with the behavioral changes, it seemed like the cruelest fate that could befall an intelligent person: Dementia. Whether it was Alzheimer's or another variant of brain deterioration, it was the worst life sentence for a woman like Lucille Desmond.

"Mr. Desmond, we need to talk about your mother. I'm worried about her living alone. Her ability to function is deteriorating and she might hurt herself. Is there anything that you might be able to do, arrange for caregivers, possibly move her to your home, or arrange custodial care?"

Astounded, he saw the glazed eyes, the lack of interest and concern on the part of the woman's son. So, he called social services and was met with the conundrum that, as long as the patient had family and represented no danger to herself or others, they could make no intervention.

And now this wonderfully brilliant mind had descended into a hell which, fortunately, it could no longer perceive.

Galen ran across the street and scooped the dancing Dresden-doll-like woman up in his arms. She continued to sing softly as he carried her to the townhouse. Luckily the door was ajar, so he quietly helped her inside to what once had been a fastidiously kept living room. Now, the decor was late disarray and the hygiene more typical of a fraternity house. He found the telephone and a worn address book, fallen onto the dirt-soiled rug. It wasn't yet 5 a.m., but he dialed her son's number and began speaking before he could be cut off.

"Mr. Desmond, I just found your mother wandering almost naked in the street. Something has to be done for her before she hurts herself. If it is not in your power to do so, I will call the county and state social services departments. She can no longer be left alone."

Curses muttered through only partially awakened lips met this statement, and then the call was disconnected. Galen sighed. He dialed the emergency county number and remained with Lucille until the ambulance arrived.

She would need a full evaluation to be sure there was no element of delirium from chemical imbalance, and then perhaps arrangements could be made by the caseworker. Maybe the agency even had the clout to move the woman's son.

Dawn broke through and Galen finished his walk, although his heart wasn't in it. *Why are people abandoned by friends and family?* It would be easy to attribute it to malignant personalities on the part of the deserted individuals, but that had not been his observational experience. Was it fear of their own mortality that led them to turn their backs on those who overtly manifested the signs of That Which Must Not Be Named?

He entered the side door of his home/office and prepared to clean up before office hours started. Halfway through, the phone rang. *It's going to be one of those days,* he thought. When things started happening this early, they usually presaged what the day would be like.

"Bob, it's Jack Basily. Sorry to call so early, but I thought you would want to know Harry Freiling passed away this morning in his sleep."

Memories of his university days returned in Technicolor along with the turns of events that led to the long friendship with his two former professors. Harry Freiling had lived a full life and went out peacefully, he thought.

How many of us will do the same?

"Jack, when are the services?"

"This Saturday. I know his family would appreciate your coming."

Galen wrote down the information, spoke a little while longer with his friend, then sat at his desk thinking. Harry would have been almost ninety by now, and he had retained his faculties of mind right up to the end. Not like poor Mrs. Desmond. He heard the toss and roll of the dice and the laughter of capricious deities in his mind.

"Barbara, I need to take a quick trip up to New Jersey this Saturday. One of my old college professors passed away and I'd like to be there for the services. How's my schedule look for Saturday morning?"

"Not a problem, Dr. G. Only a few minor things so far, and they can be put off until Monday. I'll take care of them."

"Thanks. I'll leave after office hours tonight."

He merged onto I-495, the Capital Beltway, and drove around to the intersection with I-95 north to Baltimore. Now it was a traffic-filled but fairly direct drive through Maryland and Delaware then crossing over the JFK Bridge into New Jersey. He followed the turnpike up to the cutoff that would take him to the bedroom community where the two professors had retired: Bernardsville. Even when Galen was a child, this was a place where rich people lived. Now, former farm pastures had been built over with suburban rooftops as far as the eye could see.

Looks like there's at least one dissatisfied family in God's country. That thought emerged as he passed the rental moving truck parked in front of one of the homes.

Wonder what's making them pull up stakes?

"Nancy, the truck's almost full. I think I can get the rest in, though. Four trips already. We're almost out of here."

Edison was tired, and truth be told, so was Nancy. But their dream was almost within reach. This last load would empty the house, and soon they would be heading for the promised land of Pennsylvania and retirement!

Galen pulled up in front of a compact, brick-rambler-style home. The house numbers on the lighted yard post looked over the carved wooden nameplate: Basily.

He picked up the doorknocker to announce himself but the door was already opening, and he saw his old professor and friend standing there in slippers and robe. Even in the half-darkness, Galen's trained eye caught the telltale signs. Jack wasn't well.

"Glad you were able to come, Bob. You are staying with us tonight, aren't you?"

He had thought about a nearby motel, but then nodded in agreement.

"Let me get my bag out of the car, Jack."

He turned quickly before the other man could see the concern on his face, half-ran to the car, grabbed his gear, and headed back. He followed his host into the living room and stood there, watching Basily move slowly about the perimeter.

"Jack, I know I just got here, but you know I've never been one for social niceties. What's going on with you?"

The older man faced him, smiled, then shrugged in resignation.

"Father Time, Bob. Looks like I have the Big C."

He sat down, exhausted just by the brief effort of meeting his guest.

"I knew you would spot it even if I kept the lights low. My family thinks I have a bad chest infection. But the crab is there, feeding itself and its offspring on my insides. Harry had it easy, going out in his sleep. I'm not sure what it's going to be like for me."

He stared directly at his former student.

"Tell me, Bob, how's it going to be? Is there anything you can give me to simplify my exit?"

Galen felt the dying man's eyes bore into him. How many times, in how many different ways, had he been asked the same two questions? Every doctor fears those questions, the hidden implications, the feeling of impotence at the still-limited effectiveness of present-day science and technology to cure. The burden of being fortuneteller and predictor of life and death was overwhelming.

"Jack, I'll promise you this. I'll make sure your doctor never lets you be in pain. But you know, as much as you may want me to, I can't knowingly shorten your life."

There, he had said it, the official answer to the unspoken question. But he also looked at his friend, and both understood the deeper answer. Nothing else was said about it that evening.

The next morning, he drove Basily to the funeral home. They both stood over the open casket, looking down at what once had been a vibrant gadfly of a man and Galen's one-time nemesis.

"I hope to God that no idiot says how natural he looks," Basily whispered, and both men almost laughed at the incongruity of it. "Think I'll look that 'natural,' Bob?"

Galen wanted to lash out at the gods for their perversity.

He left New Jersey late Saturday. He had called Basily's doctor and spoken at length about his friend's condition. He made sure that the other doctor, a good and caring physician in his own right, understood the importance of his friend remaining pain-free. After the war, Basily had spent many years immobilized and in chronic pain. His last days should not be a repeat performance.

As Galen exited the quiet neighborhood, he noticed the moving van was gone. There was a prominent SOLD sign on the front lawn. *Wonder where those folks are going?* he mused, as he headed back down the turnpike.

"Bob, look at the view, and it's all ours! I can't believe we finally did it!

Edison couldn't say anything for fear of choking up and crying. He stood at the top of the mountain, holding his wife as tightly as he could.

"Bill, I need another hemostat. He's got a pumper."

Peggy was bent over the body of the migrant farm worker, trying to repair a large scalp wound on the front of the man's head. He had fallen forward onto a scythe blade improperly placed in the back of a pickup truck carrying the workers back from the field. Now he looked like what Custer must have looked like after the Battle of the Little Big Horn. Half of his scalp had been sliced off and was hanging backward.

Peggy had gotten most of the area repaired when the small blood vessel decided to erupt.

"Got it, old girl." For a moment the couple locked eyes over their masked faces.

"So is this what retirement is all about, Bill?"

And they started to laugh so hard that the farm worker wondered, *¿Que loco?*

They were both tired by day's end. For some reason, there are times when every patient is an emergency, and this was one of them. But a feeling of happy fatigue oozes over one when things go well and the patient is still breathing or able to walk out afterwards.

The veranda was cooled by the evening breezes coming from the coast. They sat there, side by side, watching another sunset.

"Think it's going to rain tomorrow?"

Bill looked at Peggy, seeing through the facial creases and graying hairs to the woman he had met and fallen in love with so many years before. How had he been so lucky to have found her? With the magic that all women possess, she said nothing. She just smiled and put her hand in his.

Galen kept ruminating about the two old professors as he drove back home. *Is it really just genetics? Why does one person have to suffer at the end and another go in his sleep? Who or what decides whether we are Lucilles or Basilys or Freilings?*

His mind flashed back to that long-ago day when life ended for both the daughter of slaves and the mother of wealth and he wondered: *How does genetics preordain our passing?*

"Connie, what do you think? We'll both be ready to quit work in a few years and go on with our lives. The boys will be away by then. I was thinking, how would it be if we picked up and moved near Bill and Peggy? We could help out at the mission, and we'd still be near the beach."

Being a teacher, a doctor, and an insightful woman on top of it all, she knew what Dave was getting at. Treating "snowbirds" with more money than common sense had become the routine. They both needed to cap their careers with something more meaningful. At one time she had considered doing missionary work in Africa. But what Bill had established would offer everything they both needed in the realm of spiritual satisfaction.

"I was thinking about that, too, Dave."

They sat down together, just as they had always done, Dave the planner, Connie the moderator, outlining their escape route. It wasn't long before they called Bill and Peggy to discuss the feasibility of the move. And then it was settled: They would start the transition now.

Next came the daunting task of how to close one practice and reestablish it in another locale. They both were amazed at the paperwork nightmare and legal rigmarole involved, but somehow it seemed worth it. The boys soon would be getting ready to move on to their own lives, with their own careers ahead of them. It was time for the parents to let go.

"Don't forget, the party's tonight. I've already tied up the loose ends. All you need to do is officially turn over the hospital patients to Sam. Then come on home."

Dave felt the familiar queasy stomach of pre-exam jitters. Was today an alpha-and-omega day? Were they actually going to pull up stakes and work part-time at a medical mission in another state? Why hadn't he told Galen about the move?

Maybe this way, once it's all accomplished, the four of us can convince him to do likewise and join us. Just like old times.

What a hoot that would be: five old farts facing their twilight years just as they did the dawn.

He stopped at the lowered gate at the railroad crossing. Must be a train coming. He began to drum his fingers on the steering wheel of the old Toyota then turned on the radio. *Maybe some classic rock for the rest of the drive home.*

The construction-truck driver was tired and hungry. It wasn't easy piloting the dirt-hauling behemoth, even with power steering and brakes. But he was a careful man, going some twenty years without an accident or even a ticket. All he wanted was to get home to his wife and kids, put his feet up, and rest. What else would a man want?

Young David, Bone Man's ready fer ye.

What the hell was on that station? He reached over to press another button.

Big David and Mary waitin' fer ye.

The truck driver saw the crossing gates down and began the downshifting and braking necessary to overcome the massive momentum he was controlling. When his foot hit the pedal he immediately felt the sickening softness of no resistance. No brakes! He downshifted furiously, attempting to use the full resistance of the engine to slow the truck, but it wasn't enough to overcome the overwhelming inertia. The barrier arms of the crossing gates splintered like matches as the truck sheared through and onto the little Toyota on the other side.

Dave watched as if in a dream as the massive truck hit his vehicle head-on and felt the crushing impact as it rode over the roof, shearing it off in the process. With the last electrical impulses of his neurons he cried out, "Why now?"

Come, young David. Ye have work to do.

And everything became clear.

"Dr. Galen, that's the last patient for today. Anything else I can do?"

"No Barbara, go on home. I need to wrap up some stuff here, I . . ."

He felt the pain like a lightning strike run through him. His knees buckled and his head seemed to explode in a rainbow of light.

"Are you okay, Dr. G.?"

His other part-time secretary recoiled as her boss nearly fell across her desk, his face pale and sweat-covered.

"That was one helluva muscle spasm, Barbara. Felt like my head was being ripped off. Guess I better get some extra rest tonight."

"You haven't fooled with that computer of yours for awhile. Why don't you just do some playing with it tonight and leave the work till tomorrow?"

"That sounds like a good idea."

He went back to his office planning to finish some paperwork then tossed it down. *Barbara's right,* he thought. He got up, turned off the light and headed downstairs. He flipped on the switch of what he called his fun computer. No business on this one. It was for keeping what one of his old professors called his "diary."

He started with his e-mail and scanned the hundreds of spam messages, the majority of which offered to make him bigger and better than he was as a teenager. But there was one that tweaked his interest:

Find old friends and classmates, lost loves and experiences. Try us!

His lost loves were far beyond the reach of search engines. So, who in the world would he want to hear from again? The only friend he ever had before medical school was . . . Edison.

The way things are I wonder if he's even alive. Okay, let's give it a try.

Under the high-school category he entered the name Concepción, added the state and city, then waited the microsecond before a long list appeared on the screen.

Too many, I need to hone it down.

He entered the year Edison would have graduated and a shorter list appeared.

Akins, Bradford, Chartais, Davis, Eason, Edison!

He quickly clicked on the highlighted name for information and was confronted by the reality of the Internet world:

Please enter your credit card number so that we may start your membership.

He laughed. It reminded him of the old pay phones when the operator would come on and say, "Please deposit 20 cents to continue your call."

What the hell! In for a penny, in for a pound!

He pulled out his old sharkskin wallet. Funny, he had been with Dave in the department store when his older billfold disintegrated and he needed to buy this one. It was one of the two extravagances of his medical-school days.

Well, at least this one stayed with me.

He opened the lower drawer in his desk and stared for a moment at the ring box sitting there.

Slowly he entered the credit card number. The screen went blank for several seconds and then . . . an address and a telephone number!

"Nancy, would you grab the phone? I've got grease all over my hands"

Normal state of affairs, she thought as she picked up the handset.

Bob, you're still a little boy, even in retirement.

She heard a man's voice ask, "Is this the residence of Robert Edison who attended Concepción High School in Westfield, New Jersey?"

"Hold on," she said then cupped her hand over the mouthpiece.

"Bob, do you owe anybody money?"

Not that he would. He never spent any to begin with. He wasn't cheap. He just could do everything by himself. But he would spend his last dollar on her if she wanted it.

"Why?"

"There's a man on the phone, wants to know if you're the Bob Edison from Concepción High School."

"What's his name? It might be an old classmate of mine."

She uncovered the phone and asked, "May I say who's calling?"

The voice that replied still held a hint of New Jersey, but it was softened by a Southern lilt.

"Your husband and I were friends in high school. My name is Galen, Bob Galen."

She cupped the phone receiver once more.

"Bob, this guy sounds strange. Maybe I should hang up."

"What's his name?"

"Galen."

He snatched the phone from his wife's hands, grease smearing the handset.

"Is this who I think it is?"

He felt the excitement course through him.

"It's been a long time, Little Brother."

He was surprisingly happy that night when he finally decided to go to bed. The telephone call reconnecting him with his friend had picked up his spirits and brought back memories of the good times they shared in high school. He turned off the lights and lay there thinking of his life and wondering if maybe he should consider retiring and going to work at the mission with Bill and Peggy.

Then came that after-midnight call—that cursed, damnable call ordained by the Fates.

"Bob, it's Connie."

He could hear the strain in her voice immediately.

"Connie, what's the matter? Are the boys okay?'

Is Old Aunt Hattie calling?

"Bob," she choked out, "they took Dave to the hospital. They don't think he's going to make it. I'm here in the emergency room waiting for them to get done with him."

"What happened?"

He almost yelled the question at her through the phone.

"There was an auto accident. He was coming back from hospital rounds. It was his last day there. He didn't tell you but we were going to retire this week. We wanted to travel, maybe help Bill out at the clinic part-time. Dave even talked about getting the old team together at Bill's free clinic."

Now as she continued, she was barely breathing in, unable to stop the torrent of words. She was in shock. He couldn't get her to stop rambling.

"Connie, put the ER doctor on."

He waited then heard the receiver being picked up. But he already knew. And now he knew the cause of that terrible pain earlier in the day. His mind heard the voice of his old friend.

City Boy, Aunt Hattie was right about this, too.

"Dr. Galen, this is Tom Eastman. I'm the ER doc here in Lakeland. Mrs. Nash tells me you and Dr. Nash were long-time friends."

The word "were" rang in his ear. He felt his eyes filling.

"I'm afraid that Dr. Nash expired at the scene of the accident. We did what we could when they brought him in, but the brain damage was too massive. I'm sorry."

He slowly put the telephone receiver down and began to weep.

The church was filled with friends, patients, colleagues, all those who had been in close contact.

The minister stepped to the dais, led the group in a short prayer, then announced, "I have been asked to let another speak of the deceased. I, too, wish to learn more about him."

He beckoned and Galen rose from his chair and approached the microphone. He looked at the large group, thinking how Country Boy would have found it amusing. Then he began.

"It was a strange Mutt-and-Jeff relationship between the City Boy and the Country Boy. The Fates had decreed that we would share a room in the grueling process of our education, and no more dissimilar young men had ever been thrown together."

As he continued, he talked about Dave's humble background as a farm boy, the first in his family even to finish high school, much less college and medical school. He watched as the audience nodded at the familiar information and expressed surprise at some of the exciting points in Dave's life.

Galen paused and looked out over the crowd, seeing the capacity-filled church with standees. Connie and the boys were sitting next to Bill and Peggy, who was holding Connie's hand tightly.

He saw the back doors open. Two African-American men, tall, middle-aged, in the uniforms of the U.S. Navy and Army, removed their hats and walked halfway up the aisle to stand. Galen apologized for the length of his eulogy. But he wanted to tell one more, final story, to demonstrate what kind of man Dave had been. And as he spoke, the years slipped away and he and Dave were back on Church Hill, students once again.

• • •

"Are you sure this is okay, Dave?"

They were at the very top of the hill that looked down on the southeast side of Richmond, Virginia. Here once stood the Confederate Army Hospital, Chimborazo. And like the great works of Ozymandias, it was now rubble and brick pieces.

But the hill held another monument, this one deep underground. At one time, the railway line had bored through the hill and run tracks from the old gas works and icehouse to the very top of Church Hill. Trains would enter that nether world and exit into the light at the summit.

One fateful day, the residents of lower Richmond felt a rumble. Some thought it was an earthquake, others a great storm. But it was neither. It was the death cry of a tunnel as countless tons of earth collapsed inside, entombing the unlucky train and its passengers forever. Rescue attempts proved futile, so the city fathers sealed the lower entrance with a giant concrete slab inscribed with the date of the tragedy. That was 1926.

Thirty seven years later, two young men in their prime stood at the top of the hill, looking at the partially boarded-up top exit of the tunnel, as they picked up loose bricks to make student bookcases. They rationalized it was not really stealing. When they finished school, the bricks would be returned, as they had been by countless other students over the years, as the cycle repeated itself.

Then they heard a frantic cry.

"Mista, Mista, com hep us! Ma bruther, he in da tunnel!"

It was Marcus, one of the black youngsters in the same housing complex where Galen and Dave lived. Marcus's little brother, Jeremiah, was always getting into things and needing a rescue. But this was the most dangerous so far.

The two medical students ran to the opening where Marcus stood and pointed inward. Collapsed crossbeams and warning signs had not been enough to stem the curiosity of a six-year-old boy. Now, he was partway inside, captured by the weight of a collapsed wood strut.

Dave looked at Galen.

"Come on, Bob, the two of us can get him."

Galen remembered the old abandoned buildings in his neighborhood, deadly mousetraps for curious children. His hackles were rising, as Dave picked up a discarded length of wood.

"We can use this to pry the beam off of him."

He started to squeeze into the tunnel. Galen followed with more difficulty. He wasn't the scarecrow that Dave was. But they both reached the boy soon enough. The light from the afternoon sun penetrating through the mouth of the tunnel was just enough to give faint illumination to the scene. The young men, scientists by nature and training, saw the natural fulcrum of a fallen piece of stone.

"Dave, you grab his arms. I've got more weight. I'm going to try to lever that thing off. If we're lucky, you can pull him out. If not, I guess the three of us can spend eternity talking to the train crew and passengers below."

The drip of seeping water and something scurrying from God knows what played counterpoint with their heartbeats.

"Listen, Jeremiah, Bob is going to try to lift the beam, and I'm going to pull you out. And then we'll all get the hell outta here. Understand?"

The tearstained brown face nodded, and Galen began the counter-pressure, hoping the lever wouldn't break. He felt some bending in the old wood and then the give, as the fallen beam lifted several inches. Immediately, Dave pulled and the boy slid out from under it, just as the tension in Galen's muscles gave way, and the beam settled again.

Ominous creaking noises started, and Dave let out a "Let's move it!" He picked up the little boy, and the two young men inched their way back up and out. Galen had barely cleared the tunnel entrance when the four of them, two urchins and two foolhardy adults, heard the grinding collapse of ancient wood and a cloud of dust rise at the entrance they had just left.

• • •

"And that, ladies and gentlemen, was the type of man my friend was. I do not know why bad things happen to good people, but if I know Dave, he would come back from the afterlife if he could to help a friend."

After most of the crowd had left, Connie stood with Bill and Peggy and the boys as the minister handed her the cloth-wrapped box containing Dave's ashes. Galen saw the two military men had remained, so he approached them and shook hands. Their name tags read CMDR. JEREMIAH BAILEY and COL. MARCUS BAILEY.

CHAPTER 12

Epiphany

They were sinking!

The captain and mate had tried to save themselves in the single small lifeboat aboard the fishing vessel, making no attempt to rescue the couple and their three small children with them. Felicita and Sandoval Hidalgo watched them perish, as the lifeboat capsized under the force of the furious wind-roiled water.

The small boat had departed from Mafanzas earlier that night. The family had hidden under a fish-stench-laden tarpaulin in the back of the captain's truck, as it traversed the back roads from Havana to the side quay in the fishing-port village. Felicita had given the children honey cakes, and they remained quiet as a succession of security post guards waved the truck through. The whole country was one big military camp, Sandoval thought.

There was no moon, only the low growling of the diesel engine pushing the little boat out into the Straits of Florida. They were free!

If things went according to plan, they would reach the Florida coast in seven hours, assuming the Cuban Navy patrols did not stop them in the open sea. And the American Coast Guard would be watching at the other end to block the land arrival of any more refugees.

Sandoval had it planned, even to the small raft that would carry them within swimming distance of the crowded Florida beach. They would drop the raft over the side of the fishing boat, reach the swimmers in the water, and conceal themselves among the beach crowd dressed in swimming outfits like the rich *Americanos* wore at the Miami resorts, as they tanned and drank their *piña coladas.*

It would be easy, if his information source was correct, to reach help in the Cuban expatriate community once they got to dry land.

He had planned carefully and for good reason. Others raised questions about his loyalty to Fidelisimmo. He had risked becoming one of the "lost" and his family with him. He knew he shouldn't have disallowed the expense voucher submitted by the nephew of a high-ranking official, but he was loyal to his country and did not tolerate waste or inefficiency.

So, he was stunned when his superior at the finance office began criticizing his work output, even his dedication to his job. It did not take long to see the handwriting on the wall.

"Felicita, we have to leave. It is going to get worse. And if I am taken, what will become of you and the children?"

They both knew the answer to that. She would be offered a job as "hostess" to foreign visitors bringing desperately needed hard cash into the country. Hostess meant many things in Cuba, but for her it would mean the ultimate degradation: prostitution. And their children, no matter what they did, would always be considered outsiders.

Cuba had survived thirty years as a closed, tightly controlled society, because it was considered strategic by the Soviet Union. With all their troubles, the Russians had poured massive amounts of money into the island's economy, both directly through tourism and by outright grants for "educational development." The missiles of Soviet manufacture publicized by President Kennedy, and then by President Johnson, were part of that development.

When the Soviet Union collapsed, and with it its deep pockets, the hard-line Communist country had nowhere else to go for support. But *El Jefe* would never loosen the grip he had established on the people. The paranoia of the bearded dictator over the possibility of invasion by the United States drove him to ever-more-Draconian measures to prevent "his people" from deserting their island "paradise." He placed Cuba on permanent red alert, meaning political witch hunts and increased surveillance of the civilian population rose exponentially.

It did not deter those seeking to flee.

Now, Sandoval Hidalgo, dedicated accountant in the Ministry of Finance, loyal supporter of all that his country stood for, had decided to leave his beloved homeland. He had come to realize the greater power that love of family held over him.

The childhood memories of his own father and mother overwhelmed him.

• • •

He was born in the eleventh year of the *Revolucion*. His father would proudly announce to his barbershop clientele that his son was a true son of the revolution, born on the anniversary date of the great Fidel's defeat of the wicked Battista.

His father was a quiet man. By chance his shop was located in a section of Havana that brought the rich *turistas* and the high-ranking officials of the new government past his door, so he had never wanted for paying customers. It also led to his downfall. Success breeds envy, and this time the envious were relatives of the decision-makers. The young Sandoval never understood why his father had to close the shop and move his family into a less-desirable section of Havana.

Even then, the powers that be were not satisfied. Soon the Committee for Defense of the Revolution, the block-by-block network of spies and guardians of political correctness for the Castro regime, declared his father an enemy of the state for listening to the music broadcast by Radio Marti.

Sandoval had arrived home from school one day to find his mother crying. She told him his father had taken sick and had to go away. He was only six, so the news did not carry any of the true ominous nature his mother had tried to hide from him. He missed his father but assumed he would get better someday, and his mother agreed through the veil of her tears.

School work was easy for Sandoval. He could readily memorize the history of the great ones of the *Liberación*, recite the evils of the United States puppet Batista and the glories that Uncle Fidel had brought to Cuba. His teachers rewarded him and held him up as an example of a true believer.

He trained with the rest of the children in the military drills required of all the young, carrying wooden toy rifles and marching in step to become the next generation of defenders.

As he grew, his skills as a planner and mathematician became more evident. Everyone knew that he would be a shoe-in for classes at the University of Havana. Naturally, because education was free for all, he would not have to worry about money. Of course, he would have to take oaths of allegiance, avoid risky behavior such as listening to U.S. radio stations, and be ready to report what was considered suspicious behavior on the part of any of his classmates.

When he was fourteen, he began the required agricultural service demanded of all students. By law, he had to spend at least one month out of each year in the outlying farming areas to help with crop sowing and harvesting. His skin had toned to the golden brown gift of the sun his people were known for. And by sixteen, he was an impressive-looking young man—impressive enough to catch the eye of the young women working alongside the men in the fields.

He had seen her, skin glistening in the early morning heat, working nearby. There was something about her that made his sixteen-year-old heart beat more rapidly.

"What is the matter, Sandoval?" his friends had asked, as they saw him staring at her. They laughed.

"Aha," they sang out, "the beast has seen the beauty!"

How sly he was, shifting over, row by row, till suddenly they were side by side. He knew she saw him. The flush on her neck had overpowered even her sunlit tan.

"Hello," he said boldly. "I'm with the Revolution Brigade. My name is Sandoval, Sandoval Hidalgo."

She smiled then looked from side to side making sure her mates weren't within hearing.

"Felicita Jimenez. I'm with the Gueverra Bridgade." And in that planted field was sown the future for Felicita and Sandoval.

They both entered the university—he to study accounting and business management, she to become a nurse—and there they decided to share their lives.

• • •

Now those lives, all of the acts of life that fill every marriage, were over. They would start again for the sake of their children.

How proud they were. Carmelita, so round-faced, even as a baby seeming to listen to every word they said. A good baby, the nanas would say, as Felicita received her first state award for the act of motherhood. Federico, not the quiet little one his sister had been, entered the world with loud proclamations and never stopped doing so. He was bright, but like a magpie. And finally, Antonio, named for his grandpapa who never returned from being "sick," became the watching one, always watching, as if absorbing the world with his eyes.

Sandoval had met the boatman at a small side-street cantina. Not a place for family meals or *turistas,* he noted. He wasn't sure how to approach the subject, but his trusted friend had told him of the fisherman and his "special catch of the day."

The captain was the first to speak.

"So you would like to take a fishing trip, eh?"

Enriquez was a survivor. Whoever or whatever was in power, he knew how to stay alive and clear of trouble, but he also knew how to make the extra *peso* on the side, because he knew how to work both sides at once. He could instantly read in the face of the young man the hidden story behind the quest for escape. The system that had raised this whelp to obey had turned around and showed its fangs. Now, the truth had been seen, and it hurt too much for him to remain in Cuba.

Enriquez laughed to himself. He would get the pup's money, all of it, and he would make the extra amount, the bounty he knew would be his, when he gave the details to *Espina.*

What a joke, he thought, an American government official paying to prevent new "beach people" from arriving in his territory. No matter, money was money. Who cared where it came from? He did not know *Espina's* real name, but the money was good, and soon he could buy a new fishing trawler.

As Sandoval talked quietly with the fishing-boat captain, he realized that the man scared him even more than the act he was planning. He blanched when the unshaven, heavily jowled man, eyes moving like a wild boar, stated his fee for the "fishing trip," but there was no choice—he had to agree. He told Enriquez how he would release the raft offshore to carry his family from the boat to the beach, and the other man agreed. The plan was a go.

"Quick, Felicita! Get the raft! We can strap the children onto it before the ship sinks!"

They looked in vain but found no raft. The terrible realization hit them both: The captain had no intention for any of them to survive. The raft was gone, probably pitched overboard before they left the harbor.

Desperately, Sandoval looked for something else that would float. The cabin door! The couple pulled and kicked at the rusted hinges until the heavy wood door fell forward onto the deck.

"Come children, we are going for a very special ride. Carmelita, hold your brothers still while I help secure you to the raft."

Felicita knew in her heart what the outcome would be.

Dear God in heaven, not for me, not for Sandoval—for our children!

The two adults struggled on the pitching deck to lift the heavy door laden with the three children. They moved to the opposite side of the boat as the small fishing vessel began its fatal listing. Miraculously, the raft landed flat onto the pounding waves and the two adults leaped into the water and briefly held on to the sides, hoping for miracles.

As inevitable fatigue overcame them, one of the two things Felicita Jimenez Hidalgo had prayed for was granted. She and her beloved Sandoval saw the raft slide away safely as they held each other one last time.

Soon large fins circled and circled the makeshift raft.

They were cold, wet, and hungry. They wanted Mama and Papa.

Carmelita had seen her parents slip away from the raft and go under the gray-black waters, never to come up. Even her five-year-old mind grasped what had happened: The three of them would never see Mama and Papa again.

The currents from the Straits of Florida up to the Carolinas are some of the most erratic and reversible ever studied. The great Gulf Stream, with its triune movements can reverse itself at the slightest change in water temperature, first traveling south and west toward the Gulf, then northeast toward the Carolina coastal areas.

There are also the mysterious Gyres of the Florida Keys, which can spiral back and forth, clockwise and counterclockwise.

The third and least understood are the strange coastal-shelf tidal flows, seemingly emerging from the ocean floor, forming and reshaping daily the coastal outlines and sand barriers so treacherous to sea travel as long as vessels have plied those waters.

Maybe it simply was the whim of the gods—those gods of capriciousness who play with humanity like pieces on a chessboard, whose moves can be dictated by a cosmic flip of the dice.

She had pulled her brothers closer to the center of the raft, still drenched by the overflowing waves of water. Against all odds, the raft held its upright position, and soon the large fins relented and disappeared to seek other food for the day.

The weather had changed, too. The grayness of the storm clouds gave way to the starlit brightness of a clear night sky. Then three children heard a grinding noise and felt a bump. The raft had come to a standstill. They did not realize it, but they had been grounded on a sandbar just feet away from the darkened island that loomed over them.

"Come, Federico, Antonio."

Carmelita untied the wet, salt-spray-coated ropes Mama and Papa had used to secure the three of them to the old door. They stepped into the water, knee deep even for their height, and she led them to the beach.

There they fell to the ground and slept. Moonbeams highlighted their exhausted bodies, and during the night the tide carried the raft those final few feet to the beach. There, like its riders, it seemed to lie exhausted beside them.

CHAPTER 13

The Legend of Bald Head Island

Was it just a recurring dream, or was it a ride on the nightmare?

Galen tried to rationalize it using his professional training as a bad case of nerves and the ever-present overwork. And yet, the apparition haunted him. The loss had hit him hard. Was it all just him sensing his own mortality?

It seemed like only yesterday that he and Country Boy had struggled through medical school together. And now his old roommate was dead, the victim of a freak auto accident.

Was Aunt Hattie right? Was everything predestined?

Over and over again, a wraithlike figure materialized at the foot of his bed, beckoning with urgency, warning him—but of what?

Three of his closest friends—Basily, Freiling, and now Dave—were gone. If the dreams were warnings, then could they be foretelling potential harm to his childhood friend Edison or his wife Nancy? He knew now what the old folks at the nursing homes meant when they talked about the "slippery slope of loss."

He couldn't tell them, not then. But he had surprised Edison and Nancy when he asked to go with them to the island. It for certain seemed that way with Nancy. She thought she had figured it out right away: Galen's life was his work, his home a protective womb against the onslaught of life.

"Bob, are you ready yet?" Nancy called down to the great one's dungeon-like lair. "We need to get started now if we're going to make halfway by evening. It'll take us at least six hours to get to Galen's place."

"I'm coming, I'm coming," came the reply up the basement steps. "I just wanted to make sure I have my radio gear, tool kits, and GPS units on board. You head out to the car and I'll lock up. On to Carolina!"

"Did you call the hotel to check on the weather status? Remember, the last two times we tried this trip, we had to cancel because of storms."

"Yep, so far everything's quiet there. No low pressure areas, no tropical depressions. The last storm just washed out."

Finally he bounded up the stairs and embraced her. After too brief a moment they separated and he grinned. Thirty-five years and she still was his beautiful red-haired love.

"This time we get to see Bald Head Island!"

She smiled back, her eyes suddenly matching the glint in his.

"Maybe we can leave a little later."

"See, timing sometimes has its advantages," Edison said with a smile. They had driven almost to Galen's home in Northern Virginia and the traffic had been unusually light. The mid-July sky was a cloudless teal blue and the temperature was an unseasonably cool 78 degrees at noon. They had enjoyed open-window driving all the way from Pennsylvania.

"Look, Galen's already outside and waiting for us."

Nancy gasped as she saw the mountain of boxes stacked next to the bear-sized man. In contrast to the khaki shorts, sunglasses, and tank-top shirts both she and Edison were wearing, their friend was decked out in jeans and blue surgical scrub shirt with an old Leica camera strapped over his shoulder. His head was topped by a pith helmet that would have done the late Frank Buck justice. They pulled their old green Jeep four-wheeler up the long driveway and stopped in front of the mound.

"I thought Bob was a packrat when he traveled, but you just might have him beat," Nancy laughed as she saw Galen begin tossing bag after bag into the vehicle.

"No, these really are necessary, Nancy," Galen interjected. I'm bringing medical supplies to some friends of mine who run a free clinic that's on the way down. A five-minute stop and most of this will be gone. Now tell me again why you and Edison are so desperate to see this island resort."

Edison grumbled as he tried to figure out the logistics of packing two cars' worth of baggage into one. Finally he gave up and tied the extra boxes on the roof rack.

"It's a long story, Galen, but back in the '90s, when I was seriously planning retirement from the bank, Bob and I were both trying to decide where we wanted to live. New Jersey was too crowded and too expensive for retired folks like us. We narrowed it down either to Pennsylvania, where my parents lived, or one of the retirement communities in North Carolina. A neighbor had given us some brochures about Bald Head Island, so we scheduled a stay at one of the bed-and-breakfast spots there. Only problem was that hurricanes forced evacuation of the island, and our reservations had to be cancelled twice."

"Now that Nancy and I are very happily settled in Pennsylvania, we thought a brief trip wouldn't be a bad weekend getaway," Edison chimed in.

"And what he didn't say is that we had planned on going there on vacation before the baby . . . "

Nancy stopped herself. Even after so long, she still couldn't talk about it.

"In any event, it sounds like an interesting place," she continued.

"There's quite a bit of history. The oldest lighthouse in North Carolina, 'Old Baldy,' was built there in 1817 to protect ships in the molasses/indigo dye/slave trade from the treacherous Frying Pan Shoals. They've even found evidence of Indian settlements, and supposedly Blackbeard the Pirate had his headquarters there. Maybe we'll find some buried treasure!"

"Or, more likely, we'll all get sunburned, in which case some of the stuff I brought along might help," Galen added. "Let's get moving."

As they pulled out of his driveway Edison yelled to him in the back seat: "How does it feel to be away from the office?"

Galen couldn't lie.

"Mentally I haven't left."

His whole life had been focused on his practice since Leni, then Cathy, were taken from him. What else did he have?

Hours passed as the three traveled down Interstate 95 through Richmond all the way to the North Carolina border and into the middle of the state. Now was as good a time as any to satisfy her curiosity. Nancy turned away from the window and toward the back seat and asked point blank: "What brought about this sea change, Galen?"

She still felt awkward using his last name, but Bob had explained to her how that had gotten started so many years ago, when the two Bobs first met.

He looked up from a medical journal he had brought along to read and stared at her thoughtfully for a few moments. Her hair, naturally red, was becoming more burnished. What little lines she showed on her face came from smiling, though there were signs of suffering a long time ago. His own personal experience, and that of seeing countless patients, had honed his eye to the hidden signs of grief.

At last he replied.

"I lost a dear friend the same day I rediscovered two others."

He told her the story about Dave then turned away, staring out the driver's side window, sadness creasing his brows into an inverted V.

"I'm sorry, Galen, I didn't mean to pry."

Still, she wanted to know more. What had he done since high school? Bob had told her what the two of them had gotten into, most of which she dismissed as tall tales. But then what? Had he married, did he have children? How could she delve into that, meeting him so recently? She tried to smile and make it seem like a joke.

"So how many young ladies did you enchant?"

He looked back at her then down at the old camera that had belonged to Leni's parents, the V deepening.

She stopped waiting for the answer and respectfully turned back toward the oncoming road.

One stop before reaching the motel where they would spend the night, a side trip to that small, concrete-block building with the large red cross and Aesclepian staff painted on its front wall.

Galen and Edison already had managed to unload most of the supplies before Bill Crowley, dressed as always in doctor's white coat, strode out the front door. He smiled as he and Galen approached each other and embraced, and each man mentally compared what time had wrought in the other since the last time they had met.

"Bob, it's good to see you."

Galen heard the whispered words, felt the strength and confidence . . . no, it was more than that . . . the certainty, in his former classmate. And he suddenly sensed within himself a strong pang of emptiness and loneliness despite his career success.

As they turned and walked back to where Edison and Nancy were standing, he remembered the tortured young man who had agonized over the death of the derelict that night in the hospital. Now, rounder, bearded, and graying, Bill seemed at peace—he had found his home and his calling.

Edison had been watching the two men and kept staring at Crowley.

I've seen that face before, a long time ago, but where?

Then he remembered.

"Dr. Crowley, I . . ."

"Call me Bill," he said, extending his hand.

Immediately, the memory of the time in the maternity ward waiting area flooded in. It was the young, round-faced doctor who had sat next to him that terrible night and slowly explained what had happened to Nancy and their baby. Edison had burst out crying and the other man had put his arm around him and let him cry.

"You don't remember me, Bill, but a long time ago you rescued a young man from despair. You broke the news to me about my wife and baby. I knew that Dr. Ross had done all she could. If you hadn't stayed with me, I'm not sure what I would have done."

"I'm glad to see both of you," Bill said, as Nancy walked up and hugged him.

Dr. Ross!

Galen watched the three of them, and as he began thinking of June, his mind swirled in a symphony of irony.

"Why don't you help me convince Bob that he's too long in the tooth now for what he does, and he should join Peggy and me down here."

Before anyone could answer, Bill turned to Galen.

"We can always use another good doctor, Bob."

Galen flushed, whether in embarrassment or realization of the truth in what Bill had just said—he wasn't sure.

"You'll be the first to know, Bill. I have to admit, what you do here is very appealing to me."

Dear God! Is this my calling, too?

He still held bittersweet memories of the last time the A Team had gotten together to help Bill and Peggy with the onslaught of migrant workers. Now, with Dave's passing, it was obvious that Bill felt the same.

"Bob, you know I wish I could be asking you to join Peggy and me and Dave and Connie, but . . ."

"Yes, Bill, and the four of you would have done great work, just like old times."

"You and I made quite a team ourselves, once. Remember what the nurses used to call us?"

"Babyface and The Bear!"

"Babyface, Scarecrow, and The Bear!"

The two men began to laugh softly, until tears came to their eyes.

For Galen, they were tears of loss.

After saying their farewells, the three friends returned to a much emptier Jeep and set off for their destination. Galen looked back out the rear window at one of his few remaining friends. Even Edison remained quiet—unusual for him. Nancy sensed the tension in their passenger and said nothing.

The next morning they soon reached highway 40E then 17S and 87S. Finally, highway 33 took them to the middle of Southport, and a short drive down Indigo Plantation Way led to the ferry terminal.

"Okay, we need to leave the car behind, take our stuff on board, and be prepared to walk everywhere once we get on the island. No cars there, only legs and bicycles. Galen and I can be the pack mules, honey. Most of this is our junk anyway."

"Yeah, right, two walking heart attacks in the making," she snapped.

Nancy picked up several luggage packs and moved to the dock. The men shrugged meekly and followed with the rest of the bags.

They spent the two-mile ferry ride taking in the beauty of the water-surrounded land. The sky was that clear-sea blue, rivaling the water in its bright monocolor. The conflicting currents of salty ocean water and the freshwater efflux of the Cape Fear River caused a slight wave buffeting, as the ferry neared the Bald Head Island Marina landing.

"Think you'll get bored seeing this all the time?" Galen asked Nancy and Edison, who both smiled in response.

They headed slowly up the crushed-shell-and-gravel pathway toward the white clapboard, Victorian-style house that was to be their B&B retreat. As they neared the entrance, the proprietor approached. A gray-haired, stocky woman in blue-gray slacks and pink shirt, she wore a name badge that identified her as "Teddy." The big grin on her face widened as she looked at the overloaded threesome.

"Why didn't you folks use one of the baggage carriers?"

Embarrassed at the wasted effort, they signed in and followed her to their assigned rooms.

"Mr. and Mrs. Edison, you have the special suite," Call Me Teddy said. "Normally it's reserved as a bridal suite, but we don't have any newlyweds right now."

Edison's eyes lit up, and his face told Nancy all she needed to know about his thoughts. A few moments later, he looked in at the spacious, paneled room with its king-sized poster bed and said, "What's that on the pillow?" He walked over and picked up two gold-foil-wrapped items, one in the shape of an old doubloon, the other formed like a Folsom point arrowhead. He opened them, found chocolate, promptly ate one and gave the other to Nancy.

"Don't you folks know about the Legend of Bald Head?" Teddy asked.

"Seems that after they built the lighthouse, Old Baldy, the keeper got pretty busy trying to keep the ships away from the shoals and rescuing the unlucky sailors whose vessels didn't make it. He claimed that whenever he managed to save lives he would find a gold doubloon and an arrowhead on his bed. He thought it was a reward from the spirits of the Indians and the pirates who used to live here.

Now, of course, no one believed him, but he sure had a lot of money and Indian artifacts when he retired. At least that's what his replacement claimed—and that man never said nothin' later on!"

Nancy sat on the edge of the bolster-covered bed, sighed, and said, "Indians and pirates notwithstanding, I think we all need to rest up before dinner."

"That sea air and sunset sure do make even an average dinner magnificent," Edison commented as they took their post-meal walk along the marina. The sun was slowly sinking to the west, lighting up streaks of clouds like shadow boxes.

"I think we should take in the lighthouse and the old wedding chapel tomorrow," Nancy added. "The B&B has bikes for the guests. It'll be just like the old days, Bob."

Galen shook his head.

"Bikes and I never got along. I spent more time falling off of them than I ever did riding them. You two youngsters do the romantic bicycling bit. I'll just go on shank's mare around the island."

He turned toward the chapel area. The sky was now darkening as the last wisps of maroon highlighted the horizon. He pointed toward the marsh area and Nancy cried out, "Look at those bobbing lights! Maybe the pirates and Indians are coming!"

Then she laughed and nudged Edison.

"I don't think so," Edison replied. "They're probably will-o'-the-wisps."

Galen frowned but said nothing as they returned to the inn.

The morning sky glowed blood red the next day and the winds seemed suddenly aggressive. Edison rolled over in bed, and as he stretched like a large cat he caught Nancy looking at him.

"We should have come here sooner," he said yawning and stretched again.

"Don't you feel just like we did on Mackinac Island?"

She reached out and half-stroked, half-patted his head.

"Why don't we eat breakfast late?"

When they finally decided to get up, the sky had turned vermilion. They stared out the window, and Nancy started to shake her head.

"Not again. We just got here!"

Edison turned on his weather-band radio and tuned to the NOAA frequency for the area.

"Low pressure area building up 200 miles east of Florida with potential for storm activity within 12 hours," the mechanical voice said.

"Oh, no!" he groaned.

"Come on, let's at least see something before we have to leave in a hurry." "If all goes well, we'll meet Galen for lunch."

"He's still determined to do his walking thing?"

"Yes, and I think he needs to be alone for awhile. His meeting with Dr. Crowley seemed to upset him."

"He's trying to escape from the idea that he could do other things. I guess I'm the luckiest guy around," Edison concluded. "I have you!"

"Okay, lover boy, no more of that. Let's go—breakfast and biking!"

They ate quietly. Teddy told them not to worry. The only thing to remember was if the siren at the marina started to sound, they had to get in gear and be ready to leave the island quickly. On that encouraging note, they walked out to the bike racks.

Galen had slept poorly the previous night, but not because of the accommodations. Those had been excellent. The window of his large single room faced the ocean, and the blend of moving water and air on top of the pleasant evening meal made the right combination to calm even his nervous energy. But Nancy's instincts were right—the meeting with his old classmate had unsettled him. Should he consider making such a large change in his life?

Things had gone well career-wise. He loved what he did. And yet Bill's words nagged at him. Maybe if Leni or Cathy had lived, then he would have given more thought to taking time off—doing other things. All he had now was his practice.

Out and about now, he slowly meandered toward the lighthouse. He stared up at the great rock monument to men of the sea and wondered about the thoughts of the builders and its occupants over the years. He noted the entrance and peered in at the circular staircase to the living quarters and light bench at the top. Should he climb it? No, he wanted to see the chapel and check out the marsh area. No telling what types of birds and plants he would see there. Maybe he might even find the source of those night luminescences. Edison's will-o'-the-wisps didn't quite fit the pattern.

He walked farther east toward the wedding chapel and admired the stone beauty of the place. Conflicting memories hit him as he looked through the windows. He stepped into the doorway and stood, silent and alone, in the quiet-shadowed room meant to celebrate union and happiness. The small amount of light entering through the chapel windows cast a lavender hue in front of him, and he cried quietly in memory of what might have been.

And then, as the wind rustled through the open doorway, it seemed to whisper to him: *Hurry, Tony, it's not too late.*

He turned, wiped his face with both hands to clear away the mist then stepped back outside. A sense of purpose seemed suddenly to command his spirit. Somehow he felt compelled to check out the marsh. He headed down the path into ever increasing foliage.

"Bob, I'm worried. You've told me how Galen is always so precise about keeping appointments. It's strange for him not to show up for lunch."

"Yeah, well, let's give him a little more time before we send out the hounds."

They had done as much of the two-thousand developed acres of the island as they could during their morning bike ride. It was tiring but worth it, because it returned them to the days when they were young and just starting out together, and they savored it. After three-and-a-half decades their marriage remained fresh and, yes, exciting to them. How many couples could say that at one year, much less thirty-five?

They headed back to their bikes, which they had parked in front of the B&B, and were going to start looking for Galen when he appeared, a wild look on his face and loaded with bags.

"Come on, I need you!" was all he said, as he walked briskly down the street.

They struggled to keep up with him as he headed down the poorly marked marsh path. He said nothing for what seemed like ages until they came to a small clearing. He quickly took the bags to the edge and waited.

As Edison and Nancy joined him they saw the reason for his mad rush: three children, in rags, dirty, wild-looking and gaunt, huddled together.

"I can't get them to say anything," Galen said. "They're most likely in shock."

Nancy moved slowly toward the trio. Instinctively she started to hum a song from her childhood, softly, as the children watched her but did not move. She knelt down, looked closely at the children then started speaking in Spanish.

"Me illamo es Nancy. Estos son mis amigos, Edison y Galen. ¿Lo que son sus nombres?"

My name is Nancy. These are my friends, Edison and Galen. What are your names?

The middle child, a girl, half-whispered back, "I'm Carmelita."

Galen and Edison also moved forward then, kneeling on the ground, each in turn pointed at himself and said, in Spanish: My name is Edison. My name is Galen.

Then the two boys piped up: I'm Federico. I'm Antonio.

Nancy sat down next to the children, and Edison and Galen in turn tried gently but persuasively to ask them what happened. The three adults struggled with memories of school-learned Spanish to understand the horrors the children began to relate to them. The sea-swept life raft and the beaching far north of their destination on the undeveloped side of Bald Head Island made the adults wonder how this possibly could have happened. Was it the storm-changed currents or the whim of the gods?

The children grew silent. Their small voices suddenly replaced by the rising of the wind and the distant sound of thunder.

He was born of Gaiea and Zeus, midwifed by Poseidon in the kingdom of water and air and swaddled by all the Furies that were.

He came to life slapped by the mighty electric winds of Zeus and breastfed on the milk of moisture-laden warm air rising from Gaiea.

He entered puberty with all the angst and tantrums of adolescence, as his temper flowed in cyclonic gusts of ever-increasing speed.

Charged particles served like grains of sand within to create myriads of pearl-like moisture drops, now surfeited by Poseidon's warm ocean kingdom.

He proclaimed his presence with all the power of his one-hundred-fifty-mile-an-hour winds.

He was HURRICANE!

A god, the son of the mightiest of gods, he felt the power coursing through him. His winds rose even higher. Within the quiet of his mind's eye, he reveled at his strength and drove himself even farther, fueled by the blood of mother Gaiea and the strength of father Zeus.

He was invincible.

Again the sound of thunder shook them. The three adults looked at one another. Not this soon! A storm couldn't have moved in this fast. And then they heard the marina siren. It must be a bad one.

Galen had a thought and opened the old Leica camera. Quickly he took photos of the children and the debris of their landing site on the island. Maybe it would help identify them later.

Edison grabbed Federico and put him across his shoulders. Galen did likewise with Antonio as did Nancy with Carmelita. Feeding them and replacing the tattered clothes that had all but fallen off their bodies would have to come later.

They ran through the marsh, occasionally stumbling as the sky grew darker and more ominous. It would take at least ano-ther half-hour to get back to the marina side of the island while carrying the children.

They heard the second siren call. One more and the ferry would be leaving for the safety of the mainland.

They were within site of the chapel when the third siren screamed out, and they watched, helpless, as the ferry moved quickly from the quay into the now-roiling waters.

Galen spoke first.

"The safest place is probably the lighthouse. It's survived almost two hundred years of storms."

"But we need emergency equipment," Edison said. "You and Nancy get the kids over there. I'm going to get my gear."

He raced up the steps of the deserted boarding house.

Galen swung Federico up to his other shoulder, and he and Nancy made their way in the increasing wind toward the lighthouse. As they neared the entrance, they heard running footsteps. It was Edison with his radio equipment and tool kits in hand.

The now-locked entrance to Old Baldy gave way under Edison's pry bar, and the three adults, weighed under by kids and kits, slowly trudged up the two hundred steps until they reached the caretaker's ledge.

Edison managed a weary grin and looked at the youngsters.

"I have a surprise for you," he said as he handed each one a granola food bar.

"I found Teddy's secret stash," he said in response to raised eyebrows.

"We need to get the children settled down," Nancy said as she spread out some of the sheeting in Galen's supply pack on the floor. "This storm hasn't even hit its peak yet, and already it sounds like all the banshees on Earth are out there singing. Bob, did you bring any light?"

Edison nodded, reached into his pack and pulled out two lumilights and a book and handed them to Nancy. With a twisting motion she activated the chemical lights, sat down on the sheets, and motioned the children to sit around her. She began to read, knowing that they wouldn't understand, but hoping it would settle them down—and maybe even her and Edison and Galen as well.

"It was the best of times, it was the worst of times," she began.

Soon they all had fallen asleep. The shrieking wind had been lullaby to their exhaustion. But Galen slept only lightly and soon quietly rose, trying his best not to disturb the others. Slowly and carefully he climbed higher into Old Baldy's light portal.

Even the venerable old lighthouse trembled at the tumult of nature outside. He reached the platform and stared out at the colors of darkness. Giant fingers seemed to reach down from heaven to clutch the Earth frantically. In the depths of his rational mind, he knew it wasn't so. Electrons actually climbed the heated charged air to outline the sky.

But he couldn't shake the imagery of those hands. He slowly circled the window expanse looking outward. And then his eyes locked on one vista.

There were clouds. Seemingly out of place in the windswept darkness, their margins appeared illuminated. He watched, fixated, as the cloud rims spiraled outward, opening into a huge iris.

Galen thought he was staring into the eye of a god.

Father Zeus!

Yes, my son?

Help me to understand. I glimpsed down at Mother Gaiea and half-saw, half-felt something. It was the tiniest spark but it seemed to know me and I in turn knew it. It was not afraid.

It is called Man, my son.

He turned away from the lighthouse portals and quietly made his way back to the others, who remained blissfully under the spell of Lethe. Carefully he lay down and draped his arm over the sleeping Antonio. At long last, Galen slept.

Beloved Zeus, it is time for our son to return to us.

Gaiea, my love, ask and it is yours.

He felt it happening, slowly at first, then with rising intensity. His winds, the power of his soul, began to slow. He felt the ever-increasing weakness. He felt tired. His mind's eye questioned this change. And then he heard the call:

It is time for you to return to us, my son. It is time to join your brothers and sisters on Olympus.

Then he knew. He was a god, but he was dying, just as the gods before him.

His eye looked upward.

In one last shout he cried out:

Mother, Father, Why have you done this to me?

Apollo rode his chariot from the east and its golden-red rays lit up the early morning sky. Galen awoke to find Antonio curled up under his right arm. He saw Federico safely ensconced with Edison and Carmelita with Nancy. He coughed lightly, and the two other adults awoke to the same sight. The children, exhausted beyond belief, remained in peaceful sleep.

Nancy was first to voice what they all were thinking.

"What are we going to do with them? Are you going to contact one of your government types, Galen?"

"Like hell I will," he grumbled. "The last thing I want to see is a repeat of the Elian Gonzalez fiasco and the agents of some latter-day Janet Reno breaking down doors to send them back to Cuba."

As he uttered those words, he felt the hairs on the back of his neck prickle.

"Edison, can you somehow patch me into a telephone?"

"Why do you always ask me to do the impossible?" he groused.

"Because you can."

A few more grumbles and Edison was on the case.

"Okay, let's see if I can get someone to phone patch. You're sure you don't want to tell me to use some secret frequency and codes?"

Dead silence.

"Okay, okay, here goes."

It was several minutes before he was able to reach a ham friend to handle the patch. He handed the set to Galen, who then told the operator to call a specific number.

Galen smiled as he heard the voice say, " This is Dr. Bill Crowley. How may we help?"

They remained hidden until the ferry boat returned to bring the first of the islanders back. Quickly they mixed in to avoid arousing suspicion. They waited until another ferry was getting ready to sail back to the mainland before boarding, with the three children now dressed in bathing suits they had bought at an island store. As the ferry crew prepared to land, Galen spotted a familiar minivan, a large red cross painted on each side rising above two outstretched hands.

The three adults led the children to the vehicle and Dr. Bill, with his round bearded face and broad smile, moved toward them.

"I see the problem, Bob," he said.

"Can you get them papers?"

"You taught me all that I know about that area, Bob,"

"Good, so you have a family for them?"

"Yes—mine!"

"Come here, children," Galen spoke in Spanish.

"This is Padre Bill. He is going to take you to your new home. Padre, these are the Hidalgos."

"¿Niños, cuáles son tus nombres?" Bill said as he smiled and extended his arms.

The three answered in turn:

"Carmelita Nancy Hidalgo."

"Federico Edison Hidalgo."

"Antonio Galen Hidalgo."

Three suddenly lonely adults took the ferry back to the island in silence. They settled the bill at the B&B then climbed the stairs to their respective rooms to pack.

A shout arose from both rooms as all three rushed back into the hallway.

Each in turn opened his or her right hand.

Each displayed a solid-gold doubloon and an arrowhead.

CHAPTER 14

No Good Deed

Bob, they've arrested Bill!"

Galen had gone to bed late and was half-asleep when the phone rang.

The desperation in Peggy Crowley's voice wrenched him awake. He rubbed the sleep from his eyes and sat up.

"Slow down, Peggy, start at the beginning. First, where are you calling from?"

"I'm here in Raleigh, Bob. The state attorney general issued a warrant for Bill after the Feds charged him with obstruction of justice under the Elian Gonzalez rulings.

"Someone sent the government an anonymous tip about the children. Agents showed up at the clinic this morning, and the leader asked Bill where the kids were, but he refused to tell them. He kept saying that by U.S. law they were refugees, and Cubans constituted a special group exception to the immigration statutes.

"The agent in charge claimed that an official complaint had been filed by the Cuban government asking for the return of the Hidalgo children to their family and homeland. Bob, his men actually pulled their guns and put Bill in handcuffs! They searched our house and found the kids with our housekeeper, Mrs. Canales."

Galen found it hard to control his rage. He had learned to suppress such feelings over the years, but this was a travesty. He felt himself trembling, from a growing sense of guilt as well as the anger. He had been the one to bring Bill into this bag of worms by asking for help that day on the island.

His words echoed in his memory:

Bill, this is going to be like old times when we worked together as a team. You're not going to face this alone.

"Bob, they've taken Bill to the county lockup, and I don't even know where the kids are. What can I do?"

"Don't worry, Peggy. I'll be there as soon as I make some calls and arrange for transportation. I'll notify Nancy and Edison as well."

"Nancy, Galen just called. Bill is in trouble and needs us. Galen's arranged for us to take a charter flight from Wilkes-Barre. We'll meet him in Raleigh and head from there to the Wake County Courthouse. Let's get packed."

Edison was grim-faced as he began to assemble his gear.

A decidedly unsettled trio met several hours later at the Raleigh-Durham airport. Nancy and Edison had taken the charter flight out of Wilkes-Barre at 7 a.m. while Galen had left Dulles at 7:30. No happy greetings this time. They got immediately down to business.

Galen went over the details as he knew them while they took a taxi to the courthouse where Bill was being held. The preliminary hearing was scheduled for 2 p.m., and they reached their destination by noon. Galen clutched a large and well-stuffed manila envelope close to his chest. Nancy took note of it but said nothing.

As they waited to be escorted to the holding area where they would meet with Bill and his lawyer, Galen paced back and forth like a caged panther.

"I think he's being set up for some political reason," he said. "It just doesn't make sense that they would pick on him so suddenly. I'll bet there's some behind-the-scenes diplomatic maneuvering going on to impress the new Cuban government. That's how things are done in Washington. I also think some high-ranking government official with dirty hands is trying to conceal his or her part in this."

Nancy and Bob had never seen their friend so agitated. They both tried to calm him down by pointing out that he could hurt Bill's chances if he blustered in court.

"Okay," he finally replied. "I know you're right. Besides, I've got my little surprise for the prosecutor."

Nancy again looked at the manila envelope Galen held. Suddenly she realized what it contained. With that she smiled, relaxed, and sat down.

Edison remained puzzled. What rabbit was Galen going to pull out of his hat?

At last a guard appeared who escorted them to the holding area, where they identified themselves and were let into the room where Peggy, Bill and his attorney were seated at an old mahogany side table. Bill's eyes lit up as he saw his friends come toward him. He clasped Galen's hand and whispered, "Maybe I'm finally getting what I deserve, Bob."

"What you deserve is a medal and sainthood."

Galen turned to the attorney.

"What's the real reason for this?"

Ed Comer was a stocky man. He had lived in the county his whole life and knew the political dirt on everyone. His laid-back personality concealed a shrewd mind that had earned him respect from all sides.

"Dr. Galen, this is an election year, and our worthy attorney general is looking forward to the party slot for governor. There's also a new regional hotshot in the Federal Immigration and Naturalization Service who's pushing this as well. I'd say his neck is on the line in Washington.

"I'd bet our friends in the White House were looking for a way to break the ice with the post-Castro government. I'd also bet Mr. Thornton is bucking for promotion and an office back in D.C. Doesn't seem to like us Southern folk."

Thornton?

Edison and Galen looked at each other then Edison spoke first.

"By any chance, is this guy's first name Gregory?"

Comer stared back with lidded eyes, and the sun-darkened skin on his face seemed to glow red.

"Could be. He goes by G. Thompson Thornton. Is he a friend of yours? You folks know him?"

"Yeah, you might say that," Edison muttered as Galen stepped in.

"So what's their case against Bill, Comer? What's their trump card?"

"They say Dr. Crowley concealed three Cuban children who were rescued from a life raft off the coast. They further claim he refused to release the children to legal authorities seeking to return them to their family. That's probably their biggest point. As I said, the administration is trying to suck up to the new Cuban government and figures maybe another goodwill offering like Elian Gonzalez couldn't hurt.

"I'm not so sure about that," Galen replied. "In Elian's case, his father was still living in Cuba and really did have parental rights to the boy. But here, well, from what we've been able to gather, their parents are both dead and the Cubans can't offer any proof of immediate relatives."

"What it boils down to right now is Dr. Crowley's refusal to release the children to the authorities," Comer said. "I have to admit they have a valid point there."

Bill's face was flushed as he interrupted.

"Mr. Comer, you know even better than I do that the federal immigration statutes give special asylum status to Cubans and Haitians.

Those so-called authorities had no right to play storm trooper at my house."

"Easy, Dr. Crowley, easy," Comer said calmly. "Remember, I'm on your side. I didn't say I agreed with them. I do think you have a legitimate right of protest. Their other point is the kids never really reached U.S. soil, that they were removed from a raft while still outside the territorial limits of the United States. If that's true, then the government does have the right to intercede."

"Mr. Comer, if that's their case, we've got them by the short hairs!"

Edison saw the glint in Galen's eyes as he turned to the lawyer.

"Make sure you put us on the list of witnesses on Bill's behalf."

"Certainly you folks are welcome as character witnesses. But we have another person here for that, a Dr. June Ross Eastman from New Jersey."

Galen's eyes widened as he looked at Bill.

"Peggy called her, Bob."

Startled, Galen didn't notice Nancy blanching at the mention of the name. He caught his breath.

"Mr. Comer, we're not here as character witnesses. We're here as witnesses of fact."

He gathered them around a table, opened the bulging manila envelope he had been holding, and dumped out its contents. The attorney took one look at the pile, whistled, then broke into a watermelon grin and shook Galen's hand.

"Dr. Galen, I do believe we have us a plucked chicken here!"

The proceedings began in a courtroom filled with media types, onlookers, and the usual voyeurs. Dr. Bill was a well-loved and respected man in these parts, so most of the guests were supporters. But human nature being what it is, some in the audience inevitably regarded his life's work as "elevatin' the scum who take our jobs."

The clerk called the court to order as the Honorable Judge Samantha Todwell took the bench and sat down.

"Please be seated. Mr. Jacklin, you may present your opening argument for the State. Let me remind you all that this is a preliminary hearing."

The three friends quickly recognized Jacklin for what he was: a political hack reaching for higher office with a potentially high-profile case. They listened to him drone on about culpability in concealing children who should rightfully be returned to their family and the sovereign right of the Cuban government over its citizens. He was playing to the anti-immigration crowd as well.

Comer then took center stage. He praised Bill Crowley as a selfless individual who gave everything to others. He detailed how Bill and Peggy had cared for the needy without concern for pay or recompense.

The crowd murmured approval.

Then the judge asked Jacklin to present his first witness.

"Mr. G. Thompson Thornton, please raise your right hand. Do you swear to tell the truth, the whole truth, and nothing but the truth, so help you God?"

"I do."

Both Galen and Edison knew that face, even after more than forty years. The smugness of a childhood bully had been replaced with self-righteousness. Edison wondered if his childhood torturer had ever plucked the wings off of butterflies for fun.

"Mr. Thornton, you can prove that these children, the Hidalgos, were kept here in violation of the government policy of returning minors to their families?"

"In my capacity as regional director for the INS, I have information confirming that, Mr. Jacklin."

"Your witness, Mr. Comer."

"Mr. Thornton, you said that you have proof of violation of the refugee and asylum laws."

"Yes, certainly."

"Would you tell the Court what type of substantiating evidence you have to this effect?"

"We have an eyewitness who states that he saw the children being removed from a raft in the Atlantic Ocean. And we have the captain of the fishing boat who brought them to the Florida coast: Captain Enriquez."

"Thank you, Mr. Thornton, you may step down."

Puzzled, Nancy whispered to Galen.

"Why didn't Comer asked him to produce the witnesses?"

"Because this is only a hearing," he responded quietly. "The prosecution only has to persuade the judge that it has enough evidence to go to trial, and Thornton's statement as a government official is sufficient . . . "

He paused for a moment, as if contemplating a move.

"Don't worry."

Then Comer turned to Judge Todwell.

"Your Honor, with your permission, I would like to introduce an evidentiary witness of fact to the contrary. I reserve the right to recall the Prosecution's witness."

"Proceed, Mr. Comer."

"The Court calls Dr. Robert Galen."

Galen rose and approached the witness chair. Standing there, asked to swear the oath of truthfulness then listening to Comer prepare the judge for his testimony, he suddenly felt just like he did the first time he had to take oral exams in medical school.

"Dr. Galen, you state that you and your two friends, Mr. and Mrs. Robert Edison, were staying on Bald Head Island on the specified date, and that the three of you are the actual rescuers of the three Hidalgos. Can you substantiate this?"

"Yes, Mr. Comer."

Galen handed the manila envelope to the lawyer, who proceeded to remove the contents he had been shown earlier, describing the items to the judge: photos taken of the three children and the rescue site on that fateful day, the credit-card receipt for the three bathing suits purchased at the island general store, and the hotel receipts showing rental for three adults only.

It was a good thing Nancy was so careful about saving every scrap of payment records.

There was also a thick binder filled with papers bearing the letterhead of two unnamed government agencies.

"Your Honor, I object!" Jacklin shouted. "The Defense has not shown us this so-called evidence."

Thornton was ghost-white. He suddenly remembered where he last had heard Galen's name.

"Mr. Jacklin, may I remind you that this is not a trial, this is a preliminary hearing. The Defense has no such obligation.

"Mr. Comer, would you hand me those photos and papers?"

"Yes, Your Honor, and if you will note, they are time/date verified. I also wish to state for the record that Dr. Galen has circulated the photos among certain government friends who have determined that the children have no surviving parents or living relatives. These documents will confirm this.

"Furthermore, the captain of the fishing boat mentioned by Mr. Thornton was lost at sea during the storm that brought the Hidalgo children to the island. That, too, is described in the supporting material."

"Your Honor, may I add something?" Galen spoke up.

"Yes, Dr. Galen. Go ahead."

"There is one more interesting bit of information my sources have uncovered. The various fishing boat captains have been offered bounty money for preventing the arrival of refugees they carry to this country.

Those willing to talk have mentioned the name *Espina,* and they claim this bounty payer is an employee of our own government. They do not know his real name.

"Your Honor, *Espina* translates as 'pricklyspine'," Galen added, pausing to look at the now-deathly gray face of the government representative seated next to Jacklin. "It can also be translated as thorn."

The courtroom suddenly erupted into loud exclamations and epithets.

Judge Todwell pounded her gavel for quiet.

"Both the Edisons and I provide financial support for the three children and accept this responsibility freely and without exception."

Judge Todwell scrutinized the pictures of the three bedraggled children and their rescuers. She looked out at the courtroom and began to speak in even tones that belied her feelings of disgust and rising anger.

"Mr. Jacklin, you have wasted this Court's time and persecuted a man who has done the people of this state much more good than you ever have. I am requesting that the clerk file an official complaint against you with the state bar on my behalf.

"As for you, Mr. Thornton, as a federal official, you have perjured yourself in my court. Appropriate charges will be filed against you, and we will notify your superiors of your attempt to subvert justice. I will also demand an investigation into any connections you may have with this criminal bounty scam.

"The children are to be released to Dr. Crowley forthwith and all charges against the doctor dropped.

"Dr. Galen, the court thanks you. You may step down. Case dismissed."

Galen stepped down from the witness chair. Peggy was hugging Bill as Nancy and Bob stood nearby holding hands like teenagers. Media types fled the room scrambling to hit the airwaves and meet newsprint deadlines.

Then she walked up to him. Time had been kind to her, sparing her face the age lines that affected most women. Her silver-gray hair gave dignity to the classical aquiline features she had been blessed with. She also seemed more self-assured in maturity.

"It's been a long time, Bob. I can't believe how much time has passed."

"It looks like time forgot you, June. You look the same as you did back in school."

"Smooth line! The Bear would never have come up with that back then."

He sighed.

"That's what life does to you. Are you married?"

"Widowed. Tom died two years ago suddenly. He was a good man. You?"

"Married twice, made a widower both times. Guess I'm just a Jonah with the ladies."

He continued to look at her, seeing once again The Model of his youth.

"Any kids, Bob?"

He shook his head no and asked her the same question.

"One. Tom Eastman Jr. He's an emergency room doc in Lakeland, Florida."

Just then a voice interrupted.

"Dr. Galen would you and the Edisons and the Crowleys join me in my chambers?"

Judge Samantha Todwell had walked up to them unnoticed. The others heard her as well and shifted their focus to the late-middle-aged woman in judicial robe. She recognized their concern and smiled.

"My clerk has done some research you might find useful. I'd like to discuss the status of the children from a legal perspective."

All except June followed her through the door behind the bench. Comer had asked permission to accompany them and the judge agreed.

"Please sit down, folks."

Todwell removed her robe and sat down behind her desk. She loosened the top button on her white blouse and fanned herself with a folder then stopped and grinned sheepishly.

"Air conditioner isn't working too well."

"Sam, you've got something in mind. What's your idea?"

Comer and Todwell went back a long way.

"Still trying to second guess me, Ed? Well, you're right. Here's the story. Right now those kids have changed status from undocumented aliens to asylees."

Comer looked at the group.

"What's she saying is if the three kids had been adults, since they're from Cuba, then they would have been allowed to go about their business in the United States. The problem is they're just kids."

Todwell nodded.

"I'm going to need to pass this through Social Services, which means you three will have to undergo investigations for fitness, but I'm going to use all the connections I have to convince INS to allow the three of you to become the official guardians of these children. After what their man did, I think they owe it to you folks."

"That's my Sam!" Comer exclaimed.

Bill and Peggy walked with the four of them to the elevator. Edison was the last one in as Thornton came down the hall. He called out to them to hold the elevator. Edison pressed the "Close" button and called out.

"Sorry, Thornton, this elevator is for underclassmen!"

As they exited the elevator in the courthouse lobby they were surprised to see Judge Todwell again, now standing there ahead of them.

Comer turned to Galen.

"Sam sure loves taking that special elevator! Only judges can use it to beat me down here after a case."

Todwell stepped forward, eyes twinkling, broad smile splitting her face as she turned and motioned to the clerk.

"Jake, bring 'em out."

Three familiar young faces suddenly appeared from behind a doorway obscured by the bulk of the man and made a beeline for the Crowleys, the Edisons, and Galen. As they leaped and jumped into the arms of the adults like three unleashed puppies, Comer raised an eyebrow, which Todwell noticed.

"Oh, hush, Ed Comer," she said before he could speak. "You know I'm a softy for kids and pets. I just thought—and my friends at Social Services agreed—that the children would be better off back with the Crowleys and their friends."

As Comer took Todwell in his arms and hugged her, Galen whispered to Edison:

"I'll bet ol' Comer has ridden down that private elevator himself—and not alone, either."

The other three laughed and laughed at the happy ending.

"June, why don't you stop by my place in Virginia? I can show you Washington like you've never seen it."

"I'd like to do that someday, Bob. How would you like to join Bill, Peggy, and me next year? We're going to do a medical missionary flight to Colombia. I'd love to have you come with me."

Welcome words, but they caused the hairs on the back of Galen's neck to rise once more as Aunt Hattie's voice stirred in his mind.

Bone Man'll bite yeh and it'll sting real bad!

She had kept her promise, stopping by to see Galen after returning from a visit to her son in Florida and a stopover at the clinic to see the Crowleys and the children.

After a day of sightseeing, the two of them sat in the tiny booth of an out-of-the-way Thai restaurant, slowly sipping tea and getting reintroduced. He kept looking at her and remembering the young woman he once had loved briefly but so intensely that he even lost track of the conversation of the moment.

The years notwithstanding, June was still The Model to him. Time had just added a patina of wisdom to her classical good looks. Even more, she still had the intelligence and wit that had made working ward duty with her a pleasure.

But her next remark snapped him back to attention.

"Bob, I'm worried about Peggy. Last time I was visiting, she looked tired. I'm going to go down this weekend and help Bill out at the clinic. Want to come with me? The four of us would be unstoppable."

The four of us. Once it had been the Unstoppable Six, the A Team.

Dave, the Country Boy, was dead and Connie had never really recovered from his tragic death. She had withdrawn into an isolated existence that none of her friends could break. So, now there were four, and that fourth had left him with self-induced scars on his soul. Could things be picked up and started over again after all these years?

He felt like a schoolboy asking the prom queen for a date. Hell, he hadn't felt this awkward since . . . when? He didn't want to lose her a second time. He had had his share of loss.

"So wanna come with me?"

He smiled and nodded.

They got up before dawn the next day.

"Old training habits never die," he quipped, and she laughed as they both remembered the many times they would be awakened in the middle of the night for sick patients.

He had loaded the old Jeep with medical supplies, and they drove down to Bill and Peggy's North Carolina mission and clinic. Each wondered if this would be a new beginning for them. They didn't call ahead. They wanted to savor each other's company as long as possible.

When they arrived in the late afternoon, they went directly to the residence. It seemed a long time before the door opened. Bill stood in the hallway and looked at them without seeming to see them. He stared into emptiness.

June moved first. She slid past Bill into the house and walked back to the bedroom area. Galen took his friend by the arm, guided him to the living room sofa, and made him sit down.

"Bill, what's wrong?"

"Bob, get back here!" June's voice quavered.

He ran back to where June was examining her friend. She was crying softly even as she touched Peggy's face.

"She's dead, Bob. It looks like a sudden massive stroke."

"Madre de Dios!"

Galen and June turned at the sudden exclamation and saw Mrs. Canales, the housekeeper, standing in the doorway. Clutching her apron, the three Hidalgo children stared wide-eyed at the bed and the woman they had grown to love as Tia Peggy.

"Is Tia sick?"

Carmelita looked up at the giant who had rescued her and her brothers, but he remained silent.

"No, little one," Mrs. Canales said quietly, choking out the words, "your Tia is with the angels now."

"Will she be with Mama and Papa?" asked Federico, who went to touch the dead woman's hand.

"Yes, she will," said Galen, who bit his lip to maintain control of his emotions.

"Is Tio Bill going with Tia Peggy?" Little Antonio moved toward Galen.

"No, Tonio."

June tried to appear strong in front of the children.

"Consuela, we'll need to make arrangements and help the Padre. Will you look after the children for us until we can straighten things out?"

"Si, signora."

She opened her arms to gather the three and led them slowly from the room. Each looked back and waved good-bye at Peggy.

A few moments later, Galen and June exited the room as well, leaving her there in the bed she and Bill had shared. They returned to where Bill was still sitting, now rocking himself back and forth ever so slightly. They had to help the living. All their training cried out for that. All of their humanity demanded it.

Galen called the local funeral home to make arrangements, then he and June sat with Bill through the night.

Finally they were able to coax from him the tragic chain of events. Peggy had never quite recovered from the stress of Bill's arrest. She had worked the clinic alone the day before that terrifying court hearing. And both, in a frenzied attempt to ward off the attack on their very reason for being, had worked twice as hard afterwards.

She worked, even though fatigue and headaches began to overtake her, but she wouldn't stop, until earlier that day when she told Bill she just had to lie down for awhile. When he went to check on her a little later, he found his whole life gone. He had sat there with her, not able to move or think rationally until, like Pavlov's dog, he responded reflexively to the sound of the doorbell.

The ceremonies were quiet. Edison and Nancy had flown in to be with their friends. They were amazed at the large crowd standing silently in the early morning Carolina fog just to pay their respects to Padre Bill's wife.

Then came the hard part: going back to the house that echoed with the memories and vibrations of a fruitful life and the recent happy commotion of the children. Galen and June could sense the palpable emptiness, so they stayed a week with their friend, working the clinic and keeping a close eye on Bill, while he sat silently most of the time regardless of their attempts at encouragement.

Before he left for home, Galen contacted the regional medical school and arranged for the directors of the graduate programs to circulate their interns and residents through the clinic. Then he bundled Bill and some personal basics into the Jeep, and he and June drove the distance back to Northern Virginia. He knew the agony of being alone and vowed not to let that crushing despair permanently overwhelm his friend.

Slowly Bill did emerge from his depression. The loss still weighed on him, but he began to eat and talk more freely, particularly of returning to his clinic to continue his and Peggy's life work. But Galen recognized that pattern, too, and so did June.

"Bill, let's make that Colombia trip," she told him. "Peggy would have wanted it. It will do you some good to get away for awhile."

June could be very persuasive when she was younger, and Galen saw something else that had endured over the years as she talked with Bill, who at last agreed.

The three worked over the arrangements. June and Bill would fly down to the takeoff point in Colombia to check on the supplies and itinerary for the various stops through the outlying villages. Galen would join them later for the actual embarkation to the countryside.

The effort brought purpose back into Bill's life and renewed determination into Galen's. The night before she was going to leave, they strolled along the bike path near Galen's home. He knew it was his second, and last, chance with her.

"June, remember that day when I made a fool of myself at your apartment?"

She laughed then stopped and looked into his glistening eyes.

"You weren't a fool, Bob. I just wasn't ready for that big a step in my life."

"What about now?"

Dear God, what a stupid way to propose!

He waited that fraction of a second, expecting the same reply to echo over the years again.

"I'm ready now, Bob."

He waved to them as they left the security area to board their plane then returned home quickly. He had a lot to do before his own flight in two days. He had arranged for coverage of his patients, but Nancy and Edison would keep watch over the office and stay at his place to catch the mail and important calls. He kept checking off the items on his inventory list—including that special small box, ring size, he would carry in his shirt pocket.

He sat at his desk, looking over his passport, vaccination records, and all of the other papers he would need. The classical music from WBJC filled the room with Schubert's beautiful "Quintet in C."

Then the music stopped.

"This is a bulletin from the WBJC news room," a monotone male voice interrupted. "In what is being called a tragic accident, the Colombian government has announced that a plane carrying medical missionaries and supplies from the United States was fired upon by helicopters of the Colombian drug task force that had been tracking narcotics-smuggling operations over the central highlands. There are no reported survivors. Stay tuned for further reports."

And then there was one.

CHAPTER 15

Rebirth

He walked through the empty house next to the mission clinic that Bill and Peggy Crowley had dedicated their lives to running. He came to the small office room that both had shared and gazed at the framed documents hanging from the wall: college and medical school diplomas, board and state licenses, all attesting to the competence and knowledge of the two who had lived there. But none of that spoke to who these two people really were, what they had been, what they had meant to each other. And as his emotions twisted in agony, he spotted a small, framed photograph occupying a central place of honor among the official documents. Smiling out at him were six young faces, three couples, dressed in their senior-medical-year whites with stethoscopes hanging out of their side pockets, arms on each other's shoulders.

He took the photo from the wall, set it on Bill's desk, and sat down in front of it. Finally he did what he hadn't been able to do since he heard that recent broadcast of the accident that had claimed his two friends—he lowered his head and began to cry.

The sound of a gentle knock interrupted his grief. He sat back upright, wiped his eyes, and softly said, "Come in."

Mrs. Canales, the elderly housekeeper, once a refugee whom Bill and Peggy had rescued, opened the door.

"Doctor Galen, I have packed the children's belongings. They are outside with your friends."

"Thank you, Consuela. I appreciate all of your help these past days. I hope you will be staying on to help the young doctors coming through here."

"*Si,* Doctor. It is what the Padre and his lady would have wanted. You will take good care of the children, *si?*"

"Yes, like they were my own."

"*Signor,* they are."

He picked up the photograph from the desk and carried it with him outside, where Edison and Nancy stood by the rented minivan holding onto the three small ones now in their charge. As soon as the children spotted him, they ran to meet him, all calling out "Tio Galen! Tio Galen!"

As they surrounded him, Antonio, the youngest, quieted down.

"Where do people go when they die, Tio Galen?"

"Why do you want to know, Tonio?"

He watched the serious-faced little boy, now staring up into the sky.

"Tio Edison said that they go to heaven. Is that where Padre Bill and Tia Peggy are?"

"Yes, Tonio, I'm sure of it."

The round-faced little girl looked worried.

"Are we going to live with you?"

"Yes, Carmelita, you and Federico and Tonio are all coming with us. We're going to show you where I live, and then we'll head to your new home in Pennsylvania with Tia Nancy and Tio Edison."

"Are you going to live with us, Tio?"

Federico looked into his eyes.

Nancy and Edison also watched their friend and waited.

Stunned, Galen stared and said nothing, until three small pairs of hands took hold of his. Then he looked at his friends and said softly, "Yes, if Tia Nancy and Tio Edison will have me."

The minivan with its cargo of six lives, three young and three old, made its way back up the coast and reached the Northern Virginia suburbs shortly before dusk. It had been a quiet ride, interrupted only by meals and bathroom breaks.

Galen turned and called out, "We're almost at my house, but if everyone's not too tired, how about if we take a quick ride into the city? Washington's lights are a sight to see."

Nancy looked at the three kids in the back seat, their eyes still wide at the changing scenery. Edison, tired from the drive, stretched his arms and nodded.

"Okay," he said. "Let's do a quick bit of sightseeing."

The sun's late-summer amber light show was coming to a close as they took Dolley Madison Boulevard to the entrance of the George Washington Parkway. The road, beautifully landscaped with forest trees and plants, followed the Virginia side of the Potomac River into Washington, where the lights of Georgetown and the city's monuments formed a kaleidoscope across the darkened water.

They crossed the Theodore Roosevelt Bridge and followed Constitution Avenue past the Lincoln Memorial, the Washington Monument—a stone-block space needle, backlit by the floodlamps around it—and the White House, gleaming from across the south lawn and Ellipse.

It was late for the children to be up, but they remained excited by the stately buildings and towering monuments.

"What are those buildings, Tio Galen?" Carmelita asked.

"These are the offices of federal agencies," he replied. "That's the Department of Commerce, and farther down is the Department of Justice."

"Oh," she said, seeming disappointed.

"But here on your right is the Museum of American History, where they keep the gowns of the First Ladies, and next is the Museum of

Natural History—where they keep the giant elephant and the dinosaur skeletons."

The three kids oohed and aahed.

"Turn right here, Edison, on Seventh Street."

Edison complied.

"Where're we headed, Galen?"

He pointed to the huge gray-white building with its symbol of The Freedom of Flight, the Smithsonian's crown jewel—the National Air and Space Museum.

"We'll visit here soon," Galen promised.

They headed back to Virginia, and when they returned to Galen's home the three adults carried three sleeping munchkins inside to their beds.

"Thanks, Galen. That was beautiful," Nancy said.

Edison nodded then added, "But it doesn't match our mountain."

Galen just smiled.

It had been a while since he had slept in his own bed. He washed up and changed into the pajamas and robe that Cathy had given him when he turned forty-five. He sat on the edge of his bed for a time, trying to adjust to the rapid changes in his life. It felt strange, even more so when he realized there were five other lives in his home/office. It hadn't been that way in years. He wondered what might have been if the Fates hadn't intervened.

There might have been children with Leni. He got up and opened the upper-right desk drawer and looked at the handwritten card from long ago that had hung from the neck of the little stuffed toy dog and sighed.

Cathy and he had talked about adoption. And June, there could have been grandchildren when her son, Tom, finally settled down. Now he felt the spiritual closeness of three rescued strangers who had captured his heart. He sighed again and lay back down, the arthritic twinges in his back making him groan slightly as he tried to get comfortable. He took off his glasses, and the world blurred into the incandescence of the small night light on the shelf by his bed. He reached over and turned it off. After a while the turmoil in his mind quieted and he slept.

He had dozed off, but years of training suddenly brought him fully awake.

He wasn't alone.

He turned the night light back on and saw a small blurred figure looking at him.

Glasses, where are my glasses—ah, there they are.

He peered into the face of little Antonio.

"What is it, Tonio?"

The boy, dressed in blue bunny rabbit pajamas, climbed up on the edge of the bed. He held a stuffed toy dog in his left hand.

Galen's eyes widened as he sat up with a start.

"Boy . . . Tonio . . . where did you get that?"

He caught himself and tried to keep his voice down. He didn't want to upset Antonio, who was holding Leni's stuffed dog, the reminder of that nightmare so many years ago. Galen had kept it as a sad memento . . . no, more . . . a sacred relic of that time, but he had placed it high up on a shelf and only he knew its significance.

"The nice ladies brought it to me."

"Nice ladies?"

"I was sleeping and then I woke up and they were standing by my bed."

Galen's heart was now racing, but he knew he had to remain calm in front of the child.

"Okay, tell me about the nice ladies."

Antonio moved next to him, still clutching the toy and stroking it.

"There were two nice ladies. They were as tall as Tia Nancy. And they had the most beautiful colors in their eyes, Tio, like my purple crayons."

"That's very good, Tonio. You are a very observant boy. What did the two ladies do? Did they say anything to you?"

Galen reached over absent-mindedly and also started to stroke the sad-faced stuffed toy beagle. How many times had he sat holding it, doing the same thing?

"I don't understand, Tio. The nice ladies didn't talk to me. I mean, I didn't see their lips move. But I could hear them—and the tall man. He was nice, too."

Galen felt himself start to shake, but he fought for composure.

"What did the nice man look like, Tonio?"

"He had hair under his nose and he wore white clothes, like the pictures in the doctor book you gave me. He took my hand and told me to tell you that Country Boy was watching. What's a country boy, Tio?"

The bear-sized man suddenly felt small and weak.

"Then the two ladies and the tall man told me to tell you to follow your heart. What does that mean, Tio?"

Galen just shook his head silently.

"Can I play with the doggy? Can I take him to bed with me, please? The two ladies and the man, who are they? Do they live here, too? I didn't see them leave but then they were gone."

Galen snapped himself out of his paralysis.

"It's okay, little one. Do you want me to take you back to your brother and sister? Do you want to go back to your bed?"

"Can I stay here, Tio?"

"Yes, you can. Just let me get up so I can tuck you in."

Galen slowly rose from the bed and the child curled himself up with the toy dog on the pillow, as the old man pulled up the blankets to cover him. Antonio soon fell back to sleep, but Galen sat at his bedroom desk fighting for control of his emotions—and maybe his sanity.

After a while, he stood up and walked through the office area of his home. How many people, how many lives had he watched walk through these rooms? The babies that turned into children and then adults and having children of their own, and the old, the ones he had watched deteriorate over time, going from active to inevitable decline.

Funny he should remember just now, that first patient on the very first day he opened his office, the woman in her late sixties who had come to the door without an appointment.

She saw he was new to the neighborhood. She didn't have a doctor and wondered if he could give her a quick checkup.

He wasn't exactly busy. Actually he wasn't doing anything, so he welcomed her himself, because his newly hired secretary had not yet shown up.

He took the clipboard and began to ask for her name, address, all of the pertinent information for new patients. When he got to occupation, he had expected "retired," but suddenly she began to laugh.

"I'm a white witch."

He looked at her more carefully. She didn't seem deranged. Well dressed in a mixed floral pattern with brown pumps and matching shoulder purse, her face remained unlined, even as it creased into a smile that highlighted the mixed silver-gold of formerly all-blond hair. Her blue, highly intelligent eyes framed what must have been an attractive pug nose when she was younger.

"That's very interesting. What's a white witch?"

"Young doctor, you don't believe me, do you? You'll see."

As he started the exam, he very carefully covered each body system, until he had reached the point where he normally would do a heart recording.

"You won't be able to do that on me," she smiled.

He hooked her up carefully to the EKG machine, turned it on, and got . . . gibberish!

"Okay, now try it," she said, and suddenly the machine's printing arm moved normally, like a conductor's baton, tracing out the electrical music of her heart.

She came back two days later to go over her test results. After they concluded and he had told her how healthy she was, she looked at him.

"Dr. Galen, let me give you a gift. Think of it as an office-warming gift. Carefully she set a dried floral arrangement on his desk.

"Keep it as long as you wish to continue working. When you are ready to quit, whether in retirement or a change of careers—and only then—burn it. Never throw it in the trash."

He stared at the door, remembering her and the countless thousands of those who had passed through its portals. He walked into the living room/waiting room and opened the fireplace damper. Then he stood on a straight-backed chair to reach the high shelf and took down the small wicker basket with its badly aging dried flowers. Reverently he placed the basket on the log holder and lit a match. He suddenly yelped when a large flame jumped out at him, burning his flesh.

Galen sat up quickly as morning sunlight streamed through his bedroom window. He looked around then sighed, as he got out of bed in the empty room.

Nancy had found pots and pans, long unused, in Galen's kitchen, and she whipped up what for that house was an unusually great breakfast.

Then the kids played outside in the yard, as the three adults did the dishes and packed the minivan for the day's trip.

Six hours later they pulled off the Pennsylvania highway onto a stretch of road that wound up the side of a mountain just outside Scranton.

The wheels crunched on the gravel turnaround in front of the rustic ranch-style mountaintop house that Nancy and Edison had called home since their retirement.

Federico and Carmelita followed the couple inside, but Galen hung back to take in the scenery, and Antonio remained by his side.

"Don't you want to go in, Tonio?"

"I want to stay with you, Tio."

"Okay, let's stretch our legs a bit."

They found a narrow side path through the trees, and as they walked the large older man pointed out different colored birds and plants to the small boy, who seemed in awe of all the newness. And Galen felt something he hadn't experienced since Leni was taken. Could it be the child needed him?

He paused, his eyes misting over.

Leni, Cathy, June!

The emotion overwhelmed him. He wanted to crouch down, to bury his head in his hands. But something tugged at his shirt sleeve. He opened his eyes and felt young hands on his arm.

"Why are you sad, Tio?"

Suddenly touched, he dropped to his knees—and lied.

"I'm not sad, Tonio. I'm just very happy to be here with you."

The little boy smiled and threw his arms around the old man's neck. Galen collected himself. He picked Tonio up and held him close for a moment then put him down again.

"Come on, let's go inside. Your brother and sister are waiting for us. It will be dinnertime soon, and Tia Nancy will wonder where we went."

They trudged back up the path leading to the house, bear and cub, one trying to walk in the footsteps of the other.

A few weeks passed. Galen remained deeply troubled by the recent events. Why do such bad things happen to such good people? Was it all just a zero-sum game? Save three, lose three?

Maybe those religions that believe in capricious deities are right. Maybe Loki, Crow god, the Greek fates, and their ilk really do roll the dice and play with us like pawns.

One day he almost fell off the deck, so immersed was he in his thoughts.

Edison had been watching him carefully. Despite the years apart he understood his friend well enough to know he was still carrying the full load of the recent tragedies. *Talk about bad luck or no luck at all,* he thought. Three loves, three losses. It was almost as though Galen was meant to go through life alone.

Nancy was not so pessimistic. She had noticed how Tonio was following Galen around like a shadow—just as little Federico, who now wanted to be called Freddie, was doing with Bob. Truth be told, she had grown very happy, having quickly and comfortably bonded with Carmelita. The two of them would sit for hours reading aloud or take long walks in the woods.

The experience had planted a thought firmly inside her.

Maybe this is a second chance. Maybe in old age we've finally been blessed with the family we've always wanted.

"Dinner!" Nancy called. "Come on, guys and gals, wash up and take your places."

One by one they squeezed around the circular mahogany table, which used to be more than big enough for two but now was overflowing with the three adults and three children.

It was early August, so there still was plenty of daylight as they began the evening meal. The sky had taken on an umber hue prefacing a storm, and flashes from distant lightning faintly illuminated the expansive window pane facing the valley below. They watched as the dark clouds rolled in, and brighter streaks of light shot across the horizon. Then the rain began to shotgun-pellet its way to earth,while the flashes increased in size and intensity.

The rain performed a steady tattoo on the picture window as they ate. *Just the right background for Mussorgsky's "Night on Bald Mountain,"* Edison thought, as he popped the CD into the player then rejoined his wife and friend and the children in the dining room, where the aroma of pot roast and jasmine tea filled the air.

Thunder rumbled again, a post-prandial celebration of Nancy's good food. When a nearby lightning strike caused the power to wink out, she reflexively got up from the table and went to flip the light switch off and on. At her first try, the lights returned but only momentarily, and the ghostly flash of the light striking the table triggered a memory in the quietest member of the circle.

• • •

"Mr. Galen, hold that retractor more firmly, unless you want me to slice through this patient's aorta."

He was rotating through general surgery. Rounds—that military march of the attending surgeon, his chief resident, the other yearly residents, interns, seniors, and finally the lowest of the low, the third-year students—began at 5 a.m.

The daily routine repeated over and over, grinding away at the determination and idealism of even the most dedicated among them. Endless presentations of patients with mild or mortal conditions elicited constant pimping, a game of one-upmanship among those rounding to see who could stump the others with the most obscure journal references.

And then, OR at 6 a.m. Hour after hour, standing in gown, cap, shoe and head coverings, having learned the sacerdotal rites of hand-and-forearm scrubbing under the hawk-eyed supervision of the OR nurse, whom the students assumed was really an escaped Nazi concentration-camp guard who enjoyed tormenting them.

"Hold the retractor" was the common command, extending an arm for excruciating lengths of time between the real players bent over the spécialité du jour lying naked and unconscious atop the brightly lit table. Galen often wondered: Could he detach his arm and leave for a bathroom break without anyone knowing it?

How did the surgeons do it, standing there, hour after hour? By senior year he had the temerity to ask a chief resident that question. He blanched at the reply: "Depends on how tough the guy is. Some can hold it. Others use diapers, and the real masochists use catheters with bags strapped to their legs!"

• • •

Another zap of lightning briefly illuminated the still-darkened room.

• • •

"Galen, you have another patient to work up." The intern had called him at 3 a.m. "Oh, by the way, it's a LOL with no veins and totally out of her gourd. She's an alcoholic with terminal liver disease, heart failure, kidney failure, bed sores, and contractures of her legs and arms."

The nursing home had decided she needed help about two hours earlier. *Some place,* he thought. It looked as though they hadn't given her a bath in a week.

• • •

The power flickered on and off once more. Again Nancy got up to flip the switch, and this time the lights returned.

Galen felt a strange epiphany as he watched her rejoin the group, precipitated by the recollection the power outage had elicited.

And there you stood, Galen old boy, looking down at what was once a human being who had loved, had family, and was now being plucked apart by time. Remember what you thought? "Why is there no on/off switch to help these people?" Is that the note your own life will end on—helpless, alone and unwanted? Have the deities rolled craps on your behalf?

The echoes became deafening.

"What's your name?" . . . "Robert Galen." . . . "No, kid. From now on, it's Dottore Berto." . . . "Why do you want to know, kid?" . . . "I want to be like you." . . . "Non ho figlio!" . . . "Hi, I'm Bill Crowley." . . . "David Allen Nash, and it looks like we're gonna be roommates." . . . "June Ross, will you marry me?" . . . "Will you marry me, Leni Jensen?" . . . "Yes, Tony." . . . "Bob, Leni's spirit wants me to call you Tony." . . . "Cathy Welton, will you marry me?" . . . "Yes, Tony." . . . "Are you going to live with us, Tio?"

"Tio?"

As the lightning and thunder matched the symphony almost beat for beat, he noticed Antonio had climbed onto his lap, his little arms clutching the old man tightly.

The long-forgotten warmth of being needed, a memory buried in grief and loss, suddenly erupted in Galen's soul.

This was his family now.

• • •

• •